The elevator doors slid open and there he stood before her.

"Quay," Tykira breathed, while silently cursing herself for the sultry, needy undertone in her voice.

Quay stepped forward smoothly urging her back into the elevator car. "Did you accept the proposal?" He asked once the doors had closed behind him.

"I did," she confirmed, wincing when she noticed a smirk tilt the corner of his mouth. "It's a great opportunity," she managed to say, but found it impossible to maintain eye contact when he stood so close.

"Are you sure you can handle it?" he asked.

Ty's temper flared. "Would you ask me that if I were a man?"

"I would if you were a man who'd never done a job like this before."

"Bull," she replied. His smirk only deepened. Tykira took a step closer, dismissing the way his deep-set eyes appraised her. She would give anything to know what he was thinking.

"Good luck," he whispered, and pressed the button to reopen the doors.

Ty tried to utter a response, but the potency of the moment had robbed her of her voice.

Taking great care not to brush against any hard, powerful part of his body, she gingerly eased out of the elevator.

S0-AQE-481

ALTONYA WASHINGTON

is a South Carolina native and graduate of Winston Salem State University in North Carolina. Her first contemporary novel, *Remember Love,* BET/Arabesque 2003, was nominated by *Romantic Times BOOKclub* as Best First Multicultural Romance. Her novel *Finding Love Again* won a *Romantic Times BOOKclub* Reviewer's Choice Award for Best Multicultural Romance 2004. She presently resides in North Carolina, where she works as a senior library assistant.

A Lover's Pretense

AlTonya
WASHINGTON

To all the fantastic, beautiful readers
who never tire of asking "Will there be a sequel?"
Yes guys, prepare yourselves…

KIMANI PRESS™

ISBN-13: 978-1-58314-777-2
ISBN-10:   1-58314-777-1

A LOVER'S PRETENSE

Copyright © 2006 by AlTonya Washington

Dear Reader,

Thanks so very much for your overwhelming approval of the Ramsey family. I hope this latest Ramsey family sequel, *A Lover's Pretense,* proves to be just as enjoyable as my other Ramsey romances. Hopefully, you'll obtain more insight into this tumultuous family. Like his twin, Quaysar Ramsey was just as exciting to create, and I had a wonderful time bringing to life Quay and Tykira's rocky and intense relationship. As always, I welcome your questions and comments. E-mail me at altonyawashington@yahoo.com.

Be blessed,

AlTonya Washington

Prologue

No way. It was impossible. It was simply not possible that this man could be any more magnificent since she last saw him almost fifteen years ago.

Tykira Lowery pondered what was, to her, such a huge improbability as she headed into Damon and Catrina Ramsey's immaculate country estate just outside Seattle, Washington. Ty had given in to her mother's insistent demands that she attend the wedding of Quaysar Ramsey's twin brother, Quest. The twins were the sons of her mother's boss. In truth, she'd been almost afraid to say anything other than "yes" to the woman. Roberta "Bobbie" Lowery rarely demanded, never yelled and certainly *never* delivered ultimatums.

But she'd done just that and Ty really couldn't hold her mother at fault. After all, she hadn't set foot in Seattle since leaving for college in Hampton, Virginia, in the fall of 1990. Bobbie had abided by her daughter's wishes to not return to her home state of Washington, and had spent time with her only child elsewhere. Once Ty was financially able, she flew her mother out to one exotic locale after another. Clearly, Bobbie had simply been biding her time, waiting to play on her daughter's emotions and guilt for never visiting home.

But now, Ty owned up to the fact that it had been a mistake to give in to her mother's emotional manipulating. As her cream pumps clicked across the gray and black marble checkered foyer and into the sunken ballroom, the ruffled hem to the skirt of her roseblush crepe suit flipping flirtatiously with her every step, Ty realized that she had indeed gravely underestimated how powerfully she'd be affected by being there.

More specifically, by seeing Quaysar Ramsey again.

The overwhelming sensation should have come as no surprise. She'd suspected that she'd be more than a little shaken to see him. Though she knew he'd be at the wedding, he was actually the last person she expected to see the moment she arrived.

Tall and muscular, he had the power to make her feel incredibly small and feminine—something she never admitted to liking. But, being a woman two inches shy of six feet, feeling less dominant was quite often an exquisite luxury. Quay Ramsey not only had the ability to make her feel that way, but when he looked at her, she forgot every and anything else. Those bottomless, pitch-black eyes were set so deeply beneath the sleek brows that slanted above....

He was still fierce looking and agitatingly arrogant. Confidence personified. He'd had no idea who she was—that was clear. When he'd almost hit her SUV with his car in the driveway a few minutes ago, she'd reveled in the power of his confusion as she verbally slammed him. Of course, during her "verbal slam" she was constantly trying to hear her own voice above her heart, which beat a thousand drums in her ears. Still, she managed to coolly order him out of her way, and the look on his face was sheer delight on her part.

The smug smile curving her full mouth diminished slightly. What would happen when he saw her again later? She hadn't thought that far ahead. *Uh-oh, no time to do so now,* she told herself. A woman who looked like Catrina Ramsey was eyeing her with that *almost* certain look of recognition. Tykira smiled and wiggled her fingers in a tentative wave.

Quay was strolling back into the foyer. He jingled the keys against his palm and tried once again to place where he'd seen the woman from the driveway. He'd certainly recall having met someone like her— all that rich black hair, glossy and bouncing to the middle of her back; molasses skin just like his own. Although, he was willing to bet his last dime that her skin was supple and satiny with a soft desirable fragrance clinging to it...

Dammit! Who was she? He wondered, glancing toward the keys again as if they held some answer. She knew *him* quite well as she'd been so kind to share during their run-in—no pun intended—out in the courtyard.

Then there was her height. He liked his women tiny and curvaceous. Of course, that was a preference he'd developed in yet another vain attempt to keep his mind off of...

Hold it. *No way.*

"Can't be," Quay breathed, his eyes gleaming with a fierce determination as he bounded toward the ballroom.

He scanned the crowd, knowing she'd stand out. After all, how many Amazons with silky midnight skin, amazing tresses and the most entrancing doe eyes could there be in the world? And suddenly, there she was, swaying to the soft classical tune the quartet performed from the alcove. His steps were halted just briefly before they resumed and he headed straight for her.

How could he have not known it was her? They'd been in one another's lives since infancy. Tykira Lowery had taken an immediate, surprisingly intense liking to the overtly sensual and clearly outspoken Quay—as opposed to his quieter, more serious twin brother, Quest. She'd loved him before he even admitted to liking girls, was Quest's usual tease. Quay loved her, too, but a small voice warned him of the danger. He couldn't let anything happen to Ty especially when his feelings for her were just as deep and overwhelming. He'd felt the need to protect her no matter the cost. Still, over the years, the man in him had daydreamed of Ty. He wanted just a moment, just one moment to allow himself to pretend they could be a normal couple—loving and living without fear. Quay knew she'd hate him forever afterwards, but he believed he could take that for just another minute in her arms.

Tykira was laughing and slapped her dance partner's shoulder.

Yohan Ramsey, the groom's cousin, feigned surprise. "Ow," he uttered playfully.

"Ow, is right if Mel walks in here and sees us. Stop holding me so tight. I don't want her upset with me," Ty teased, referring to Yohan's wife.

Like someone had pulled a plug, the happiness on Yohan's dark face drained away. His eyes pooled with a sadness not to be ignored.

"Han? What is it?" Ty whispered with concern, noticing his reaction.

"It's okay," Yohan assured her in his deep voice. "Melina and I are separated. Hmph," he gestured and shook his head slightly as though he were in a state of disbelief. "It's been six years. We should be divorced."

Ty closed her eyes as recollection dawned. Her mother had informed her of the couple's troubles and subsequent separation long ago. She searched his eyes with hers. "You wanna talk about it?" she asked.

Yohan's easy expression returned. "Some things are best left alone. Besides, I think my cousin wants to cut in."

Ty blinked and turned to find Quay standing right behind her.

"Not quite, Han," he said, curving his hand around Ty's upper arm and leading her from the ballroom.

Ty swallowed, trying to remain unfazed by the feel of his fingers snug around the crisp material of the tailored crepe cutaway jacket.

"What are you doing here?" Quay muttered as they walked.

"It's your brother's wedding day," she reminded him. "Mama threatened to stop visiting me altogether if I didn't show up."

At last they were on the balcony. Quay leaned against the doorjamb of one of the French doors and watched her. "Q's wedding, that's the only reason?" he asked, looking completely unconvinced as he settled his hands into the pockets of his black tuxedo trousers.

Tykira's temper flashed and she opened her mouth to retaliate. The sound of approaching guests stifled her remark.

Quay must have figured they would be less bothered if they hid in a crowd because he took her arm again and led her to the dance floor. He pulled her into a snug, arousing embrace. Reminding herself how much she despised him, Ty tried not to get lost in how fantastic she felt in his arms.

"How long do you plan to stay?" he asked, effectively casting a sour element to the dance.

Ty rolled her eyes while silently warning her hands to remain firmly planted against his chest and not to venture upwards to choke his neck. "I'll be here long enough to visit my mother and your family."

Quay tugged his bottom lip between his perfect teeth. "But not me?" he probed.

"Why you?" she threw back.

"Tyke…" he almost purred.

When his right dimple flashed, Ty realized that he was taunting her. "You still enjoy hurting me, don't you?" she asked, hating the way her voice wavered on the question.

Something flickered in Quay's black eyes but he masked it before it grew too telling. "Hurting you isn't what I had in mind…unless you're into that sort of thing now."

In a flash, Ty jerked out of his arms and laid a cracking slap on the side of his face. Infuriating her more, Quay only grinned while brushing his knuckles across his jaw.

Ty shoved his chest. "You're still the same conceited jackass you've always been," she said, sounding as though the discovery really didn't surprise her. Pressing a hand against her pearl choker, then brushing her fingers across the single button that secured her chic double-breasted jacket, she turned and made a regal exit from the dance floor.

The room was alive with laughter over the scene and as Ty exited the ballroom, she heard someone remark that she and Quay were like fire and gasoline—a volatile combination. Amidst all the amusement, however, she never saw that Quay's eyes were filled with the darkness of regret.

Chapter 1

Two years later...

The penthouse office of Ramsey Group was alive with conversation and cheer. The executive members of the real estate conglomerate had gathered to discuss final matters concerning their largest project to date. Holtz Enterprises of Vancouver, Canada, had commissioned the group to construct a state-of-the-art, yet old-world style ski resort. The organization had purchased property in the mountainous regions just outside Banff, in the neighboring province of Alberta. They wanted a mammoth-sized, impressive, unequalled castlelike resort to sit high atop one of those mountains. The organization wanted no ex-

pense spared—nothing but the best. And Ramsey
Group was the perfect choice. It was well equipped
to oversee all aspects of the project including con-
tracting and construction. The development division
began working diligently two years prior and now
the project was nearing completion. Another six to
eight months would produce a destination like no
other.

While the actual completion of the resort was
going smoothly, there was one aspect that still
needed to be addressed: transportation. Holtz wanted
a nonstop service to shuttle passengers from Calgary
to the resort by train. The rail would travel up the
foreboding mountainside to its peak. Ramsey didn't
build trains, so the question before them now was
who could they entrust with such a gargantuan task.

Quest, who was assigned with finding the rail
design company for the project, believed he'd found
his choice.

"I'm leaning toward a design company out of
Colorado," he said, standing at the head of the long
rectangular conference table. "They're very well
known in the rail community in spite of the fact
they've only been incorporated for five years. I want
you guys to look over their portfolio," he said,
passing a stack of packets around the table. "I'd like
your decisions by Wednesday's meeting."

Everyone at the table nodded their agreement.
Some were already tearing into the packets and reviewing the enclosed material.

"If there are no other questions…?" Quest

prompted, his sleek brows rising as he paused for reactions. "In that case, meeting adjourned," he said
when no one spoke up. "Quay? Wait up, man," he
asked, before his brother headed out with the rest of
the group.

Quay shook hands with Russ Anderson, one of
Ramsey's chief architects. They made plans for
drinks later that week. Then Russ left, closing the
door behind him.

"What's up?"

Quest watched his twin perch on the corner of the
long table. Then, bowing his head, he cleared his
throat softly. "I'm leaning toward Tyke Designs to
build the rail," he announced.

"Tykira?" Quay breathed, his black eyes narrowing as he spoke. Sure, he was well aware that she was
in the business. Aside from Quest and perhaps Mick,
no one knew how closely he'd kept tabs on the woman since seeing her two years ago at his brother's
wedding. "Why?" he asked, watching Quest shrug.

"Her company is impressive as hell. Innovative
and fresh," Quest raved, taking his place on the
opposite corner of the table. "They're a highly
sought after group and I don't think we'd be disappointed."

"Cut it. You know that's not what I meant."

"Well that's what *I* meant," Quest countered, his
gray stare sharpening as he stared down his mirror
image.

Quay uttered a quick, humorless chuckle. "You,
better than anyone, know what the situation is here.
Why would you suggest this?" he whispered.

"Quay, no one's seen or heard from Wake Robinson in almost three years."

"Is that supposed to reassure me?" Quay threw back with cocky sarcasm. "Because it doesn't."

"Get over it," Quest suggested while shaking his head and reaching for the chocolate-brown suit coat on the chair behind him. "Once I hear from the rest of the team on Wednesday, I'll be putting in a call to Ty."

"And you're so sure they'll go for this?"

"I'm positive."

Quay gnawed the inside of his jaw, his dark eyes following his brother's every move. "And you think the family is going to support this?"

Quest's knowing smile triggered his left dimple. "They all love Tykira, you know that."

Quay waved his hand. "It's not about that," he said, moving off the table.

Quest studied the invisible pattern his index finger traced on the cherrywood finish. "Well maybe it's about the fact that you've lived like a virtual hermit for over two years now?"

"Dammit, Quest, does it matter that her life is at stake if this fool ever discovers how I feel about her?"

"Ah Quay," Quest sighed, not wanting to tell his brother that he was overreacting. That he felt his worries were unfounded. After all, it had been fifteen years since he and Ty had had any semblance of a relationship. Fifteen years since Quay had pushed Tykira away believing that he was saving her life.

For that reason, he had no sympathy for his brother. He knew how deeply Quay felt for Tykira. "Have you ever thought of protecting the woman you love by keeping her close instead of shutting her out?"

Quay's hearty, contagious laughter filled the room. "Damn, you're one to talk. Hell, Q, I said almost those same words to you back when you were about to lose Mick for good."

Quest smiled. Stepping close to his twin, he patted his shoulder. "Then I guess you already know what you have to do, right?" he challenged, and then left his brother alone to think.

Quay sank into one of the hunter-green armchairs in the boardroom living area and pondered this new upset. Tykira could not come there. While he had no doubts concerning his ability to say enough of the wrong things to keep her at arm's length, he was *full* of doubts about his ability to actually go through with saying those things.

He smiled, smoothing a hand across the front of the black banded collar shirt he wore. He thought about how incredible she'd looked two years ago at Quest's wedding—especially when she angrily shoved her hands against his chest. He recalled her storming out of the ballroom. Men's eyes followed her until she was out of view and then sometimes, further still. Tykira was viewed by Quay and, he suspected, most every man she met, as the epitome of Amazon. Tall, strong, exotic and erotically proportioned—she was a woman who could take care of herself, while still being feminine enough to elicit

a need to protect in any man she met. At five foot
ten, her height advantage added to her seductive, intimidating persona. Aside from her mahogany-
brown doe eyes and glossy mane, her voice was
low—shockingly husky and womanly.

Quay closed his eyes. He'd almost kissed her
when he took her out on that balcony during the reception. And when he'd pulled her into the dance,
every part of him ached to drag her off somewhere
and make love to her until she was too weak to leave
the bed. She couldn't accept Quest's job offer, he
thought. No one would buy that Quay only regarded
her as a quick lay, a brief dalliance. Fifteen years
ago, she'd been a girl who had been kind enough to
take the hint and steer clear of him. It had made it
possible to stay away from *her*. Now, she was a full-
grown woman. *Boy was she,* he thought. She would
be coming here with a job to do, a job that would
include working with him, and he couldn't pretend
he'd have strength enough to hide his feelings for
her.

Quay shook his head. He couldn't allow Ty to stay
there. She'd left Seattle once because of him. Surely
he could make her leave again.

Denver, Colorado

"I mean it, lil' lady. I'm gonna git you out here if
it's the last thing I do! You ain't lived till you take a
ride on a private train 'round the grandest ranch in
Texas!"

Tykira wiped a tear from the corner of her eye as she listened to the ravings of Henry Rose. The gregarious petroleum tycoon had commissioned her company to create his specialized rail earlier that year. It went without saying that he was more than pleased with the finished product.

"Henry, are you forgetting I've already taken a trip around your ranch?" Ty said, shaking her head as she envisioned the man chugging around his massive El Paso estate/ranch/oil field. The christening of the train car had been a grand society event and now the rail was hard at work traveling from one end of Henry's empire to the other.

"Bah! That was for work. I'm talkin' sheer relaxation."

"Mmm-hmm," Ty remarked, smiling at the man's charm. He'd made no secret how "interested" he was throughout the time she'd spent in Texas designing the rail. "I promise to try and get away for a visit soon," she said, chuckling when Henry uttered a "hot dang" and boasted about how fine a time he'd show her.

Used to such offers, Tykira had perfected the art of accepting them with a cool head. Her light, inviting responses never placed her in a position of being obligated to accept proposals from her adoring clients. While she had no intentions of providing them with anything but the finest in rail design, they were each left feeling that they were unique in her eyes.

Once the call with Henry had ended, Ty closed her eyes, pulled a hand through her hair and swiveled her chair around to take in the view of downtown Denver. Simultaneously calmed and energized by the environment, she thought about her life there, which began the year after she'd graduated Northwestern with a master's in engineering. Denver had been her home ever since.

Ty's vibrant brown gaze clouded over momentarily as thoughts surfaced about the reception two years ago. *Lord, why am I thinking of that?!* Because, she admitted with a sigh, *that* involved Quaysar Ramsey. And Quaysar Ramsey came to mind whenever she thought of her life in Denver. It was a great life, but it would never include the man she loved.

Ooooh! He'd been so arrogant at the reception. Apparently, age had had no effect on his tact or reason. Perhaps hitting him and storming out in the middle of the celebration had been a tad over the top, but Quay could incite such a reaction by doing little more than stepping on her toe.

He'd actually thought she'd come there to see him. What nerve! She continued to rant. Deep down she knew he was right, of course. She could finally admit that. No matter how much her mother had pressured her, she still could have said no. Giving in to her mother was just an excuse—Quay was the real reason for visiting home.

In spite of the cold way he'd treated her, she'd still nearly melted for him. And how had he reacted to her? She'd discovered that after all those years sex was still the only thing he wanted.

Sadly, she knew if he had pressed just a little more, she'd have quickly and happily indulged.

"Choose quick, Michaela, 'cause my bags are waiting to be packed. I've had it with you."

"Sweetie, just bear with me a little longer, I know how much you need me, but I have to see this through."

Contessa Warren, Michaela's friend and owner of Contessa House Publishing, rolled her eyes and leaned back in the majestic black suede desk chair she occupied. Focusing on one of the three diamonds adorning her right hand, she prayed the glimmering sight would calm her as it usually did. Unfortunately, these phone conversations to her top author were growing increasingly annoying. Sure, she wanted Mick hard at work on her next smash family biography, but more importantly, she wanted her to stop wasting her time on a dead end.

For Michaela Sellars Ramsey, however, nothing stirred her juices like the subject she'd embarked upon more than two years ago. Although the Sera Black case had virtually come to a standstill, Mick had been like a bloodhound sniffing out every new lead—no matter how minute—on the case of the murdered teen.

"I mean it, Mick, I can pack and be there before the end of the day," Contessa warned before a quick laugh escaped her. "I don't know what good *that* would do. Hell, if Quest can't keep you busy enough to take your mind off this damn case, I don't know what makes me think *I* can."

Mick's brows rose as she tapped her fingers against the polished oak arm of the chair she lounged in. "Believe me, the man keeps me plenty busy," she shared, thinking of her husband then.

In truth, she'd had very little time to do any real work since becoming Mrs. Quest Ramsey. True, most of their *busy* work resided in the bedroom, but Quest was determined to have his wife be part of every aspect of his life. He sought her opinion on business, family and every other interest he held. Michaela found that she was just as happy doing the same.

"Listen, I promise I'll begin research on another family soon." Mick tried to assure her editor in hopes of stifling the woman's weary sighs on the other end of the line.

"Mmm-hmm," came the doubtful response.

"Contessa, please. Look, I even have my own office space here at home. I've got everything I need to thoroughly research anything and anyone I want," Mick boasted. "Courtesy of my husband," she added adoringly.

"Hmph." Contessa was unimpressed. "Your hubby's just full of great ideas."

"I haven't used this office just to investigate the case, you know," Mick whined.

"The hell you haven't. Mick, I'm not a fool. You've done an incredible job on this case. Wake Robinson hasn't reared his head in a long time, but still you've given Johnelle Black a peace she's never known. Sera's mother finally has someone she can point a finger at. That's more of a solid lead than she's ever had before."

But what if Wake Robinson is only part of the story? Mick inquired silently. She had no idea why she felt that way, but the reporter in her had that nagging doubt which rarely led her astray.

"I promise I'll let it go soon," Mick said at last, trying once more to reassure her best friend.

Contessa swung her legs from her desk and stood. "Because I'm damn tired of debating with you and damn sexually frustrated, I'm going to accept your promise."

"Good," Mick said in a laughing tone as she ruffled her blue-black curls. "Go get a massage or something and try to relax," she suggested.

"Hmph, that would depend on the *kind* of massage."

"Goodbye, Contessa," Mick retorted, shaking her head over the suggestive reply. Setting aside the white cordless, she returned to her notes. She'd been in the midst of rereading her interview with Johnelle Black when Contessa called. Her brows drew close when she scanned something she'd overlooked before. A moment later, she was snatching up the phone and dialing furiously.

Quay had taken a drive out to his parents' home instead of heading straight into the office that morning. He'd taken solace in the den where he sat lounging on one of the overstuffed black cushioned sofas. In his lap was a photo album dated 1979. His mechanical turning of the plastic-covered pages, halted when he found the photo he'd been searching for—one of he, Quest and Tykira sharing a "school's out for summer" party after their 2nd-grade year.

Quay and Ty sat closest to one another in the picture. They looked so happy and, even then, everyone thought they'd one day fall in love and live happily ever after. Then, some years later, things began to happen, Quay recalled, his black eyes growing impossibly dark. There were mishaps, disappearances, murder...and happily ever after became an impossibility.

Catrina Ramsey waltzed into the den, humming a low tune. Her mind was on changing the potting soil in her vases, when she spotted her son—younger by three minutes—on the sofa. Setting aside her gardening basket, she removed her gloves while watching him curiously. Her Reebok Classics padded softly across the fuzzy champagne carpeting until she stood close enough to the sofa where Quay sat. Peering over his shoulder, she saw him with the album.

Quay smiled when his mother's perfume drifted beneath his nose. Turning slightly, he tugged on her wrist and kissed her cheek when she was close enough.

"Reminiscing?" she asked, smoothing her hands across his shoulders beneath the burgundy shirt he wore.

The melancholy returned to Quay's handsome dark features. "More like regretting," he admitted.

"Yuck," Catrina replied, making a face. "That's no fun."

"Ma, how can situations just suddenly fall so far

off track?" Quay asked, once again staring intently at the photo.

Catrina perched her slender frame on the arm of the sofa. "It's the nature of life, sweetie. Our job is to ride the waves until they subside and then snatch up as much happiness as possible when they do."

"What if the happiness only leads to more pain?"

Catrina pressed a kiss to the top of Quay's head, then propped her chin there. "Better to have *some* happiness than none at all, right?" she reasoned and then dropped a quick kiss to her son's temple. It was then that she noticed the picture that his hand hovered over. "She certainly was beautiful at the reception," Catrina remarked, smiling down at the young woman who had once been like a daughter to her. "Not surprising, though. Ty always was such a beautiful child. Bobbie says she's still not married, though." Catrina shared, referring to Tykira's mother. "I'm sure she has a special man," she added.

"She doesn't."

Quay's brisk reply caused a light to flicker in Catrina's gaze, but she offered no comment. Instead, she moved from the arm of the sofa to take a seat on the cushion near Quay. "That's so hard to believe considering how lovely she is. I can't imagine a man who'd let such a beauty run around unattached," she said, staring down at the album and pretending to have no clue about how her words were affecting Quay.

"Quest plans to offer her a job," he said, needing the conversation to shift from the allure of Tykira Lowery.

"I heard," Catrina responded with a nod. "How do you feel about that?" she asked, without looking away from the family photos.

"It's not a good idea," Quay snapped, tension suddenly tightening every muscle he possessed. "Tyke needs to stay where she is, which is as far away from me as possible."

"And how would that solve anything when you two still love each other?" Catrina slyly inquired, setting the album to the stand beneath the coffee table. Silence met her question and she glanced across her shoulder to find Quay watching her with a stunned expression. "What? What's that look for?" she asked.

"We still love each other," Quay repeated in a flat tone of voice.

"Oh, baby," Catrina sighed, slapping her hands to her jean-clad thighs, "everyone knows how you two feel about each other. Anyone paying close attention to you at the reception could've seen it."

"That might've had to do with another emotion, Ma." Quay spoke pointedly, hoping his mother understood what he meant.

She did, and waved off the suggestive reasoning. "It was about more than that. Simple desire has a look you can spot a mile away. Desire mixed with love, well, that's seen with more of the heart than the eye."

Quay shook his head. "You're a deep woman, Trina Ramsey."

Catrina shrugged. "I know a lil' somethin' somethin'. You could've had her, you know? Ty loved you so much, but then you went completely crazy and you started to treat her so coldly."

Quay's dark gaze faltered. He didn't want his thoughts to take him back to that time, but it was unavoidable.

"Anyway," Catrina said with a quick toss of her bouncy silver-gray tresses. "I couldn't blame her for wanting to get as far away from you as possible. Do you think she'll come all the way back here just to take this job?"

Quay's trademark sly grin flashed in an instant. "It's a challenge, it's something most people would expect a man to do and most importantly, she knows I won't like it. Yeah, Ma, she'll most definitely take the job."

Chapter 2

A shiver touched Michaela's spine as she stretched lazily. The sensational kisses showering her back made her want to snuggle in bed forever.

"Quest," she sighed, feeling his fingers becoming a more potent part of the scene. She pressed her face into one of the pillows littering the headboard and began to grind her hips in sync with his thrusting fingers.

A second later, he was turning her to her back and they were kissing madly. Soft moans filled the darkened space of the spacious bi-level bedroom. Mick arched into her husband's hard frame, her nails grazing his neck where his soft hair tapered.

The subdued, yet noticeable ring from the phone on the nightstand chilled the moment. They groaned simultaneously, but the passionate kissing continued.

"Leave it," Quest growled into her mouth when she made a reach for the phone.

Mick was happy to comply and snuggled back into the erotic embrace. Quest broke the kiss to trail his lips down the line of her neck and lower still to the swell of her cleavage.

"Good morning, Michaela, this is Johnelle Black returning your call..."

The sound of the voice rising from the answering machine had Mick's undivided attention. Wrenching away from Quest, she snatched the phone off its hook before Johnelle could finish her message.

"Good morning!" Mick greeted breathlessly while slapping at her husband's groping hands.

"Michaela? I know it's early. Is this a bad time?"

"No, Johnelle," Mick assured, pausing to slap at Quest's hands again before flashing him a warning look. "No, this is a great time. Thanks for getting back to me so fast."

"Well, it sounded urgent," Johnelle noted, a slight twinge of uneasiness coloring her words. "Have you had a break in the case?"

Mick winced, pushing herself up in bed. She should have been more clear in her message. The last thing she wanted was for Johnelle to get her hopes up unnecessarily.

"Not exactly, Johnelle. I mean, yes, there could be something. What I really need is the other diary you said Sera might have written. The one you said might be missing," Mick explained.

Johnelle sighed. "I could be mistaken about that. I really never had solid proof that another existed, but from reading the one I did have—"

"You have a strong suspicion there may be another one," Mick finished. "Johnelle, it's important that we try and find it."

Johnelle uttered a shuddery sigh on the other end of the line. "I have to tell you that's not something I'm looking forward to. Going through Sera's things again...it just makes me miss her even more."

"I understand," Mick whispered, pressing her lips together and fearing to say more lest she be responsible for making the woman break down in tears. "I can't even begin to imagine what it really feels like to go through something like this. Take your time in deciding and think about what it could mean if we *do* find the other diary."

"You're right," Johnelle replied, drawing a deep breath and releasing it in a refreshing sigh. "I can't stop searching now. We've uncovered too much."

Mick's amber eyes sparkled with emotion for the woman's strength. "I still want you to take your time with this," she cautioned.

"I know, I know," Johnelle promised, her voice sounding more firm. "But if there is another diary, I'll find it. I mean that."

"I'll let you go, then," Mick said, leaning close to the nightstand.

"All right, and thank you, Michaela."

Setting the phone back on its cradle, Mick stared at it for a while. A weary smile touched her mouth, though, when she heard Quest clearing his throat. "I've already heard your upcoming lecture from County," she said, flashing him a knowing glance across her shoulder.

"And it obviously did no good."

"Quest—"

"I'm not going to ask you to stop trying to solve this thing," he promised, folding his arms across his bare chest as he leaned back against the pillows. "I just don't want you so obsessed with it that you forget about everything else."

Mick's smile softened then. She took in the stubborn set to his gorgeous profile before snuggling closer to tease his earlobe with a brush from her lips. "Baby, are you trying to say that you think I'll forget about you?"

Quest rolled his eyes. "You could never forget about me."

"Oooh, confidence," she laughingly replied. "I like it," she murmured against his cheek.

"Hmph."

Leaning away, Mick decided to try a different approach. "Honey, I know how you feel about this, but it's so important that I find more answers. For Johnelle, yes, but especially for Quay. He needs this and I'm really concerned for him."

Quest shook his head. "Yeah, I'm concerned, too. I thought if he at least knew who might be responsible for this it'd be something of a comfort."

Mick grimaced. "Not when that person is running loose and preventing you from going after the woman you love."

"Tykira?" Quest took a guess.

"Tykira," Mick confirmed.

"You know, everybody except Quay wants her on this project for the rail. I'm calling her as soon as I get to the office."

Mick propped her chin on her husband's shoulder. "You think this'll work?"

Quest's heavy brows rose momentarily in a gesture of uncertainty. "My brother won't be too happy, that's for damn sure."

"But you're hoping he'll be too mesmerized by Ty to argue?"

"It's happened before," Quest shared, his gray eyes narrowing mischievously.

"Mmm," Mick returned, snuggling back into the crisp, sandlewood-colored linens, "but that was years ago—before he felt her life was in danger."

"I have to try," Quest whispered, his hand flexing into a fist. "I want him happy. He's been like a zombie since he saw her at the wedding reception," he said, turning to face her. "Besides, it's because of him that I have you," he murmured against her lips as he settled next to her and felt her nails grazing his spine.

The conversation silenced and the moment segued into a sweetly erotic interlude.

A group of five men sat stonefaced and silent, staring at the woman who sat at the head of the table.

Their handsome faces were rarely void of grins or full-blown smiles. As usual, however, their boss had succeeded in catching them off guard.

Tykira kept a calm smile on her face as she sought to judge reactions from her crew chiefs. Their expressions gave away nothing. Well, that wasn't exactly true. Ty could clearly see that they weren't a happy bunch. Folding her arms across the front of her V-neck tan sweater, she waited. Not known for her patience, she cracked a second later.

"Will you guys please say something?" she demanded.

"You're kidding, right?" Frank Royers finally spoke up.

"She better be," Morton Garner added, his blue eyes snapping with frustration.

"You're just a little tired," Samuel Bloch added.

"Tired or going crazy," Kenny Sutton teased.

Gary Charles ran a hand through his curly blond hair. "We haven't taken a break in our project lineup in five years," he argued.

"That's why this is the perfect time," Ty pointed out, her brown eyes sparkling with encouragement. "We've been working nonstop and that's not healthy."

"Making money is always healthy, Ty," Kenny challenged.

"What's really going on here, Ty?" Morton asked, his green eyes narrowing as he studied her more closely.

Finally, Ty let her facade drop. She stared down at her hands and began to fiddle with the thumb ring she always wore. "I guess I'm bored," she admitted at last, peeking beneath the heavy fringe of her lashes to see her crew frowning out of sheer confusion. "Yes, we've made a great name for ourselves, but now I'm ready for a *real* challenge. Frankly, I think I'll scream if another choo-choo to go 'round somebody's house comes our way," she complained, her low voice still resounding in the room.

The guys exchanged closed looks.

"I think you're oversimplifying what we do, love," Samuel chastised quietly.

"I'll say," Gary agreed. "Our projects range, Ty, you know that."

Closing her eyes, Ty relaxed against the black leather chair she occupied. "I know," she conceded, rubbing her arms through the overlong sleeves of the mohair sweater. "I don't know what's wrong with me," she added in a weary voice.

"Maybe Sam's right," Frank was saying, "maybe you're tired. All this on-the-go work, traveling, up all night...maybe it's starting to wear you down."

"Yeah, Ty, maybe you should take a week—or three—off. Go home, visit your mom, get some rest," Kenny suggested.

Tykira leaned back in her chair and considered the suggestion. It would be nice to get away and her mother would be quite surprised to see her prodigal daughter arriving home out of the blue. But then, those unwanted warnings of seeing Quaysar Ramsey—and anything associated with him—resurfaced and she began to silently talk herself out of it.

"Ty?" Morton called. "What do you say?" he prompted.

After another few seconds of silence, Ty graced the men with her most dazzling smile.

"Yeah, Jason?" Sam called when the phone buzzed amidst their laughter.

"Hey guys," the intern greeted, "Ty, I got a Quest Ramsey on the phone for you."

Her laughter vanishing, Ty's heart jumped to her throat. Calls from Seattle from anyone other than her mother or her business associates were about as common as a warm winter in Denver. Immediately, she feared there might be a problem with Bobbie. She was berating herself for not visiting more when she picked up the phone.

"Quest?"

"Hey girl, what's goin' on out there?"

"Is my mother all right?"

Quest hesitated. "Yeah, why wouldn't she be?" he asked finally.

"Dammit, don't scare me like that," she hissed softly, glancing back to see her crew involved in another conversation. "I already feel guilty enough for not seeing her more."

"Honey, I'm sorry. I didn't mean to upset you," Quest said, though laughter still colored his voice. "Maybe we can do something about your not visiting. I have a proposition for you."

Curious now, Ty perched on the edge of the small desk in the conference room. "Continue," she urged.

Quest chuckled. "Afraid I can't. To find out what

it is, I'll need you in Seattle before the end of the week."

Shaking her head, Tykira fiddled with a bouncing curl from her ponytail and turned to fix her crew chiefs with a wide grin. "I think that could be arranged," she told Quest.

"Are you getting anywhere with this stuff?" Quay asked, eyeing the screen of Michaela's laptop with decided skepticism.

"Wake Robinson is a very educated man," Mick reminded her brother-in-law, her eyes focused as she scrolled the screen. "I never know when an idle search might pay off. It's been close to three years—maybe he's snagged a high-level position somewhere. It never hurts to check," she advised.

"I guess it's a good idea when you put it like that," Quay admitted, leaning back in the chair he'd pulled behind the desk where Michaela was working. "I never realized Wake was so resourceful—making his way through college with no help from family."

"Hmph, it can be done. Trust me," Mick confirmed, a rueful smile curving her mouth. "If you are resourceful you can slip under the grid by using cash and disposable cell phones."

"I know," Quay said, knowing his sister-in-law had done the same and probably had a rougher time of it. Leaning forward, he squeezed her knee. "I'm surprised you never thought to check the Net for business ties before," he said after a while.

"Actually, I have," Mick confided, with a quick toss of her unruly curls.

Quay slanted a narrow, dark glance her way. "What's that tone about?"

"I've been at this for weeks. It's almost become a daily ritual for me. A ritual that produces no results," she groaned.

Quay's handsome features were a picture of concern. "Mick, I want you to let go of this."

"What?" she retorted, whirling around to face him.

"I don't want you to keep wasting your time on a dead-end case," he told her, pointing his index finger toward the laptop.

"Quay—"

"I mean it. Hell, you've already discovered more in less than a year than it's taken a league of detectives."

Mick inched closer to him. "That's because I really want the truth."

Quay's eyes narrowed with suspicion. "You think they didn't?" he asked.

"I think it could've been a show to make people think the Ramseys were after the truth. A pretense," she suggested.

Quay leaned back in his chair, not bothering to hide his grim expression. Yeah, he knew all about pretenses.

"I'm dedicated to you and Johnelle," Mick told him, inching closer still to rest her hand on his forearm. "The truth is out there and I'm like a dog after a bone."

Quay grinned, his right dimple flashing adorably. "Wake better watch it."

"Damn right," Mick confirmed, "especially once Johnelle finds that diary."

Quay blinked. "What diary?"

"That's right," Mick sighed, realizing she'd never told him. "In reading Sera's other diary, which was quite short because of her murder, there was no mention of the man she was interested in by name. Johnelle is under the impression that the diary was just a continuation and that there's a previous one out there somewhere."

Quay scanned the spacious second-floor corner office his twin had constructed onto his home. "You think it could shed more light?"

Mick shrugged, her amber gaze as pensive as Quay's. "Did Wake ever say he liked Sera or wanted to get to know her?"

Quay knocked his fist against his knee and reminisced. "If he did, he didn't tell me and he told *me* everything. Or so I thought."

Mick massaged his shoulder, a knowing smile tugging at her mouth. She understood his unease. "Honey, do you think he could've been responsible for the situations with the other girls?" she asked in the tiniest voice.

Quay shook his head, but he was one hundred percent certain of it. "It'd make perfect sense. You know, after this all came out, I started recalling things I never paid any attention to before. Ways he behaved. He'd disappear for days and no one heard from him. I knew he and his mom had it rough, but he never wanted any help. Then, he up and disappears when he realizes you're onto him." Quay looked at Mick and shrugged again. "What other explanation could there be?"

"Well, I'm determined to find out," Mick declared, leaning in to tap her finger to the end of Quay's nose. "We gotta do something to bring the dazzle back to this handsome face," she teased, hoping to make him smile. It didn't work. "Say, why don't you come out and have dinner with me and Quest tonight? How does Marone's sound?"

Quay rolled his eyes and grimaced. "I don't know, Mick." He tried to decline.

"Aw come on, it'll be fun. The three of us haven't been out in a long time. Please?" she cooed, pouring on the begging extra thick. "Please?" she repeated, this time blinking her long lashes in rapid succession.

"Enough," Quay ordered, with a wave of his hand. "I may be late for dinner but I'll definitely be there for dessert."

"Yaay!" Mick playfully responded, sounding every bit the little girl given the green light to play in her mother's makeup. She threw her arms around Quay's neck and kissed his cheek. "Eight o'clock, Marone's," she told him.

"Mmm-hmm," Quay tiredly drawled, tousling Mick's curls before he stood and left the room.

Tykira laughed when she stepped off the elevator and into Quest Ramsey's waiting embrace.

When Quest pulled away, he uttered a light whistle.

"You know, if I weren't a married man, I'd—"

"Still treat me like I'm your little sister," Ty finished for him, joining Quest in laughter as he hugged her again.

Another whistle sounded in the gorgeous penthouse office, this time from Ty. "Wow," she blurted, her doe-shaped eyes growing wider as she studied the exquisite decor and masculine aura of the dwelling. "Mommie always told me this place was somethin' to see," she shared while easing her hands into the side pockets of her wine-colored pleated-hem skirt. "I see business is treating you very well," she complimented with a saucy glance across her shoulder.

Quest threw his hands in the air. "We do all right," he said, intentionally trying to downplay his pride.

Ty caught on. "I'll say, Mister Fortune Five Hundred."

"And you're right there beside me, Miss Only Been In Business Five Years," he challenged.

"Thanks. We do all right," Ty repeated his earlier words with a graceful tip of her head.

Quest waved his hands in the direction of the inner office. "That's why I called you out here," he told her.

Ty folded her arms across the chic, short-waist blazer she sported. "Ah yes, the proposal," she sighed, taking a seat in one of the deep armchairs before the desk. The easy expression that lightened her lovely features faded slowly as she cast several nervous looks around the soft-lit room. "Are we alone?" she asked finally.

"Quay isn't here," Quest softly assured her.

"But he *is* still with the company?"

"He is."

"And I assume your proposal is business related?"

"It is."

"And how does he feel about that?"

Quest lowered his gray stare to the pine desk. "I believe you can guess."

Ty fiddled with the lone curl that dangled outside the high chignon she wore. "Unfortunately, I can," she replied.

"Honey, even my foolish brother can't deny you'd be perfect for this."

"And what exactly is *this?*" Ty asked, crossing her long legs as she became wholly focused on her reason for being there.

"Ramsey was commissioned by a group out of Canada for a ski resort in Banff. A state-of-the-art castle sitting on a mountain was what they wanted," Quest explained.

Ty's dark face brightened with humor. "And I thought I had some outrageous requests."

"It gets more outrageous," Quest promised, tugging on the cuff of his gray checkered shirt. "They want a private rail service to shuttle guests from Calgary to the resort."

Tykira uttered the third whistle of the morning.

"Yeah," Quest confirmed, acknowledging that the project was quite an undertaking.

"People work for decades and never get a chance to work on something like this," she testified. "It *is* impressive, Quest."

"But?" he prompted, sensing her hesitation.

"*But,* the last thing I want to do is bring tension here," she said, fiddling with the sleeves of her blazer as she stood. "Quay is a very important part of this business and if he isn't on board—"

"Hold it," Quest commanded, raising his hand as though he were about to ask a question. "Follow me," he urged, standing behind his desk and leading the way into the display room on the other side of the office.

Inside the room of maps and boxed models of Ramsey projects, the Banff construction sat in the midst. It was indeed a breathtaking creation and was complete with a replica of the desired rail chugging its way around the mountainside.

"Damn you," Ty muttered to Quest. She was thoroughly mesmerized by the sight. Without a doubt, the real thing would be an even more magnificent accomplishment. The opportunity to take on this assignment was one in a million, and seeing the project this way had truly sealed her fate.

"Is that a yes?" Quest asked when he heard her groan.

"When do we start?" she asked, turning to shake hands before they shared another hug.

Tykira trailed her fingers along the collar of her blazer as the elevator from the penthouse office made its descent. She was already at work envisioning possible designs in her mind. True, Tyke Designs had undertaken some major endeavors. Still, she knew they were all preparations for this one. Of course, this particular undertaking would catapult her business to a level even she hadn't dreamed of. Life was good, she thought. Business was great. Now, her only question was what to do about the dark cloud that loomed above it all.

As if on cue, the elevator doors slid open and said "dark cloud" stood before her eyes.

"Quay," she breathed, while silently cursing herself for the sultry, needy undertone clinging to her voice.

Uttering not a word, Quay stepped forward, smoothly urging her back into the elevator. "Did you accept Q's proposal?" he asked, once the doors had closed behind them.

"I did," she confirmed, wincing when she noticed a smirk tilt the corner of his mouth. *A sensuous pleasure-providing mouth. Ty...* she warned herself and cleared her throat as though that would help her to gather her wits. "It's a great opportunity," she managed to say, but found it impossible to maintain eye contact when he stood so close.

"Are you sure you can handle it?" he asked, pretending to be concerned with something on the lapel of his hand-tailored black corduroy sport coat.

Ty's temper flared she was so peeved. "Would you be asking me that if I were a man?"

Suddenly Quay brought his sinful onyx stare to

her face. "If you were a man who'd never done anything like this before—yes."

"Bull."

Quay's smirk deepened.

Tykira took a step closer, dismissing the way his deep-set eyes appraised the scoop neckline of her blazer. "I'll admit my team has never designed a train to go up a Canadian mountainside before, but we've taken on some pretty major assignments. I'm sure you know that."

Quay was solely focused on Ty, but he didn't hear a word she said. He was, however, focused on how good she smelled, how beautiful her face and body were... He could scarcely take his mind off what it'd feel like to have her long legs locked around his back as he pressed her against the elevator car and—

"Quay?" Ty called, her heart doing fanatical somersaults inside her chest. The intensity of his look was too intoxicating and she would've given anything to know what he was thinking.

Breaking his stare, Quay ground his teeth and focused on the short carpeting covering the floor of the car. "Good luck," he whispered, and then moved to press a button which reopened the doors.

Ty tried to utter a response, but the potency of the moment had robbed her of her voice. Taking great care not to brush against any hard, powerful part of his body, she gingerly eased out of the elevator.

She was in her car before she realized she'd been holding her breath.

Chapter 3

Quest, Michaela and Tykira had just finished a fantastic Italian meal at Marone's and were waiting on coffee and biscotti for dessert. Tykira and Michaela became instant friends the moment Quest introduced them. He barely had been able to get a word into the conversation as the two new acquaintances talked nonstop. Of course, Mick was quite intrigued with Tykira's strong interest in what she'd always deemed a male-dominated profession. Likewise, Ty was just as interested in meeting the author whose family-saga biographies graced both her living room coffee table and her office bookshelves.

"You've got to tell me what it was like growing up around Quest," Mick urged, knowing Ty must have had some fascinating stories about her husband as a youth.

"Let's see," Ty sighed, leaning back in the cream leather armchair she occupied. "If you'd like me to put it in one word, that word would have to be 'crazy,'" she said, joining in when Mick burst into laughter.

"Hey," a wounded Quest called from his spot at the table.

"Shh," Mick retorted. "Go on, Ty."

"Well, I say that in the most loving way, Quest."

"Mmm," was the low reply.

Ty shook her head. "Anyway, I didn't have any brothers or sisters, so any child that was near was a welcome and needed playmate. My mom lucked out on snagging not only a job at Ramsey Group but she also snagged the *guesthouse* they owned just a ways from where Quest and Quay lived with their parents."

Mick's light eyes narrowed. "You say guesthouse like it holds special meaning?"

"Honey, guesthouse is not an accurate description of the place. It was incredible, and believe me when I tell you at least fifty guests could've lived comfortably in that place."

"My family believes in treating their employees well. But Ty and her mom were more than that— they were practically family," Quest explained.

Ty smiled. "Thanks, Q. I always felt that way even before my mom actually went to work for Ramsey. My grandparents both worked for Quest's grandparents, then my mom worked for his dad and now *I'm* working for Quest…it's somethin' to wrap your head around," she said, brushing a tendril of hair behind her ear before propping her chin to her fist. "We've grown up together for generations."

Mick was nodding. "So, when the Ramseys moved to Seattle—"

"Oh, Mr. D asked my mom to relocate and she didn't hesitate," Ty said, referring to Damon Ramsey. "It was easy for her to do it since I was on my way to college in the fall. They even constructed a house close to the estate. Aside from us being in Seattle instead of Savannah, not much else changed," Ty said, although a bit of the light had dimmed in her eyes.

Mick noticed. "Sounds like you had a pretty wonderful childhood," she said, hoping to improve the mood.

Ty's expression turned mischievous. "Let's just say I'm glad I didn't have to suffer Quest's shenanigans around the clock. I could escape and go home at the end of the day."

Laughter erupted once more, but quickly silenced when Quest caught sight of his brother across the dining room.

"What the hell…?" he breathed, drawing both Ty and Mick's attention.

Mick shook her head when she saw what caused her husband's outburst. Obviously Quay had decided to join them for dinner. Unfortunately, he didn't come alone.

Ty noticed Quay and his date as well and prayed she'd pull off a convincing job of looking cool and unfazed. Though they were quite a distance from one another, Tykira knew the black, unsettling stare was focused right on her.

"Dammit," Quest muttered, standing when Quay and his companion headed toward the table.

"What's she doing here?" Quay's first words were snarled in his brother's ear once the distance closed between them.

"We invited her to dinner," Quest shared, his usually low voice sounding a bit harsh.

Silence settled then and it was quite uncomfortable. To break the ever-thickening ice, Mick stood and extended her hand in a gesture of welcome to the woman at Quay's side.

"I'm Michaela Ramsey, Quay's sister-in-law," she said with a smile.

The short, voluptuous beauty was completely oblivious to the disconcerting silence at the table. Clearly she was in awe of the devastating dark twins she stood between.

"Oh!" She gave a start, before giggling at herself. "Lisa—Lisa Melvin."

"Lisa, so nice to meet you, and this is Tykira Lowery," Mick introduced, smiling as the two women shook hands.

"Have a seat, Lisa," Quest urged, already pulling out the one vacant chair at the table. "We need to talk," he grated to Quay once Lisa was comfortable.

"What's she doin' here, Q?" Quay demanded to know as the two of them bounded across the golden-lit dining room.

Laughter lilted somewhere in the distance and they both glanced back to find it was Tykira, Mick and Lisa. "Obviously they hit it off," Quest remarked in a sour tone.

Quay rolled his eyes. "Goody," he remarked in an equally sour manner.

Quest stopped in an area just off from the lobby and folded his hand across the sleeve of his brother's medium-blue wool blazer. "What the hell are you doing here with a date, Quay? After two years of actin' like a hermit, you pick *tonight* to go out with a woman?"

"Nobody told me she'd be here!" Quay snapped in a soft, vicious tone, and wrenched his arm from Quest's grasp. "I'll be damned if I play third wheel for the fiftieth time and watch you and Mick play touchy feely all night," he vowed.

Quest uttered a soft, humorless laugh. "Right, Quay, if we'd told you Ty would be here, you'd have probably shown up with two women instead of one," he predicted.

"That hurts, Q," Quay said, pressing one hand to the front of his white open-collar shirt.

"Truth always hurts, Quay."

Quay stopped Quest from turning away by catching the cuff of the tan sport coat he wore. "Q, man, do you really think I'd do that to her?"

"This is a trick question, right?"

Quay released his brother. The spiteful remark sent his infamous temper to simmer. He knew he was merely a few seconds away from crashing a fist into his twin's gut. Instead, he shoved that fist deep into his trouser pocket and pressed the other hand to his chest. "Q, I swear I'd never do that to her."

"You did it before."

"I was a stupid kid," Quay excused, his midnight gaze filled with disbelief. "I thought I was protecting her. You know that. Tonight...I just wouldn't have come at all."

Quest looked away as he gnawed the inside of his jaw. Of course he knew that. He could look at Quay and almost feel the honesty radiating from his words, and yes, he could see that his brother appeared genuinely distressed over what had just happened.

"Hey guys," Tykira said when she breezed over.

Their conversation was effectively stifled. Quay was speechless, enjoying the scent of Ty's perfume that wafted beneath his nostrils.

"I just wanted to say good-night. I'm on my way back to the hotel," she told them.

"What about dessert?" Quest argued, hating that his plan to bring his brother and Ty together that evening had unraveled.

Ty lifted the foil duck she carried. "I asked them for a doggie bag. I can't eat another bite," she sighed. "Anyway," she whispered, leaning close to hug Quest, "good night. I'll talk to you tomorrow," she said. She spoke a hushed good-night to Quay and was about to ease by.

"Tyke, wait," he softly urged, his hand folding across the overlong cuff of her emerald-green off-the-shoulder sweater. "I'm sorry for what happened back there," he apologized once Quest had walked off.

"Sorry?" Ty parroted, appearing confused.

Quay blinked. "Walking in here with a date," he clarified, tilting his head as though he didn't quite believe she'd misunderstood him.

Ty shrugged. "She seems very nice."

"But I shouldn't have come up in here with her on my arm. I'm sorry," he went on.

"You don't owe me any apologies, Quay," she assured him, barely able to hear herself over the ringing in her ears. Clearing her throat, she flashed a pointed look toward his hand smothering her wrist.

Slowly Quay followed the line of her gaze. He winced, stunned by the rush of sensation he felt from the simple touch. Brushing his thumb across the pulse point below her wrist, he finally released her.

Tykira turned and left the restaurant. She ignored her desire to look back, knowing she'd never leave if she did.

"We already ordered dessert," Mick was telling Quay when he returned to the table.

"Thanks, Mick, but, um, I can't stay," he said, fixing his date with a soulful, remorseful stare. "I'm sorry, Lisa, but something's come up," he told her, kneeling next to her chair as he spoke. "Would you be too upset with me if I took you home now?"

Thoroughly charmed by Quay, Lisa was far from upset. "It's perfectly all right. But I'll expect a rain check, and soon," she softly requested.

Quay only nodded, brushing his index finger along the curve of her cheek before he stood. Quest and Mick could only shake their heads at the man's suave demeanor. Clearly living the last two years like a hermit hadn't affected his way with the ladies.

"Michaela, Quest, it was so nice to meet you," Lisa was saying as Quay helped her from her seat.

"Oh, same here," Mick replied, smoothing both hands across her black suede front-split skirt when she stood. She carried on the conversation with Lisa while her husband spoke with his brother.

"Where is she?" Quay asked.

"The Sorenson, room seventeen-thirty," Quest supplied.

Ty literally let her hair down when she returned to her suite at the Sorenson. She exchanged the elegant off-the-shoulder sweater and slacks for more comfortable nighttime apparel of an oversized T-shirt and soft cotton shorts. Settling down in the living area with a bowl of the sinful Italian cookies from Marone's on the coffee table, she started searching the TV listings for a suitable movie. She was about to turn on the impressive plasma screen when the doorbell rang.

Munching on a mouthful of the crunchy cookies, Ty grimaced and reluctantly left the sofa. She helped herself to another bite of the treat and was chewing heartily when she opened the door.

"Quay!" she cried, crumbs spewing past her lips.

Having worn a fierce scowl for the better part of

the evening, Quay couldn't help but laugh at the picture she made. Her hair was deliciously tousled, eyes wider than usual, her incredible legs bared by the Broncos T-shirt and short athletic shorts she sported. A pang of emotion struck someplace deep in his stomach and he admitted that he didn't think he could let her walk away from him this time.

"What—" she paused to swallow a mouthful of cookie "—what are you doing here?"

Instead of a verbal reply, Quay took her arm, closed the door and led her inside the suite.

"I wanted to apologize," he told her once they'd returned to the living area.

Ty rolled her eyes and shuffled past him. "For the second time, Quay, you don't owe me any apologies," she said.

Quay didn't hear her. "Mick and Quest invite me to dinner almost every week. It's sweet and I love 'em for thinking of me," he said, his smirk striking a gorgeous right dimple, "but I spend the better part of the night watching them play the 'newlywed game' at the table, if you know what I mean," he added.

Ty nodded in response to the suggestive remark. "I do," she confirmed, pressing her lips together.

"I had stopped going, but today Mick made a huge deal about my going out with them and how long it's been. Anyway, that's why I showed up there with Lisa tonight," he continued, smoothing a hand across the back of his wavy, closely cut hair. "It was a last-minute thing. I hardly even know her," he finished, then focused his deep onyx eyes on her face as though waiting for her to utter words of forgiveness.

Instead, Ty was moved to ask a question. It was a question her powerful voice of warning demanded she *not* ask. Of course, she didn't listen. "Why are you going to the trouble of telling me all this?"

"I just don't want you to think I'd hurt you that way," came Quay's soft response.

Ty couldn't look at him. "You've done it before," she reminded him. With an edge to her voice she added, "Not that you have to worry about having done that tonight. As much as you seem to love believing that I spend all my time pining for you, I can assure you that isn't the case."

Hearing the words spoken from her lips instead of his brother's didn't fill Quay with anger as they'd done earlier. Instead, he felt sick—sickened by himself and the way he'd treated her all those years ago.

"Listen, Quay, all this is in the past, you know? Let's not rehash it, okay?" Ty decided quickly, shaking her head as if trying to rid her mind of past dramas.

Quay watched her take a seat on the sofa and decided to join her. "Why aren't you staying with your mom?" he asked.

"She's on vacation," Ty shared, taking the TV listings from the coffee table and scanning them again. "Anyway, you know how I hate being alone in that big house," she added.

Quay's chuckle caused his deep-set eyes to crinkle adoringly at the corners. "Yeah, I remember. Damn, how many times did you stay at our house when your mom was working late?"

"Lots," Ty replied, with a flippant shrug. "Besides, your house was just over the hill. If that wasn't a convenient babysitter, I don't know what was," she reminisced, not wanting to remember those happier times. "Anyway, that's why I'm here," she sighed, feeling his unwavering gaze focused her way. He made no further comments and his stare never wavered. Ty began to grit her teeth from agitation. Even the delicious biscotti she'd been snacking on was starting to leave a sour taste in her mouth.

"Did you just come here to apologize again?" she finally asked, losing her battle at patience.

Quay nodded. "I did."

"Well, I'd say you've done that," Ty decided, and stood.

Quay tried to keep his hands away, but couldn't. Slowly, his fingers brushed the lush curve of her thigh left bare where the hem of her shorts ended.

Ty could feel her every nerve ending charting a path toward the most sensitized part of her anatomy. Her lashes fluttered and she lingered close to the touch, savoring the fire igniting there. The simple, barely noticeable caress almost forced a moan to her parted lips.

"Good night, Quay," she told him suddenly. The danger of remaining close for a second longer had become all too real.

Standing then, Quay blocked her way. "Not yet," he cajoled, his fingers trailing just a fraction higher.

Ty closed her eyes. "Don't do this," she urged,

hating the pleading tone of her voice. The soft huskiness of her voice made the simple request sound desire-filled and needy.

Quay lowered his head, his cheek brushing hers gently as his thumb began to graze the swell of her bottom. "I missed you," he whispered next to her temple.

"Mmm, I figured, judging from all the calls I've gotten over the last fifteen years," she said, celebrating the firm tone of her words even as her nipples tensed against the fabric of the jersey. Finally, uttering a quick sound of frustration, she surprised herself and pushed him away. She smiled when the shove she supplied to the unyielding breadth of his chest caused him to stumble a little. Capitalizing on his momentary imbalance, she sauntered around him and headed for the front of the suite.

"Get out," she ordered, flinging open the door.

Quay was slow to comply. Eventually, he straightened and moved forward.

Ty kept her brown gaze averted, knowing he'd never believe she was serious about him leaving if he looked into her eyes. Quay stopped just at the threshold, invading her space once again. He brushed his thumb along the curve of her cheek. The intense dark of his eyes practically smoldered with need. He saw her blink once, twice, three times and knew her feelings were still there—as powerful as his own and surging just below the surface.

"I did miss you, Tyke," he said, and then he was gone.

* * *

After leaving the Sorenson, Quay drove around for a while trying to clear his mind of Tykira Lowery. God, she was still everything he'd ever wanted. Every woman he'd known since had barely scratched the surface of ruling his heart and soul the way she did. And he was confident that it would be easy to coax her into bed.

Flexing his hand around the wheel of the Navigator, he gave a smirk. Coaxing her into bed would be *more* than easy, it would damn well be satiating as hell. But what would it solve besides a hoard of raging male hormones that he barely managed to conceal to a state of semiarousal in her presence, rock hard and throbbing when he was alone with thoughts of her rampaging his senses. No matter how many times he took her, it would do nothing to drive her from his mind, he'd simply want more. No matter how many women he had, it would do nothing to force Tykira from his thoughts. His quest to find *the* woman would never end until he had *her*.

The long, thought-provoking drive eventually led Quay back into the city and to Double Q. The upscale jazz and R&B club/restaurant he'd opened years ago with Quest was growing more successful every month. Seattleites and tourists alike made a point of visiting the elite dwelling. As usual, the place was packed, with even more waiting outside, hoping for an opportunity to party inside.

Quay spoke with the security crew who usually collected in the state-of-the-art surveillance booth just off from the club's entrance. Later, he headed for the bar and took a glass and a bottle of Hennessey to his office nestled far in the back. Preparing to dim Tykira's image from his mind with the power of the dark drink, Quay was already breaking the seal on the bottle as he headed for his desk. It wasn't long before he discovered he wasn't the only one who'd sought refuge in the solitude of the paneled office.

A big grin flashed on Quay's face when he saw his cousin, Yohan. "As I live and breathe, history is being made this night."

"Don't start, man." A slow, canyon-deep voice rose from the depths of the room.

Quay wouldn't be discouraged. "Now, wait a minute, wait a minute. A moment like this calls for recognition. It ain't every day I see the notoriously reclusive, antisocial Yohan Ramsey daring to grace our humble place of biz with his presence."

Yohan couldn't resist his cousin's contagious humor. A smile brightened his unforgettably gorgeous face as he tilted his glass of Jack Daniel's in greeting.

"What's up?" Quay inquired, while shrugging out of the wool blazer he'd worn that evening. "Something's gotta be goin' on to bring you out," he added, knowing that his cousin's preferred choice for an evening escapade was a night of movies at home, listening to music in his library or, if he was feeling especially claustrophobic, high seas fishing.

Yohan's dazzling gold herringbone chain sparkled at his neck when he shrugged. "Just wanted to get out, man."

"Mmm-hmm, right," Quay threw back, rolling the sleeves of his eggshell shirt above his forearms. "We need to mark this one on the calendars," he continued to tease. "What's the date?" he asked, already headed for the huge wall calendar behind his desk.

Yohan massaged his temple. "Quay—"

"Come on, man, what's the date?"

"My anniversary."

Quay tugged on his bottom lip and winced. Closing his eyes, he uttered a muffled groan. Damn, this was his second screwup of the night. He was rollin' now, he thought.

Glass and bottle in hand, he took a seat across from Yohan. "Sorry, man," he apologized, setting his burden onto the coffee table.

"Forget it," Yohan instructed slowly. His very deep-set brown eyes seemed to cloud as they filled with a question. "How long does it take to get over the only woman you every *really* gave a damn about?" he asked finally.

Quay's long brows rose briefly. Of course, he couldn't answer the question, since the reply would have been "never." Somehow he didn't think that would have done his cousin any good. "Why don't you give Melina a call," he suggested instead.

"And say what, man?" Yohan snapped, the mere mention of his estranged wife's name stirring his frustration. "What do I say to her, Quay? I miss you?" he probed, his syrupy slow voice holding minute traces of humor. "Does it work, Quay?" he added. The look on his first cousin's face was answer enough. "Thought so," he threw back, propping his feet against the coffee table. "Hell, Quay, what right do I have to say something like that to her after the way I treated her? I got no rights at all after the way I did her."

"You still love her, man," Quay argued in a soft voice. "You still got a right to love her and that gives you the right to change where things stand between y'all."

Yohan's chuckle could chill a spine as quickly as it could incite the need to laugh. "Is that what you tell yourself about Ty, man?"

Quay shook his head, grinning as he swallowed a bit of his drink. "I've never told myself that about Ty, but I think it's damn time I started."

"My team should be arriving within the next few days and then we'll be able to get firm ideas down," Ty shared during a morning meeting with Quest and the top executives at Ramsey Group. Quay wasn't there, which in Ty's opinion made the gathering far more enjoyable.

"Well, unless anyone has more questions…?" Quest stood and posed the usual request, pausing to give time for anyone to speak. "In that case, meeting adjourned," he said, when the group remained silent. "Ty? Stay as long as you like. I'm heading out," he said.

"Thanks!" she called, already sealing her notes in the chic, black leather portfolio she carried.

Alone in such spectacular surroundings, Ty took

the time to stroll around the fantastic office. She'd never had the opportunity to do so before and was determined to give herself the grand tour. Bobbie had often told her daughter that the office was the inanimate replica of its owners: dark, darkly overpowering and then some. Tykira was studying a painting above the gas fireplace when the elevator doors opened.

"Quest?" Ty called, hearing someone move about in another part of the office.

Quay stilled, having retrieved a stack of mail from his desk. After last night, he figured it was best that he not attend the meeting that morning. He hadn't planned on Ty still being there, but no way was he about to complain. Tossing the mail aside, he followed the sound of her voice.

Tykira left the painting and went to say her good-byes to Quest. Her steps slowed, then drew to a complete halt when she spied the man in the doorway.

It wasn't the olive plaid suit coat he wore over a coordinating gray-black shirt and no tie that made him appear such a force, it was his stance. Quay's demeanor always struck her as silk sheathing a sword. It was as though he were ready for confrontation, always on guard in spite of the easy aura that followed him like mist. Unconsciously, she took a step backward.

"Looks like I missed the meeting," he noted.

Ty glanced down at her black suede boots and

smiled. "I get the feeling you planned it that way," she challenged softly.

Quay nodded, easing one hand inside his trouser pocket. "I didn't know you'd still be here," he told her.

Ty cleared her throat and tucked the portfolio beneath her arm. "That's about to change," she said.

"Tyke," he called, smoothly hindering her progress to the door.

Just as smoothly, Ty evaded his grasp. "What do you want, Quay?"

He didn't mean to allow his desire to flash so quickly but he couldn't help it. She was like a drug he'd only sampled once and was dying to try again. His thoughts were almost totally centered on what it would be like to have her now.

"Incredible," Ty breathed, her lovely doe eyes narrowing with disbelief. "You have no real feelings at all where I'm concerned, do you? It's just like yesterday to you, isn't it? The way you treated me so long ago?"

"Could you accept an apology based on the fact that it *was* so long ago?" he asked quietly, stepping forward, his dark eyes studying her face.

"The things you said at the reception weren't so long ago."

Quay winced as though she'd slapped him. "I can't believe you remember that," he whispered, humor lacing the revelation.

Ty's lashes fluttered. "I remember everything," she said, refusing to break eye contact. By then, Quay was standing right before her. She had dressed for business, stylish and impeccable in the straight, front-split skirt and matching one-button blazer. Still, the familiar feeling of being diminutive and sweetly feminine and powerfully aroused all swirled together.

Quay's piercing eyes studied hers as though he could read her mind and knew how he affected her.

"You remember everything, hmm?" he taunted, simultaneously tugging her close and taking her mouth in a throaty kiss.

Ty couldn't think to resist, only to curl her fingers weakly around the lapels of his jacket.

"Quay," she moaned helplessly when the kiss broke for a split second. She needed him more in this basic way than he could ever know. Moaning again, she began to mimic the motions of his tongue. She thrust hers deeply into his mouth and trembled when he groaned in response.

Their bodies were a perfect fit; always had been. The kiss was like heaven. His hands roamed her body, skirting her hips then traveling upward to mold her torso beneath the snug blazer. He touched her with the patience of a skilled, giving lover who possessed the power to make her swoon, gasp and beg for fulfillment.

This was the man, Ty thought, crying out softly when his big hands cupped her breasts. He was the *only* man she'd ever felt even remotely compelled to give herself to. For her there was no other, she admitted, feeling his fingers slipping inside the front of her blazer to stroke the lush cleavage rising over the top of the lace camisole she wore.

The realization chilled her suddenly. No, for her there had been no other. Sadly, he didn't feel the same. And never had.

Quay could sense a change in the way she responded to his touch. Something had chilled and he knew she was having second thoughts about her participation in their encounter. He released her slowly and with great reluctance. As though it were the most important task, he removed the lipstick smudged at the corner of her mouth with the pad of his thumb.

When he walked away, Ty pressed her hand to her heart as though that would slow its rampant beating. She prayed her legs would support her until she made it to her car.

Chapter 4

Quest's gray stare was focused toward his laptop, which was perched on the coffee table. "Maybe we should have a dinner party," he suggested absently, while trying to concentrate on his game of online chess.

Mick shook her head, her own eyes focused on a computer screen. "Haven't you done enough meddling?" she responded in a voice that held an absent tone similar to her husband's. Seated behind the massive cherrywood desk in his study, she performed her daily Internet scouring for possible leads in the case.

Quest grimaced at his wife's mention of the dinner fiasco earlier that week. "Just bad communication," he excused. "Besides, you should've told Quay not to bring a date when you invited him to be there."

Mick's lips parted and she looked up. "I told him it was just going to be the three of us. How was I supposed to know he'd bring a date? As far as we know, he hasn't been out with anyone in two years," she argued gently, her eyes narrowing mischievously as she focused on the desktop screen. "Anyway, *you're* his twin. You should've psychically tapped in and realized he was going to do something stupid," she pointed out in a naughty tone, and was promptly hit in the side of the head by the pillow Quest threw.

"Her crew's coming in today," he sighed, folding his arms across the Seahawks jersey that emphasized the striking breadth of his biceps and chest. "It might be a nice touch to throw a dinner party for the group. It's sure to be a grueling project and everyone should start off as comfortable as possible."

"Sounds like you've already put a lot of thought into this," Mick noted, still focused on her screen.

Quest shrugged. "We could have it here, make it very relaxed. We could cook all the food."

Mick finally looked toward her husband where he sat before the coffee table. "We? You *and* me? Hmph, you're just full of bad ideas today, aren't you?" she criticized in a teasing voice, leaning back in his chair as she crossed her bare legs. "Do you know what'll happen if we're tied down in a kitchen together?"

Quest blinked, his gray eyes settling on his wife. "Tied down, huh?" he reiterated, appraising the line of her shapely chocolate form, much of which was left bare by the cotton short suit she wore.

Mick shook her head. "Stop, Quest."

"Not unless you come over here," he challenged.

Her lashes fluttered and the familiar stirring someplace unmentionable told Mick that was a challenge she would definitely not back away from. "If you insist," she sighed, leaning close to the PC. "Just let me shut this thing down...can't be," she whispered then, her head tilting just slightly.

Quest's brows drew close. "What?"

Mick was already reaching for the phone and dialing the number to the Savannah Police Department.

Quest left the floor and came to perch his tall frame against the side of his desk.

"Jillian Red, please." Mick was speaking to the person on the other end of the line. She chewed her bottom lip as her nails tapped out a quick tune along the desk.

"Jillian Red."

"Michaela Sellars," Mick said, hoping her name would sound familiar.

There was a slight pause, and then laughter filtered through the receiver. Mick realized she had indeed reached her former contact during her reporting days. Of course, Jill refused to part with any information on herself until Mick shared what had been going on in her own life.

"Girl, what are you doing down South? Was the windy city too much for you?" Mick was asking.

Jillian was laughing. "That is a very long and dramatic story."

"Well, are you still in forensics?"

"Hmph, the powers that be at my *lovely* former precinct didn't seem to appreciate the fact that I was good at my job."

"Uh-oh."

"Mmm, anyway it seemed that I was getting too close to solving my last case and they trumped up some cause to remove me from my team and the force altogether."

"Damn," Mick whispered.

"Story of my life. So now, I'm in charge of the cold cases for the SPD," Jill explained. "It was the only position I could find that was even *remotely* stimulating," she confided.

"So are you working on anything now?" Mick asked.

"Just finishing up reports on a case I just closed."

"Congratulations."

"Please! I should be congratulating *you*," Jill said, referring to the self-history Mick gave earlier in their conversation. "Successful author *and* happily married woman? Sounds like life is good."

"Oh, it is," Mick confirmed softly, tugging on Quest's hand as she spoke, "but even a happily married woman could use a helping hand every now and again."

"Do tell."

"Are we still close enough to exchange professional favors?"

"Of course. What'cha got?"

Mick smiled and scooted closer to the desk. "Actually, it's something I think *you* have—a cold case."

Jill laughed shortly. "Yeah, I've got tons of those."

"Well, if you can crack this one, I'll bet the SPD would create a forensics position for you."

Jill was silent a few moments as she processed the possibility. "Well, don't keep me in suspense, girl, what's the case?" she demanded eventually.

Mick looked up at Quest. "It's a who, Jill. Sera Black."

Ty stretched, luxuriating in the security of crisp, petal-pink cotton sheets and thick quilts. Her eyes opened to thin doe-shaped slits as though she were uncertain what she might see. The sight of her mother, caused a smile to widen on her face.

"Good morning," she called. Seeing her mom brought a rush of warmth to her entire body.

Roberta "Bobbie" Lowery looked up from setting out breakfast in the small alcove in the bedroom. Seeing her daughter nestled in bed brought laughter lilting to the air. Tykira looked every bit the little girl and Bobbie realized then how much she'd truly missed having her home.

"Good morning, baby. Did you sleep well?" Bobbie asked.

Ty stretched again, curving her fingers around the edge of the pillowcases. "I slept very well. Even though my room doesn't look the same," she added slyly.

Bobbie's head, full of thick natural tresses, bounced merrily when she laughed. "Honey, please, don't scold an old lady for trying to spice things up."

"Isn't your life spicy enough, Miss Jet-setter?" Ty teased.

"You're right," Bobbie sighed. "I'm hardly ever here. Those Ramseys got me flying from one part of the world to another."

Ty threw back her covers. "*Anyway*. You love it."

Bobbie's look was pure cunning. "Sure I do, but they might stop sending me on these all-expense-paid things if they knew that."

The room filled with laughter.

"Now, I've got coffee and Danish," Bobbie announced, clasping her hands together as she looked down at the cozy table. "We'll finish the rest of our breakfast downstairs," she decided.

"Mmm, coffee and Danish…conversation food," Ty guessed, having left the bed to stroll toward the alcove. Obviously her mother was in the mood to talk—and she had a pretty good idea about the subject. Taking a seat on one of the cushioned cream armchairs, she leaned forward and smelled the pot of coffee. "Mmm…hazelnut. You want to discuss Quay," she surmised coolly.

"Stop being a smart aleck," Bobbie ordered, with a roll of her eyes as she took a seat. "I know you've seen him."

"I've seen him," Ty replied, her easy expression changing a bit.

"And?"

Ty helped herself to coffee. "He's gorgeous."

Bobbie rolled her eyes again. "I know *that*. What else?"

Ty kept her gaze averted. "What do you mean, what else?"

"Have you talked?"

Ty eased a stray lock behind her ear. "About what? We haven't seen each other in fifteen years." *Well, actually more like two years,* she added silently, recalling the reception.

"Exactly," Bobbie said.

Groaning, Ty focused on choosing one of the heavenly Danish pastries from the white, floral-print China plate. "Mommy, have you forgotten the way things ended between us? Sorry, but that's not a conversation I want to replay or a memory I want to relive."

Bobbie broke a cinnamon Danish in half. "You're still in love with him?" she asked knowingly.

Ty wouldn't deny it. "What good will it do?" she asked, tucking her long legs beneath her on the chair. "Nothing would change. Quay isn't as outwardly mean to me as he used to be, but there's still a distance. I feel it in myself. I feel it in him, too. It's as though he wants to be warm, but then…I don't know," she shook her head and concentrated on adding sugar and cream to the hazelnut blend. "Something always changes and that's when I pull away and start to remember. Then I get angry with myself for—"

Bobbie leaned over to pat her daughter's hand. "I understand," she assured her. "Do you think there's a chance that he's trying to make things right between the two of you?"

Ty frowned at her mother's question. "I don't know why."

"Oh boy," Bobbie muttered, with a shake of her head. "So beautiful and successful, but still so dense at times."

"Mommy!"

"Is it possible that he still loves you as much as you love him?"

"After fifteen years?"

Bobbie waved her hand. "What's so crazy about that? Your feelings haven't changed."

"But this is Quay we're talking about," Ty reminded her mother, her brown eyes firm with agitation. "And if he loved me, then why would he have treated me so coldly all those years ago?"

"Honey, you two were babies and Quay was just young and stupid. But now, maybe he sees what he's missed and he doesn't want to lose you again. Personally, I've wanted to kick his butt for the way things ended between the two of you. But a part of me believes there was more to that entire mess than he ever let on to you or to anyone else."

Ty shook her head, refusing to let her spirits soar over Bobbie's assessment. "I just can't see that," she said, blowing at the surface of the coffee in her mug before helping herself to a taste.

"Have you ever just come right out and asked him why he treated you that way?" Bobbie challenged.

Ty's lips parted, but she couldn't respond. She wanted to tell her mother that she already knew why.

Unfortunately, telling Bobbie that Quaysar Ramsey had gotten what he wanted from her and was done with her or that she'd given him her virginity and he'd given her his ass to kiss didn't seem like prime info to be shared in a mother-daughter talk.

Thankfully, Bobbie felt that she'd given her daughter enough to think about and decided to leave her be. "Get showered and come on down for the rest of your breakfast," she said.

Tykira stepped outside the express elevator and into the Ramsey twins' dark, posh penthouse office. She cleared her throat purposefully, hoping one of them—preferably Quest—would appear and they could get the meeting underway. In spite of her dramas with Quay, she had become very involved and inspired by the monumental project.

Ty received her wish when Quest stepped from the elevator car a short while later.

"Where's your crew?" he asked once they'd finished hugging.

Ty set her black portfolio onto the credenza. "They called from the plane to tell me they were just landing," she explained, tossing her thick locks across her shoulders as she secured another larger portfolio beneath her arm.

"Sounds good," Quest said, nodding as a curious light brightened his gray eyes. "So does the project have your creative juices flowing yet?" he asked, folding his arms across the oatmeal heather polo shirt he sported.

"Does it?" Ty cried, patting the portfolio under her arm. "Ideas started flowing as soon as I walked out of this office after our first meeting."

Quest's sleek brows rose. "Impressive."

"Let me show you," Ty urged, waving Quest toward his desk. The portfolio housed several preliminary sketches, which she spread out on the huge polished surface of the desk. "I'm not sure if the group prefers something more old-world style or a more modern look for the rail," she explained, motioning toward the sketches as she spoke. "Maybe they'd like a mix of both styles to show in the finished design."

Quest tugged the long sleeves of his shirt above his forearms. "This is somethin'," he marveled, his gaze intent as he studied the work.

Tykira and Quest were still reviewing the drawings when Quay arrived in the main office.

"Man, you gotta see this. Ty's got some really good sketches for the rail here," Quest raved, glancing at his brother from across his shoulder.

Quay remained silent, unbuttoning the raspberry suit coat he wore over a jet-black shirt. Instead of joining the twosome at the desk, he took a seat at the back of the room and watched from afar.

Almost a week had passed since he and Ty had kissed in that very room. Since that time, his well-known and well-feared temper had begun a slow simmer. Quaysar Ramsey was not a man known for his patience—especially when it came to wooing a woman. He'd never had to be patient when the women came tumbling at his feet. A kiss, a soft-spoken compliment or glance usually did the trick. Many times it had taken far less. As usual, Ty had him stumped. Clearly, she didn't trust him—that was for sure. He knew if he could win that back, she would be his.

Of course, something as precious as winning back trust didn't happen overnight. Therein lay his problem. His thoughts were progressively filled with images of them together so long ago. They were just kids then and still that encounter was the standard by which he'd judged all others. There had been no equal, and he knew the only other encounter that could compete would be with her.

Ty tried to keep her mind on Quest and what he was saying, but all she could do was curse herself for wearing her most feminine suit for the meeting. The beige lightweight tweed skirt suit didn't do a damn thing but call attention to her thighs thanks to the high split in the back of the skirt. Not only could she feel Quay's ebony stare on her, she could see it each time she cast a casual glance across her shoulder to see if he'd left the room. No surprise, he hadn't gone anywhere. He just sat there and continued to roam her body with so much familiarity, as though he'd become her lover that morning instead of fifteen years ago.

"These are terrific, Ty, just terrific. I can't get over it."

Quest's excitement over the sketches roused Ty's amusement. "I can't wait to see your reaction when you see the real thing," she teased.

"Quay, man, you should see this!" Quest once again beckoned his brother. He'd already turned back to scour the sketches further and didn't hear his twin's reply.

"I'm sure it's as good as it looks," he'd said. His eyes were unwavering and trained on Ty, who heard every word.

Quest was shaking his head. "You can really make somethin' that looks like this?" he marveled.

Ty laughed aloud. "I can't believe you're so taken by this when Ramsey creates such phenomenal stuff."

"Mmm-hmm, but our stuff is stationary. Not moving from place to place," Quest pointed out.

"Haven't you traveled by train before?" Ty asked, folding her arms over the tailored mocha shirt with its cuffed sleeves.

"I haven't been on a train since me and Quay went to visit our grandparents in Savannah during our sophomore years in college. Remember, Quay?" he called.

"I remember," came Quay's slow response, but he was more interested in Ty's reaction. Quest mentioning their grandparents' estate had definitely affected her. Yes, she was remembering, too.

The silence caught Quest's attention and he tuned into the heaviness of the moment. Clearing his throat, he backed away from the desk and rubbed his hands together.

"I better go check on the refreshments for your crew before they arrive," he said, before making his way out of the office.

Ty turned and leaned against the desk, her head bowed. Quay finally relinquished his seat in the back of the office and came to take his place next to her.

"Remember how much fun we used to have at my grandparents' place?" he asked.

Ty let out a deep breath and nodded. "Almost everything fantastic that happened to me when I was young happened there," she admitted.

Quay inched closer, his shoulder brushing hers. "Remember that week?"

Ty wouldn't pretend to misunderstand. "I remember it. I could never forget it."

Quay had been aching to touch her since he'd seen her there in the office. Now, he gave in to his desire and trailed his fingers across the line of her cheek.

Ty leaned into the touch only briefly, before she bristled and moved away. "I'm sure many girls remember that place," she said, tossing her head back.

Quay winced, the barb causing a flash of hurt to appear in his dark eyes. "I never took other girls there," he denied in the softest tone.

"Hmph, unless they were virgins, right?" she threw back, not wanting to believe the place had been as special for him as it had been for her.

Quay eased away from the desk and moved to stand before her. "You're the only one I ever took there," he swore, staring directly into her eyes. "You're the *only* one I ever wanted to take there."

Tykira tilted her head back, hoping to prevent un-

expected tears from spilling. Quay's eyes locked in
on the thick glossy fullness of her hair tumbling
down her back.

"You only took me there once," she quietly reminded him.

He cupped both hands around her neck and
propped his thumbs beneath her chin. "*That* was the
biggest mistake I ever made."

"Quay…" she breathed, her words ending on a
moan when he stepped between her legs.

His hands lowered to her thighs, cupping them
gently as his lips trailed the curve of her jaw. The kiss
was slow and unhurried and every bit Quaysar Ramsey being something he never was—the giver instead
of the taker. He taunted her mouth with slow lunges
that were light and teasing. His hands massaged the
firmness of her thighs, loving the feel of strength
mixed with the female allure he felt there. How he
wanted to show this woman that his very last intention was to purposely hurt her. Protecting her was
what drove him, loving her was almost driving him
mad. She was everything to him and, in trying to do
the best thing, he'd wound up losing the best thing
he'd ever known.

Ty, on the other hand, was intent on being the
taker, taking everything Quay had to give. She
yearned for him to touch her with demand but he was
gentle, and that was just as sweet. He caressed her,
skirting her breasts, brushing the backs of his massive hands across nipples that strained against her
blouse. When his fingers disappeared beneath her

skirt, she cried out softly in pleasure. When he simply plied the satiny inner walls of her thighs with his touch and went no further, she arched and rubbed against him in hopes of encouraging him to move on.

Quay ended the kiss, pressing a soft peck to the corner of her mouth. Not wanting the moment to end, she reflexively tightened her thighs about his waist. Quay only nuzzled the soft flesh below her ear and smoothed his hand across her hip to persuade her to release him. Knowing it wouldn't be long before Quest returned, he wanted to give Ty—and himself, for that matter—the chance to catch her breath and become presentable.

It was almost impossible for Ty to accomplish. Everything shook uncontrollably. Finally, she braced her hands against the edge of the desk and took deep gulps of air until the feeling had passed.

Quay had returned to his seat just as the elevator doors opened and Quest returned with Tykira's crew in tow. The not-too-nice side of Quaysar's demeanor had subsided to a happy place during his time alone with Ty. Now, it was returning at a boil this time as he watched her run to greet the group of men. Of course, they each had to hug, kiss and hold her close, far longer than he thought was necessary.

Since Quest had already met the guys, Ty turned to make the introductions to Quay. Only Quest caught on to his brother's mood when Quay simply waved from his place at the rear of the office. Closing his eyes for a brief prayer, Quest only asked that they make it through the meeting.

But Quay was in no mood for a meeting. He was more interested in surveying Ty with her group of design engineers. He was especially interested in the one who had been holding her hand since he'd stepped into the office. Quay didn't like it and had no problems admitting that. He disliked it so much, in fact, that he went over to Ty and intruded on the cozy conversation she was holding with Samuel Bloch.

"Why don't we get this meeting started," he suggested, keeping his hand at the small of Ty's back while escorting her from Sam's side.

The group took their places in the conference room, also nestled within the penthouse office. Ty remained cool and poised while spreading the railcar drawings on the table, but inside her mind was racing. She was more than curious about Quay's mood—she was downright dumbfounded. She could barely go five seconds without him touching her someplace and his unsettling dark eyes practically bored holes through Sam. Thankfully, only she and Quest noticed.

"All right," she began, clearing her throat as she leaned close to the table. "Quest's already taken a look at the preliminary sketches I faxed to you guys last week. He seems pleased," she noted, smiling when Quest nodded. "Still, these are only preliminary mock-ups, we've got a long way to go."

Her words prompted hearty discussion then. Obviously, everyone was stimulated by the demands of the project. Even Quay let go of some of his mood-iness to offer his own suggestions regarding the rail. In truth, he found it incredible that Tykira had such a flare for the gritty business of railcar design. However, he knew if he were to compliment her on her expertise, she was likely to think he was patronizing her. The discussion was definitely productive, but Ty couldn't deny how pleased she was when Quest brought the meeting to a close.

"My wife, Michaela, and I will be having a dinner party to get you all acquainted with the rest of our executive team," he was saying. "We'll be in touch with the particulars, and if there's nothing else pressing right now—" he paused for last-minute comments "—we'll meet back here in the morning," he finished.

"Tyke? Would you stay?" Quay asked in a voice only she could hear.

Suspicious, she flashed him a guarded look but offered no comment. The rest of the guys were preparing to leave and she had no desire to be alone with Quay then. Still, she managed a nod in response to his request. The last thing she needed was to draw attention to what was going on between the two of them.

"Guys, I'm staying with my mom now, but we'll meet later at the hotel, all right?"

"Sounds good," Morton Garner called in response to Ty's question.

"We'll meet you in the hotel lounge," Gary suggested.

"I'll just ask for you at the front desk," Ty added.

The group said their goodbyes and Quest offered to show them out. The instant Ty heard the elevator doors slide shut behind them, she bolted from the chair she occupied next to Quay.

"What are you doing?" she demanded to know.

"What's goin' on with you and Sam?" he asked, appearing unfazed by her anger.

"Sam?" Ty parroted, rolling her eyes when Quay only stared in response. "He's the head of my crew."

"And what else?"

"He's also my friend."

"And what else?"

"It's none of your business," she interjected, her lovely face contorted into a harsh glare.

Quay focused on the silver pen he manipulated with his fingers. "Have you slept with him?"

"What if I have?" Ty challenged, folding her arms across her chest. Her glare lost a bit of its intensity when Quay snapped the pen in half. Dismissing her unease, she stepped closer to the conference table. "What if I sleep with a different one of them every night? It's none of your damned business!" she raged, sick of being sweet and civil. "You had your chance. I gave you everything and you used it to make me feel lower than dirt," she whispered then, turning away lest he see an emotion other than anger fill her eyes. "I doubt you've got any real interest in this side of the project, Quay, so why don't you just stay away from it?" she suggested, her back still toward him. "Otherwise, I might be entitled to inflict a little pain of my own." She turned to face him then.

"I think I've damned well earned that right, don't you?" she inquired softly, and then swiped her belongings into her portfolio and left the room, cursing that there was no door for her to slam.

"Small piece of advice, Quay. Our waitress is liable to spit in both our salads if you're more rude to her than you've already been."

Quay slanted his twin a black glare before tossing back what remained of his drink.

"Just a little advice," Quest said, his hazy gray stare still focused on his menu.

"You're enjoying this, aren't you?"

"Damn right."

Obviously stunned by his twin's quick, honest response, Quay slammed his glass to the table.

Quest's left-dimpled grin deepened as he used his napkin to wipe away the remnants of the brown liquor that sloshed from his brother's glass. "You deserve exactly what you got and more. I'm surprised Ty waited this long to tell you to go to hell."

Quay's fist slammed to the table in response.

Quest finally ceased his taunts and leaned back in his chair. "You wanna talk about it?" he asked.

Quay shrugged. "Why should I when you're right?"

"Give it time, Quay," Quest urged, tossing his napkin to his twin's side of the table. "You hurt her. Bad."

"There were reasons."

"That's right. There were reasons. Maybe it's time to live in the present, hmm?"

"And that would serve what purpose?" Quay queried in his cockiest tone.

Quest rolled his eyes and focused on his menu again. "Tykira's like family. The purpose it would serve is you'd be acting civil toward someone we've known all our lives."

Still brooding, Quay lost a bit of his agitation and considered his brother's words. As soon as his mood began to mellow, he felt his frustration began to mount again. His midnight stare narrowed with murderous intensity toward a couple who'd just entered the dining room.

"What are you having? Quay?" Quest called, finally glancing up. Seeing the expression his twin wore took Quest's mind totally off eating. "Quay?" he called again, sitting a bit straighter in his seat. He knew the look well. Any second now, Quay would be pounding some poor fool's face in. Quickly, Quest glanced around to determine what had gotten his twin's jock in a bunch. Then he saw Tykira, beautiful and glowing, laughing at something Sam Bloch had just whispered in her ear.

"Son of a bitch," Quaysar muttered, his hand too weak to even clench a fist.

"Quay…" Quest called in warning, already poised to stop his brother from storming across the restaurant.

Quay, however, didn't have the strength to stand, let alone *storm* anywhere. A cloud had settled across his brain, rendering him dizzy and completely helpless. His entire body felt weak. His heart was in his throat.

"What's she doing with him?" he whispered.

Quest opened his mouth, then closed it, trying to put his opinion into the most calming terms. "They're business partners, man. I'm sure it's just something to do with the rail," he explained, knowing he probably wouldn't have believed that either.

"I need to get out of here," Quay decided, tugging fiercely at the banded collar of his shirt.

Quest was already reaching for his wallet. "You need me to go with you?"

Quay grinned. "Hell, yeah, if you expect me to leave without makin' a fool of myself."

Tossing a few bills to the table, Quest stood and, keeping a firm grip on his brother's upper arm, escorted him from the dining room. Of course, the twins never went anywhere unnoticed. Such was the case that day, as every woman who caught sight of them helped herself to an intense study of their heavenly good looks and powerful, lean muscular frames. Not surprisingly, Ty saw them as they walked by.

Quest jerked Quay to a halt and nodded before closing the distance between himself and Ty.

"Hey, love," Quest whispered, drawing her into a hug.

"Quest," Ty greeted, her lashes fluttering as she tried to keep her eyes off Quay.

"You two got time to join us?" Sam asked while shaking hands with Quest.

"Nah, we gotta run, but thanks," Quest said, winking at Ty when he noticed her relieved expression. Then, catching Quay's arm, he and his brother left the restaurant.

Chapter 5

"You know, we've got food here, too."

Ty smiled at Mick's query and responded with a mock toast of her glass. "This is insurance," she shared.

"Against?" Mick probed.

"Your brother-in-law."

Amused now, Mick leaned next to the bar. "What's going on? And is it the reason why he's yet to show up to our little gathering to get your crew acquainted with Ramsey?" she asked, unmasked laughter coloring her words.

Ty studied a curl dangling from her high ponytail. "You're a smart lady," she said, tossing away the curled lock.

"Will you give me a few details?" Mick asked, smoothing one hand across her form-fitting ecru trousers as she took a seat on one of the barstools.

Ty helped herself to another sip of her second martini. "Please, Mick, I know Quest has told you the story of my pathetic involvement with his twin."

"I know it didn't work out," Mick said, taking the glass from Ty and placing it on the bar. "I know you were hurt," she added.

"Hmph, hurt," Ty retorted, and then rolled her eyes toward Mick. "And I should get over it, right?"

"Ty—"

"Hell, you're right. It's been, what? Fourteen, fifteen years? Oh, Mick, every day I tell myself the same thing. Do you know what it's like to pine for a man as long as I have and know you probably *never* cross his mind?"

"Oh, sweetie," Mick whispered, pulling Ty into a hug. "Honey, have you ever wondered if Quay acted the way he did for a reason?"

Ty sighed, and then pulled away. "You sound like my mother," she said, shaking her head. "I guess the man is just damn good at charming his way into the heart of a woman."

"Seriously, Ty, do you think there could be more going on here than you're aware of?"

"Then why wouldn't he just tell me what it is and stop playing these games? It's gone on long enough, don't you think?"

Mick agreed and hated that she couldn't do more to reassure Tykira. Her amber eyes lit up, however, when she looked across the room. "Maybe he'll tell you if you just ask him," she said. Ty noticed Mick's expression and followed the line of her gaze. Seeing Quay sent her heart jerking ferociously beneath the toffee-colored off-the-shoulder blouse she wore. When Mick patted her hand and walked away, Ty finished the last of her martini. She was accepting her next refill when she felt him standing behind her.

"I'm sorry," he said, standing there with his hands pushed into his chestnut trousers as he waited for her response.

Tykira tapped her nails along the sides of the glass she held before turning around to face him. "Do you realize you've already apologized to me twice and I still have no idea what's really going on?"

Quay bowed his head, his brows rising briefly as he acknowledged the truth in the statement. "I guess I'm jealous," he confided finally.

Ty couldn't have appeared more shocked. "Jealous? What could you possibly be jealous of?" she asked in an incredulous tone. It never occurred to her to ask *why* he was jealous when he'd pretty much shunned any meaningful involvement between them.

Quay hiked his thumb across his shoulder. "Let's try how close you are to your crew, for starters."

"Yes, we're close, but that's all," Ty swore.

"What about Sam?" Quay softly probed.

Ty rolled her eyes. "He wanted it to be more, but I didn't."

Choosing not to show how pleased he was by her words, Quay simply nodded once.

Laughter fluttered past Ty's lips then as she observed him. "You're something else to be jealous of five men," she said, folding her arms across her chest. "What's five men compared to what? Two, three hundred women?" she noted.

Quay shook his head, allowing his unease to show. "I guess it would take about that many to drive you out of my head."

"Why would you want to drive *me* from your head?" she demanded to know. The simply spoken comment affected her more sharply than she realized. "What did I do to make you want me out of your life, Quay? I mean, I know I was a virgin the last time we slept together, but was I *that* pathetic in the sack?"

Quay's darkly handsome features tightened with the regret he felt. "You're wrong," he whispered, moving a step closer. "There were reasons why—"

"What reasons?" she cried, frustrated that after all this time he still couldn't just come right out and tell her why he'd treated her so coldly. Setting an unfeeling mask in place, she fixed him with a level glare. "I can understand you not wanting to be my man, Quay," she began, "but after all the years we've known each other, how close we'd become long before sex ever entered the picture, I can't believe you won't even be friend enough to tell me the truth." She waited, hoping her words might penetrate the wall around the explanation she truly felt he wanted to give. Unfortunately, he refused to give in and, rather than beg, she moved off the barstool and walked away.

* * *

Ty's head was bent in concentration as she sketched a quick design that had come to her while she'd picked at her soup and salad. She was practically oblivious to all else around her, but managed to look up in time to thank the waiter when he freshened her tea.

"Everything all right, ma'am?" The waiter asked, having heard her gasp soon after she'd thanked him.

Ty swallowed and managed a nod. "Yes, yes, thank you," she whispered.

The waiter nodded and moved on as Ty set aside her pad. She'd glimpsed Quay across the room and was momentarily stunned by his presence. Common sense won out after a while and she decided it was too much of a coincidence, him just *happening* to be there. Leaning back in her chair, she beckoned him to her table with a steady gaze. She tilted her head back slightly when he stood and began to head in her direction. Ty's gaze faltered only a few times as she observed the blatant stares of want that followed him. A man with that sort of power over women is a man with no interest—or need—for *one* woman.

Keep things cold, Ty. Get your job done and get the hell out of here, she told herself.

"May I?"

Ty offered no reply, but gathered her things when he sat down.

"I only wanted to apologize again," he said, smiling softly when she fixed him with a confused look. "For dinner," he clarified, suddenly appearing uneasy. "And the cocktail party the other night. I'd like to take you out and make up for it."

"Make up?" Ty whispered, clearly surprised by his nerve after all that had happened between them. "No," she refused.

Leaning close, Quay blinked when he noticed her flinch. "Are you afraid of me, Tykira?"

"No, never. It's just easier to keep our…whatever this is between us…it's easier to keep it going," she decided, while reaching for her portfolio. "Let's not try to go back and make up for anything. I don't think I have the energy," she almost laughed.

"Good afternoon, Mr. Ramsey. Will you be dining with the lady?"

Ty stood before Quay could answer the waiter, who'd returned to the table. "The lady is done," she said, adding before she walked away, "but Mr. Ramsey will be taking care of the check."

Ty cursed and mumbled below her breath as she stomped back to her rented Jeep Cherokee. She'd just thrown her portfolio and tote bag into the back seat, when her arm was caught, stifling any further movement.

"Don't walk away from me, Ty," Quay said while making her face him.

Thoroughly amused, Tykira's full laughter lilted into the air. "Walk away from *you?* You're one to talk, Quay Ramsey, and get your damn hands off me!" she demanded, slapping at the hold he had around her arm.

Quay did as he was told, yet stepped closer to invade more of her personal space. "I can't handle this," he confessed, his nose outlining the curve of her jaw as he inhaled her scent. "I can't think straight having you around...and that's dangerous, Tyke."

Ty allowed herself to lean into his frame, desperate to indulge in a moment of the warmth residing between them. "Then please do as I asked, Quay," she managed after a while. "Distance yourself from the project and—"

"No. I can't do that," he snapped, shaking his head.

"You mean you won't," Ty argued, forcing herself to resist crying out in response to his mouth trailing the line of her neck. She tried to move, but he held her against the side of the Cherokee. "You don't want me, Quay—not really. It's just your guilt...and hormones talking."

The arrogant dimpled smirk appeared. "And I suppose *your* hormones are on vacation?" he taunted, unbuttoning the champagne suede blazer that outlined her bosom adoringly.

"Pig," Ty huffed, shoving both her hands against his chest. "What is it with you? You think you're so fantastic no woman could get over you once you've had her?"

Quay kept his head bowed. His dark eyes were on his hand where it cupped a plump breast. "I don't know about that, Tyke," he said, studying the mounds, partially exposed where he'd undone her blazer. "But I do know *you* haven't gotten over me," he said, applying a proprietary squeeze to her cleavage.

Ty slapped him so hard her palm burned. Yet it was nothing compared to the satisfaction that coursed through her. Her glee was short-lived, though, as he caught both her wrists and held them together at the small of her back.

"Can't you just let me do my job and go?" she urged, trying a softer approach. Her doe-like gaze was wide and pleading. "Quay? Can't you at least do that for me? At least that?"

Jerking her forward, Quay smothered her mouth beneath his. Tiny whimpers fluttered within Tykira's throat at the sensation of his tongue plundering hers, rotating and thrusting deep. Ty felt her eyes sting with tears as she kissed him back. In spite of it all, he could still reduce her to a pool of nothing with just a kiss.

Quay pulled back, then treated himself to just one more taste of her lips. *No, I can't,* he wanted to say. *Letting you go is something I don't think I can ever do again.* Then he pressed his forehead to hers and walked away.

Tyke Designs began their project with all the gusto they were known for. The railcars would be a dazzling sight, everyone was sure. Ty had been working round the clock not only to ensure the team would meet the deadline, but also in hopes of avoiding Quay and of keeping her every waking thought off him.

She was passing the receptionist's desk one day

when a thought came to mind and she began to sketch right there. About five minutes passed before she was interrupted.

"Hey guys," she said to the three Ramsey Group VPs. She recognized them as easily as everyone else she'd come to know during the last five weeks. "What's up?" she slowly inquired, setting her pad aside as she observed the strained, yet polite expressions each man wore.

Steve Owens glanced at his colleagues when they nudged him forward. "Tykira, we, um, we hate to come to you with this…"

"What?" Ty prompted, shaking her head when no explanation was forthcoming.

Bailey Gardner chuckled nervously. "Sorry, Tykira, we're just trying to be tactful."

"I don't think there is a *tactful* approach here, guys," Matthew Clark shared before focusing his brown eyes on Ty. "This is about Quay," he told her.

Her gaze wavered briefly, but she nodded. "Go on."

"Well, Ty…we know the two of you were close. *Are* close," Bailey corrected.

"We need you to talk to him," Steve urged.

"If you would," Matthew added.

Ty fidgeted with the hem of the red cardigan she wore over a matching knit top. "Talk to him about what?" she asked in a hesitant manner.

The three men exchanged quick glances. "His temper," Matthew finally spoke up.

Ty, who'd always known Quay to be teasing and

laid-back, fixed the VPs with suspicious looks. "I know Quay can be a bit...difficult...but certainly he's not *that* bad..."

"We're glad you've been lucky enough not to see that side of him," Steve said.

"Well, what's he upset about?" Ty asked, clasping her hands in her lap while she sat perched on the edge of the desk. "Is he upset about the project?"

"We think it might be about something going on between the two of you," Bailey guessed.

"A disagreement," Matthew suggested.

Ty smiled and waved off the perception. "I haven't even spoken to Quay in a couple of weeks."

Again, the three men exchanged glances.

"We know, Ty. It's pretty obvious the two of you are going out of your way to ignore each other," Bailey said.

"He may be willing to try to ignore *you*, but the rest of *us* haven't been so fortunate."

Ty almost laughed at Matthew's words, but noticed how solemn he appeared. "Well, what's he done?" she asked.

"When Quay's on a rampage, he's like a monster. Quest's the only one who can calm him down."

"Probably 'cause they've both got tempers that can leave grown men quaking in their boots," Steve offered and stepped closer to Ty. "Quay will come down on you—"

"Hard," Barely interjected.

"For next to nothing," Steve went on. "Leave the office too early, feel his wrath. Spend too much time chatting at the water cooler, feel his wrath. Disagree with him—"

"You don't wanna know," Matthew interrupted his coworker.

"Guys, I'm sure he'll cool off soon," Ty tried to reassure them.

They responded with a bellow of laughter. "He sure will!" Barry cried.

"And Heaven help the poor soul who's in the way when he does!"

"He's about ready to snap, Ty. Would you just talk to him, please?" Matthew implored.

Knowing nothing but a promise would soothe Bailey, Steve and Matthew's worries, Tykira nodded. When they'd thanked her and walked off, she closed her eyes and groaned.

"If only I weren't about to leave for the day," she whispered once the guys were out of earshot. Ignoring the voice calling her a coward, she collected her things and left the building.

That evening, Michaela had ordered Ty to take a break and they headed off for a girl's night out. Double Q was set to be their final destination.

The two beauties received tons of nods and even more attention when they entered the club. Of course, everyone knew Mick was strictly off-limits. Ty, on the other hand, appeared to be fair game. Still, she had loads of fun talking and laughing with the scores of interested men who approached her. Unfortunately, every man Ty met wasn't so gentlemanly, as she discovered when one of her dance partners got a little too friendly.

"So, what will it take for me to get you to wrap those gorgeous legs around my back tonight?" the twenty-something overconfident male whispered against Ty's ear.

Prying his fingers out of the back pockets of her snug-fitting jeans, she fixed him with a knowing look. "It wouldn't take anything at all," she told him, humor filtering her brown eyes. "You've got about a snowball's chance in hell of that ever happening."

The remark left a sting that caused momentary surprise to flicker in the young man's eyes. Not about to be bested, he eased his arm about her waist, pulling her close again. "Feel that? Impressive, huh?" he asked, curving his fingers into the small of her back to settle her more snugly against his aroused state.

Not terribly shocked, but very peeved, Ty easily removed his hands from her back. "At this very moment it's more endangered than impressive," she breathed, rolling her eyes as she prepared to turn away.

Sadly, the determined younger man wasn't willing to let his partner go so easily. His grip tightened in an attempt to force her compliance. The push Ty applied to his chest sent him stumbling and his confidence wavered when a few people laughed.

"Bitch," he hissed, reaching for her again.

This time, Tykira curled her fingers into the front pockets of his jeans and tugged him close. "Your prized possession down there is about to be bruised and terribly battered in about the time it'll take me to raise my knee. Then you'll see how powerful these gorgeous legs are."

Swallowing noticeably, the man raised his hands and decided not to tangle another minute with the statuesque beauty. He decided to back off a little too late. A split second after he raised his hands, he was jerked away.

It was a moment or so before Ty realized that it was Quay who had pounced upon her dance partner. Then, watching the crowd part as he dragged the man away, she recalled what the vice presidents had told her about his temper.

"He'll kill him," she breathed, pushing her hair away from her face as she rushed after them. "Quay!" she called, her voice effectively drowned by the thick crowd. Ty had to fight her way through the mass of bodies that had gathered to witness the vicious scene.

There was Quay, beating the man to a bloody mess. Ty could hear Quay tell his victim to leave her alone and asking why he'd been bothering her in the first place. Of course, every word Quay uttered was followed by a vicious blow to some area of the man's face. Security intervened at last and it almost took Quay's entire staff to pull him off the battered club hopper.

"Call an ambulance!" someone ordered.

"Ty!"

"Mick!"

"What happened?!" Mick shouted over the melee.

Ty ran a shaking hand through her tangled hair. "Quay almost beat some guy to death."

"What?!"

"Mick, I can't talk right now. I gotta find Quay!" Ty called, already sprinting in the direction she'd seen security take their boss.

Mick was about to follow when she felt her cell phone vibrate in the breast pocket of her denim jacket. "Yeah?" she greeted hastily.

"Mick? What's goin' on there?"

"Jill?" Mick called, hearing Jillian Red's voice come in faintly beneath the noise from the crowd.

"Can you talk?" Jill bellowed.

"Gimme a sec," Mick advised, hurrying back inside the nearly deserted club to take solace in a quiet corridor. "All right, what's up?"

Jill laughed. "First, let me thank you for dropping such a hot pot of a case in my lap. Her death could've been solved years ago and I damn well intend to do so now."

"Have you been able to turn up anything?" Mick asked, taking a seat on one of the royal-blue velvet settees lining the hallway.

"Let's just be thankful that the SPD of old hadn't tossed their old case files—dusty and cobweb-riddled as they were," Jill teased. "There's definitely evidence missing," she added, her tone firming.

Mick nodded, having already told Jill about the Ramseys' shady dealings regarding the case. "Will this missing evidence put more of a stump in the investigation?"

"Well," Jill sighed, sounding strangely optimistic, "that's what's strange. Even though actual physical evidence gathered at the scene was missing, the files were still there—*detailed* files."

Mick leaned back against the wall. "*How* detailed?" she asked.

"An autopsy was performed, as were the crime-scene workups."

The beginnings of a frown furrowed Mick's brow. "What are you saying?"

"According to this file, samples were taken from Sera Black's body. There was saliva from the breasts, skin under her nails and semen from the vagina as well as trace amounts on her clothing."

"Who did it belong to?" Mick asked, straightening on the settee.

Jill sighed. "The investigation reached a halt after that. There's no record of the samples ever making it to the lab for analysis."

"Damn," Mick grumbled.

"Obviously there's still more investigating to do."

"You said it."

"At least we know we've got a definite case to solve."

"What's your next move?" Mick wanted to know.

"I'm going to speak with the county M.E. He's retired and word is he's in poor health. It may be a long shot to even *try* to get a face-to-face with him, but I'm gonna try like hell," Jill vowed.

"Thanks, girl," Mick breathed, her lashes fluttering. "I feel a lot more positive about this thing knowing you're on it."

"We're gonna bring down whoever's responsible for this. Look, I'll let you know what happens with the medical examiner, all right?"

"Sounds good, Jill. Talk to you soon," Mick said, pressing the phone to her forehead when the connection ended.

Tykira was approaching Quaysar's upstairs office when the double doors opened and several men hurried out. She could hear Quay roaring for them to leave.

"You may want to give him a minute, miss," one of the security guard advised.

"*Several* minutes," another stressed.

Ty nodded, waiting for the group of men to disappear around the corner before she turned back to the doors. It was now or never, she realized. Besides, she couldn't handle knowing Quay was lashing out at people because of her. Taking a deep breath, she trailed her fingers along the silver door lever before pushing against it and stepping inside.

The office was dim and mellow, of course, but Ty spotted him easily. He leaned against the wall next to the tall windows overlooking the downtown area.

"How's your hand?" she softly inquired, taking short, awkward steps closer.

"Fine," he replied just as softly.

"Quay, what were you thinking?" she asked,

folding her arms across the apricot-colored crop jacket she sported. "I could've handled that," she informed him.

Quay smiled, triggering his right dimple. "I know you could handle it. I was watching you the whole time."

Something about the admission made her breath catch in her throat. "Then what were you thinking?" she managed to ask again.

"He shouldn't have been touching you," Quay blurted, smoothing a hand across the cobalt blue shirt that hung outside his sagging jeans.

Ty bowed her head and smiled. "People touch when they dance, Quay."

"And you shouldn't have been dancing with him."

"Why not?" she couldn't help but ask.

"Mick wasn't dancing," was Quay's response as he pushed away from the wall.

Ty shook her head. "That's because nobody dared to ask her."

Quay grinned. "Yeah, I taught Q well," he boasted playfully. "He staked his claim and everybody knows she's his."

Ty rolled her eyes. "Well, the same doesn't go for me. Men will always approach a woman in a club," she reasoned, hooking her thumb through the empty belt loops on her jeans.

Quay's smoldering black stare raked her body with unmasked possessiveness. "That's because they don't know you're mine," he said in a low voice, sounding as though he hadn't meant to speak the words aloud.

"Are you serious?" Ty whispered, tilting her head as she stepped closer to the desk he stood behind.

Quay shrugged, appearing as though what he'd said was no great revelation.

"I'm yours," Ty parroted, her eyes narrowed in suspicion as she rounded the maple desk. "I suppose that's why you've treated me so coldly all this time? Or why you're not being straight with me right now?" she challenged.

"I don't want to do this now, Ty," he groaned, and began to massage the back of his neck.

"Oh, to hell with you!" Ty snapped, bringing her palms down hard upon the surface of his desk. "I'm sick of all this damn beating around the bush. You're attacking and snapping at everyone who gets in your way. Is it all related, Quay?"

"Related to what, Ty?" he bellowed finally.

Ty stood unruffled. "Related to what's happening between us," she clarified softly.

"Nothing's happening between us," Quay countered as he massaged his nose. "You've kept that clear," he added in a muffled tone.

"Please, Quay," Ty spat, throwing up her hand as she whirled away from the desk. "Since I came back you've run hot and cold and I know there's something you're keeping from me. I've always felt it," she quietly admitted, smoothing her hands over her arms to ward off a sudden chill. "What is it?" she asked, facing him again. "Are you trying to spare my feelings? You never cared about them before. Hurting me, humiliating me seemed to be your preferred activities."

At last, Quay slammed his hand against the window. The thick glass vibrated in response. "Damn, Ty, hurting you was never the intention!"

"Then what?!"

"Hell, I was trying to protect you!"

The response stopped Ty cold. "Protect me?" she whispered, heading toward him when he turned away. "From what?"

"Tyke, I—"

"No. Not this time. You tell me everything," she demanded, standing boldly before him. Again, Quay made a move to retreat and she took hold of the hand he'd bruised during the fight. He winced when she added a bit more pressure. "How painful do you want it?" she asked.

"Don't make me go into this, Ty," he pleaded, setting his other hand into the pocket of his caramel trousers. "It's irrelevant, anyway," he added.

Ty smiled, her doe eyes narrowing. "Good, then you should have no problem telling me about it."

Quay started to turn away once more. "All right, all right," he conceded, when her grip tightened on his injured hand. "You know I always had a lot of girls around me, right?" he asked, seeing the guarded look that flashed on Ty's face. "You also know that none of those relationships ever worked out."

Ty nodded again, not liking the drawn look beginning to cloud his features.

"A lot of that was my fault." Quay sighed, taking a seat on the corner of his desk. "But Tyke, a lot of it had nothing to do with me."

"What are you saying?" she asked, not altogether certain she wanted to know.

"Things began to happen to 'em. I always felt there was more to it, like it was more than just coincidence."

"What *things?*" Ty probed.

"Out of the clear blue, they'd move away, their parents' jobs would be phased out and they'd relocate or some just up and disappeared." Quay shook his head then. "It was all so smooth no one really questioned it or felt there was anything strange about it. I began to think I was cursed with girls or something." He laughed, then sobered the instant his eyes met Tykira's. "I never had a relationship with Sera. We almost kissed once before you and I were ever intimate. After she died, I knew somehow it was all connected to me and there was no way in hell I'd let the same thing happen to you."

Ty closed her eyes. "Are you trying to tell me that my life is in danger?" she asked finally.

Quay folded his arms across his broad chest. "I didn't say anything because I didn't want to upset you but I knew as long as we were together...if Wake ever knew—"

"Wake? *Wake Robinson?*"

Quay nodded. "We think he killed Sera, and I think if he knew how I really felt about you, you wouldn't be safe."

Ty felt the pressure in her chest rising as though she couldn't breathe. It wasn't a disturbing feeling, it was exciting, expectant, and slowly she proceeded with her next question. "Quay, were you only pretending back then? Were you only pretending not to care about me?"

Before he could tell her yes—yes, he'd been pretending and doing a piss-poor job of it since his feelings for her were written all over his face. Before he could tell her he loved her, that it had always been her, the desk phone buzzed. Ty shook her head and turned away when he answered.

"Hey, Mick," Quay greeted.

"Are you all right? What was that fight about? Is Ty up there with you?"

Quay chuckled over his sister-in-law's rambling. "I'm fine. The fight was my fault—I lost my temper, and yes, she's right here."

"Good. Listen, something's come up and I need you to give Ty a ride home. I have to leave right now. You don't mind, do you?" Mick finished, devilment in her every word.

Quay heard it clearly. "I know what you're up to and you're no good at it," he said, hearing Mick suck her teeth over the line.

"I don't care how good I am at it. I just want it to work," she admitted.

Quay ran a hand over his face and groaned.

"Listen, this might put a smile on your face. I got some very interesting news from my contact in Savannah."

"Talk to me," Quay urged, turning to study Ty as she stared out the window. Mick rehashed her conversation with Jillian Red, and what she told Quay removed any chance of him telling Ty how he really felt. Wake Robinson had killed Sera like she was nothing and he was still out there somewhere. Wake also knew that his supposed old friend was helping to fuel an investigation that could put him behind bars. Now, while confessing all to Tyke had been right and necessary, Quay knew it was dangerous. Wake was dangerous, and so was he, for that matter. Wake Robinson, however, was willing to kill and clearly he didn't care who. Quay did. He cared— loved—who very much. He couldn't risk it. He couldn't risk having Wake turn up and catch him off guard when he least expected it.

His onyx stare narrowed as he watched her. Oh yes, his guard would most definitely be way down. He'd have nothing but Tykira Lowery on his mind and in his bed. Hell, he'd probably never come into the office and there it would be. Yet another beautiful life for Wake to snuff out and fulfill whatever sickness motivated him.

He tuned in to the sound of Mick yelling for him to confirm he'd give Ty a ride and not have one of his men do it. They needed to talk, she said.

"I'll take her home myself, Mick, I promise. I'll call you. Bye."

"Well, Quay?" Ty was saying the instant she saw him set the black cordless phone to the desk and stand. "Will you answer me? Were you only pretending not to care?"

"It's late," Quay was saying while he rummaged around in his desk drawer until he found what he was looking for. "We can finish this on the way. Mick asked me to take you home."

Ty hated being alone in her mother's too huge house, but she was glad Bobbie wasn't there when she and Quay arrived. He was gentleman enough to see her inside and check around for her, but Ty wasn't about to let him off that easy.

She was determined to receive an answer to her question and called herself a fool for wanting to hear his response so desperately. She tried to dismiss the flutter of her heart, which anticipated hearing what she most wanted—that she wasn't just another toss for him, and what had happened was as special for him as it was for her.

"Well, Quay?"

Massaging his heart through his shirt, Quay bowed his head. "Ty, what the hell do you want to hear?" he sighed.

"The truth!" she cried, not caring anymore that her emotions were bared to his gaze. Her heart jerked when he turned and fixed her with an incredible smile and look. *That* look...that look which had the power to make a woman physically ache with the expectation of a night in his bed.

In spite of the look, it took Ty a full thirty seconds to realize an answer to her question would not be forthcoming. She heard herself moan before his arm encircled her waist, before his head lowered, before his incredible mouth melded with hers. Answers be damned, she decided silently. *This* was what she wanted, to be satisfied by this man and only this man. The low, needy moan ended on a gasp that Quay used to his total advantage. Thrusting hot and deep, he thoroughly ravaged her mouth, making love to her with slow wet lunges of his tongue, reducing her instantly to a mass of sensitivity.

Feeling her melt against him, Quay knew she was his for the taking and taking was exactly what he intended to do. He lost every coherent thought in his head except one: after that night, she'd want nothing more to do with him, he'd see to that.

The kissing continued, growing lustier every moment. Tykira was lost and shameless in expressing how desperately she wanted him. Her fingers sought every exposed area of his molasses skin not covered by his clothes. Breaking the kiss, she let her lips glide across the powerful cords in his neck. Her fingers stroked the back of his head, her nails savoring the feel of his soft, close-cut hair. Wantonly, she rubbed herself across his muscular athletic form, telling him with every movement how deeply she desired him.

For Quay, it was sheer heaven; the feel of her touching every inch of him in perfect alignment. No other woman came close to feeling the way she did in his arms. Taking a fistful of her thick tresses, he kissed her again. Tortured, helpless moans passed his lips every time he stroked the sweetness of her mouth and felt her suckle his tongue in response. Overcome by a need so powerful, his manhood swelled to the point that his pants felt uncomfortably snug.

"Tell me to leave," he whispered, breaking the kiss to graze her jaw with his perfect teeth.

"I can't," she sobbed, her fingers curled so tightly into the crisp fabric of his shirt she could have ripped it apart. The next thing she felt was him lifting her and walking in the direction of the spiral stairway.

"Where?" he asked against her cheek as he kissed her there.

Softly, Ty gave directions. Her hand cupped his jaw as she arched deeper into the embrace. Quay shouldered open the door to her bedroom and the shiver that brushed her body had nothing to do with the temperature of the house. Ty was so affected, so in tune to his every move she trembled as much from arousal as she did from anticipation.

Quay's magnificent features were sharp and focused. He'd imagined her bared to his gaze since he'd seen her two years ago. He prayed nothing would rob him of the treat now. Dexterous fingers unfastened the button fly of her jeans. He bowed his head to kiss her as his hand disappeared below the lacy waistband of her panties.

Ty felt her legs give when his middle finger curled inside her. The pleasure—so desired and so missed—left her gasping his name and shifting her leg to take more of the thrusting caress. Her reaction to him was satisfying, yes, but there was more. He drew pleasure from *her* pleasure. His intense dark gaze followed her every reaction to his touch. Smoothly, he added his index finger to the caress and Ty clung to him as her forehead fell upon his shoulder.

"Quay, please," she begged in the tiniest voice.

"Tell me," he urged, moaning at the flood of moisture he felt against his fingers.

"I need more, please," she unashamedly admitted.

His hormones thundered at her breathless confession and he continued to undress her. The buttons on her crop jacket gave way beneath his manipulations and he shuddered her name at the realization that she wore absolutely nothing else. He weighed her generous breasts, worshipping their firmness and the way they molded to his palm.

Ty's lashes fluttered when he practically ripped the shirt from her back and hoisted her against his powerful form. She felt faint, scarcely able to breathe she was so overwhelmed by the strength and smell of him. Unable to verbally communicate her need, her fingers went to the fastening of his trousers.

Quay stopped her, gripping her bottom that was barely concealed within her jeans. Lowering her to the center of the queen-size bed, he quickly relieved her of what remained of her clothing. Her breathing was rapid and he was mesmerized by the beauty of her dark body. How many times over the years had he awoken hard and aroused—his dreams filled with her? Dreams of them making love had both tortured and exhilarated him.

"Quay…" Ty groaned, wanting total fulfillment.

"Shh…" he breathed against her thighs. "You'll have it," he promised, knowing what she yearned for.

Ty relaxed upon the coverings which were now a

tangled mess thanks to her uncontrollable writhing. Quay held her in place then, his tongue plundering her femininity with all the devastation he'd used when he'd treated her mouth to the same pleasure. Ty couldn't remain still beneath the long, sultry lunges, but had no choice as he kept her hips firmly upon the bed. Eventually, he allowed her to arch herself closer to his mouth, his grip tightening in warning when she moved too much. He wanted complete control and Ty had no strength to refuse him anything.

He alternated, nuzzling his nose within the fragrant walls of her womanhood and exploring the treasure inside. Ty raked her fingers across his head and cried out into the air. Quay carried her to the edge and past it. He ravaged her senses, whispering words of desire, providing the dual caress of seductive strokes to her sex as his fingers rubbed and squeezed her ever-firming nipples. He was relentless in his task of pleasuring her and only gave her respite when she climaxed and trembled to no end.

He gave her but a moment to absorb the deep sensations, removing his clothes as he watched her twist and arch upon the bed in the throes of her orgasm. He took her before she came down off the high. He took one of the condoms he'd pulled from his desk at the club and put protection in place. Mercilessly, he drove the stunning length of his desire deep. Ty was caught between twin sensations of pleasure and pain. He gave her no time to grow accustomed to his size and her body began to tremble anew as she felt

her inner walls being stretched relentlessly. Quay
didn't want to feel anything accept the part of her
he'd craved far more than he realized. He pulled her
hands away from his body and pressed them high
above her head. With her legs wrapped high around
his back, he penetrated deep; branding her with his
touch.

Ty flexed her fingers above his grip and drove
herself against him in a wild display of desperation.
Suddenly, Quay broke contact and pulled her up. He
turned her, bringing her back against his chest and
burying his gorgeous face in her hair. Ty turned her
head and kissed him, jerking in delight when she felt
him take her from behind. He held her hips firmly,
pummeling her body with lunges that made her want
to melt into the covers. Slowly, he began to chant
her name. The chanting grew more forceful and rapid
as he reached his own peak of fulfillment. They remained locked in position for the longest time. Ty felt
him heaving against her back as he struggled to catch
his breath. Her hair was a tousled mass that covered
her face when she bowed her head. Slowly, he eased
her down to lie on her stomach. He covered her completely and she fell asleep surrounded by him.

Quay helped himself to the beautiful woman who
slept so soundly next to him. His fingers played a
tune across the flat plane of her stomach. He toyed
with one nipple while his lips nibbled on the other.
His intention was to awaken Ty and he took as much
pleasure in the task as he did regret.

In her gorgeous eyes that night, he'd seen love and devotion in addition to desire and lust. He wanted everything Ty had to give, but knew if his wants cost Ty her life, everything inside him would shut down.

Ty woke and stretched, smiling lazily in happiness and the stirrings of arousal. She tugged at Quay's shoulders, snuggling beneath him when he rose to cover her body. Outlining the curve of his mouth with her thumbnail, she leaned close to kiss him lustily.

Say it! a voice demanded inside Quay's head and he reluctantly acknowledged the magic was at its end. Breaking the kiss, he looked down at her and smiled. "Must've taken quite a few men for you to be as good as you are now," he said.

Tykira's easy smile faded, a furrow beginning to appear upon her forehead.

"You were so lost in the bedroom back in the day," he continued, stroking her from hip to thigh. "Don't get me wrong—you were still a good hit," he clarified, a slow smirk sharpening his features. "These legs make a brotha hard at first sight," he added cockily.

Ty could feel her heart sinking to her stomach as she listened. His words, so casually hurtful, were things no woman should have to hear after making love to the man she loved.

Quay's heart wasn't sinking, it was breaking. Still, he continued, deciding he'd rather have her hate him than to have anything tragic befall her. He could tell his plan was producing the desired effect.

The warmth in her enchanting doe eyes turned cold with disgust in the wake of every word he uttered.

Tiring of the idle caresses he lavished on her thighs, Quay leaned down for something more substantial. His mouth brushed the smattering of curls shadowing her womanhood. A heavy slap fell across his cheek just then.

"What are you saying?" she whispered, watching him as though he were a stranger. "What are you doing?" she snarled, this time shoving her hands against his chest.

"What?" Quay returned, feigning confusion.

Ty began to shake her head.

"Hey," Quay prompted, brushing his knuckles across her jaw, "I'm complimenting you here, girl."

"Compliment?" she could hardly pronounce the word.

"Oh, I get it," he said, nodding slowly as his dark eyes feasted on her breasts, spilling over the sheet she clutched to her chest. "You prefer action to all this talk."

"Stop," Ty ordered when he whipped away the sheet to cover her with his body. "Quay, don't," she tried.

He didn't hear her and was far more interested in cupping her breasts as he buried his face in the valley between. His tongue began to stoke the lush curves surrounding his face. His fingers began a dual assault on her nipples.

Ty wanted to argue, but could manage only one last faint "stop." She felt his powerful body shake when he chuckled and settled himself more snugly

against her. Slowly, the fight drained and she was left
with an empty feeling. That is, until sadness rushed
in. She lay there feeling his mouth glide across her
body and cursing herself for reacting to his touch
when he'd succeeded yet again in reducing her to
less than nothing.

Quay's long, sleek brows were drawn together in
complete concentration as he suckled madly at one
nipple. He glanced up in time to see a tear slide from
the corner of her eye.

"What the hell's the matter?" he quietly demanded, bracing his weight on his elbow as he
looked down at her.

"Just go," she asked in a lifeless voice.

"Tyke—"

"Just go, I don't want to see you again," she said.

Again, the dimple-triggering smirk appeared.
"That's gonna be impossible," he said, kissing her
collarbone, then the swell of her breast, "since you
work for me," he explained.

"I work for Quest," she corrected, stiffening beneath him.

Quay finished his teasing nips at her body. "You
work for Ramsey. Don't forget it."

Ty rolled her eyes. "Get out."

Grinning broadly, he nodded, agreeing to the
order. He lavished one last, wet kiss to her jaw, neck
and breasts before leaving the bed.

From the corner of her eye, Ty saw that he was
donning his clothes. She looked away when he cast

a glance at her from across his shoulder. She waited for him to close the bedroom behind himself, and then allowed herself to cry.

Outside the door, Quay slammed his fist to his palm and blinked away his own tears.

Chapter 6

"Did she say why?" Quest was asking Samuel Bloch two mornings later when the group met at Ramsey for its weekly meeting.

Sam's light blue eyes reflected concern. "She said something came up and she just couldn't be here. She sounded tired, though. *Too* tired. I couldn't get her to tell me there was anything wrong."

Quest grunted in response, stroking his jaw as he listened. He, too, was growing concerned.

"Anyway," Sam sighed, glancing back at his crew, "it's been two days so we're gonna head out to her mom's place and check on her after the meeting."

"Good idea. Maybe you'll get more out of her with a face-to-face meeting," Quest figured.

Sam shrugged. "I hope so," he said doubtfully.

"Listen, keep me posted," Quest urged, slapping the side of Sam's arm before nodding toward the breakfast buffet across the room. "You better get over there before they clean it out," he teased.

Sam grinned, then shook hands with Quest and went to rejoin his team.

Quest turned and found his twin standing a short distance away. "What did you do?" he asked, knowing his brother had been listening in on the conversation with Sam.

Quay didn't bother to play dumb. "I did what had to be done."

"What the hell does that mean?" Quest snapped. "Dammit, Q, don't you ever talk to your wife about this case?"

Squeezing his eyes shut tight, Quest hissed an obscenity. "Not this damn case again. I'm sick of hearing about that thing," he muttered, massaging the bridge of his nose.

"You and me both," Quay muttered, folding his arms across the gray plaid wool suit coat he wore. "It's keeping me away from Ty even after all these years, so how the hell do you think I feel?"

"It doesn't have to be like that," Quest argued softly.

Quay waved his hand. "As long as that fool's runnin' loose this is exactly how it has to be."

Quest stepped closer to his twin. "I can't believe you of all people, runnin' scared."

"Listen, Q, the only thing that kept Ty safe before was that Wake didn't know I cared about her that way."

"I'll buy that," Quest said, pushing his hands inside the deep pockets of his brown tweed trousers, "but how do you explain Sera? You never made a play for her."

Quay cleared his throat while slanting his brother a coy look. "Actually, she approached me quite a few times. I told Wake about it."

"You told Wake, but not me?" Quest complained, fixing his twin with a wounded look.

Quay couldn't resist smiling at his brother's jealousy and shook his head. "Nothin' personal, man. It just wasn't somethin' I wanted the family to know. Especially when Sera and De were such good friends," he explained, referring to their cousin Dena. "Hell, Uncle Houston walked in and almost caught us at their house once. I was this close to kissing her," Quay shared, positioning his index finger above his thumb. "That made me think, Q. I knew if things didn't work out between us—which they probably wouldn't—I'd be in for it from the family since she and De were so close. Besides, Sera was a sweet girl. She deserved better than me. So does Tyke."

"There's just one problem," Quest began, bringing one hand to his brother's shoulder. "Ty loves you, fool."

"Hell, Q, I love her!" Quay swore in a vicious whisper, his black eyes sparkling with emotion. "I love her with everything in me, but that doesn't matter here since two days ago I did everything I could think of to make her hate me." He took a deep breath, his gaze faltering. "I'm positive I succeeded," he said finally.

"Quay—"

"Let's get this meeting started, all right? I'm ready to get the hell out of here," he grumbled and left his brother staring after him.

"Just a few moments, Ms. Red. He's very weak," the petite Asian nurse warned as she escorted Jill to Raymond Patillo's room in the stately Savannah mansion he called home.

"I'll be very brief," Jill promised, just as the nurse opened the door to the bedroom suite.

Raymond Patillo had served a lengthy term as county medical examiner in Savannah. Jill could still detect the passion in the man's voice when they'd spoken over the telephone. It was obvious he still missed his former position very much.

"Ms. Red!" a large, intimidating man greeted in a surprisingly warm and friendly voice. From his appearance, she could never tell how great a toll the lung cancer had taken on his well-being.

"Mr. Patillo, thank you so much for agreeing to meet with me," Jill said, reaching out to shake hands. "This is about the Sera Black case," she announced, recalling the nurse's instructions to be brief.

The glow in Patillo's eyes dimmed a little. "Sera Black," he recited. "She seemed to have been a lovely girl. At the scene, I remember thinking that she was a smart young woman," he smiled in spite of himself. "I don't know how I knew that, I just had the feeling there was great potential there."

"You were the C.M.E. when the accident occurred," Jill confirmed, taking a seat in the armchair near the bed.

"It was no *accident*," Patillo corrected quickly, his warm expression fading completely. "That poor girl was murdered and those people covered it up."

"The Ramseys?" Jill probed, crossing her trouser-clad legs. "Did you have any thoughts on who may've been responsible?" she asked.

Patillo's smile was sour. "Someone in that family covered this up and I'm still certain that someone in that family was responsible. But not the boys," he added.

Jill's eyes narrowed. "Why?"

Patillo rested his head back against one of the oversized pillows behind him. "I met them, spoke with them at length. Every boy at that party was tested and questioned. They were confident, very sure of their appeal and their capabilities. But murder…I never saw them as murderers." He shrugged. "A hunch, Ms. Red. Do you know what I mean?"

"I do," Jill nodded, understanding those feelings quite well. "I've been a cop for many years. Forensics was my specialty," she shared.

Patillo nodded slowly, his dark eyes gleaming with deeper respect for her. Suddenly the look grew troubled as his cough reasserted itself.

"I'm sorry," Jill whispered, already standing from the chair. Patillo grabbed her hand before she could move too far.

"Check the body," he said, amidst the roaring cough.

Jill's brows drew close. "Mr. Patillo? The body, I don't—"

"The evidence will be there!" he insisted, struggling to smother his coughing. "Please, I'm an old man and I've prayed the girl's killer would be brought to justice. I took the Ramseys' payoff...first there was a phone call from someone saying he represented certain parties in the family. A few days later, a wad of cash was mailed to my office. I let the child's killer get away scot-free. This is an injustice that must be corrected."

Jill moved close to pat his back when the coughs once again roared to life.

"I'm sorry, Ms. Red, I'll have to ask you to leave now." Patillo's nurse hurried in issuing the order.

Jill offered no argument. "Thank you both," she said, patting Raymond Patillo's hand before she moved back from the bed. She returned his wave and nodded at the determination in his eyes.

Construction on the railcar for Holtz Enterprises began one month after Tykira and her crew finished the designs—a record. Everyone raved. The people at Holtz had already approved the final layouts via satellite conferencing. Still, vowing the importance of communication, the group decided to meet Ramsey's team about a month and a half into construction.

The group of forty-something businessmen arrived one afternoon and toured the site. Then, it was off to Gabron's for an authentic French meal.

During the entire affair, Louie Danoue, CEO of Holtz, kept Tykira close to his side. He raved as boldly over her creativity as he did her beauty.

Quay had no intention of attending the lunch, but knew he'd draw Quest's wrath if he tried to back out. Additionally, once he'd discovered Ty would be in attendance, he knew he wouldn't want to be any-place else. A clear wall had been raised between them. While a wall of some form had always existed where they were concerned, this one was different. Ty was openly cordial and responsive to everyone in attendance accept Quay. She treated him as though he weren't even there—directing her questions to Quest or any other member of Ramsey. Her mood was so cool, no one except Quest really noticed how she'd tuned out his twin.

Still, Quay didn't mind letting his agitation show over Louie Danoue's interest in Ty. She certainly wouldn't notice, neither would any member of her crew. The five men appeared just as agitated by Danoue's adoration as Quay.

Lunch was a lively affair. The executives of Holtz had the opportunity to review color layouts of the project firsthand. They also enjoyed a video presen-tation via laptop featuring a computer animated replica of the finished railcar making its way up the majestic mountainside to the towering sky village in Banff.

"Exquisite!" Louie Danoue raved while his col-leagues clapped. "We are greatly anticipating your arrival at the resort. It will be quite the celebration," he boasted, and then favored Ty with a meaningful smile. "I look forward to showing you the village firsthand," he told her.

"It sounds wonderful," Ty replied, gracing Louie with a dazzling smile before she cleared her throat. "If you gentlemen would excuse me for a moment," she said then, pushing her chair away from the table and smiling as every man stood.

Quay's onyx stare followed her until she left the dining room. That stare narrowed with murderous intent when Louie Danoue excused himself from the table less than a minute later.

Tykira and Louie had only been gone a short time. It was far too long for Quay, who went after them without so much as a word to anyone who remained at the table.

Ty was on her way back then, having stopped to speak with one of her mother's church friends. She was inspecting the chic pinstriped skirt she wore and literally slammed right into Quay on her way back to the main dining room.

"Sorry," she whispered, before realizing who she'd run into. Rolling her eyes, she went to move past him but felt his hand on her forearm.

"What?" she snapped, keeping her eyes on his hand.

Quay's features were drawn into a closed mask. "Just wanted to see where you and Lou disappeared to," he admitted.

"Why?" her voice rasped as she looked up at him finally.

Quay shrugged. "You've been gone awhile."

Ty had the strongest urge to connect the tip of her spike-heeled black leather boot to his shin. "What are you getting at?" she inquired knowingly.

His hand flexed around her forearm. "I think you know," he said, tugging her just a bit closer.

"What do you want?"

Quay's smile was devilment personified in response to her question. "I think I already got it," he sighed, appraising her breasts, outlined so prominently against the black turtleneck she wore.

The slap she sent to his cheek turned the heads of the servers who whisked along the corridor. Quay barely felt the sting to his face, but in his heart the blow vibrated a thousand times.

Quest had witnessed the scene, but waited for Ty to storm off before making his presence known. Quay turned when he heard the "tsking" sound across his shoulder.

"Don't start, Q," he groaned, preparing to walk away.

"Not so fast," Quest coolly requested, drawing his twin toward a quiet corner of the corridor.

"What, Q?" Quay snapped, tugging at the cuffs of his mocha suit coat in an agitated fashion.

"I can't afford to have her distracted by this drama, Quay."

Quay hissed a foul curse. "There's nothin' goin' on," he said finally.

Quest folded his arms across the hunter-green shirt he wore with burgundy suspenders and almost laughed. "Nothin's goin' on? Then why the hell are you always up under her?" he challenged, walking away when he saw that his brother had no comeback.

"I honestly don't have a clue," Mick was telling Jillian, who had just told her about the meeting with Raymond Patillo. "None of my research turned up any other evidence, but then I'm not privy to every bit of legal documentation," she noted.

"Check the body, check the body," Jill was repeating, hoping it would force some sort of clarification.

She heard Mick gasp. "What?" she demanded.

Mick hesitated only a moment. "Do you think he could've been telling you to *check* her body—that the evidence was buried *with* her body—actually buried with it?"

"Impossible," Jill breathed, "are you serious?"

"It's a possibility, Jill."

"But why would Patillo risk his career that way?"

"Jill, you have no idea the kind of power the Ramseys wield down there," Mick shared, crossing her legs at the ankles while relaxing on her bed. "I got a healthy taste of it when I was in Savannah trying to connect pieces of this damned puzzle. Money is a powerful temptation and Patillo pretty much admitted he'd been persuaded by them right after the murder."

"Murder," Jill repeated, massaging her forehead. "So you're certain that's what it was?"

"That's what I believe and I think after what Mr. Patillo said, it's safe to say it's been confirmed."

"So what's next?" Jill sighed, grateful to have someone to bounce ideas off. Almost the entire station had deemed her a pariah for delving into the case.

"We'll have to contact her family to get an order to have the body exhumed. After such a long time, they may not be willing to have her grave disturbed. It could be quite a burden."

"It may not be as big of a burden as we think."

"Care to elaborate?"

"I think it's time to give Johnelle Black another call."

At Gabron's restaurant, the meeting was nearing its end. The members of Holtz Enterprises, who had flown down from Canada, were a sociable bunch. Ty was very pleased since she needed something laid-back and easygoing to keep her mind off Quay, who unfortunately had decided to rejoin the meeting following their episode in the hallway.

"How long do you all plan to stay?" Jeffrey Naven, one of Ramsey's chief architects, was asking.

"We hadn't decided before leaving," Louie said, "but now I think maybe a longer stay might be a nice idea," he added, focusing an appraising look toward Tykira.

Quest slanted his twin a warning look when he heard the heavy sigh Quay uttered.

"We hope to take another tour of the train before its completion," Louie announced.

The Ramsey group was delighted and plans were discussed to nail down a date and time.

"This is fantastic," Ty was saying, especially pleased by the plans. "We really want to get your input on every phase of the project, but right now at the beginning is the most critical stage. I really want to be sure you get exactly what you're looking for."

"That sounds nice and I'm sure we will," Louie replied.

Quay could tell by the way the man's eyes traveled over Ty's upswept hairstyle and exquisite face that he wasn't just referring to the train. He felt Quest's hand close over his knee and gritted his teeth while praying for an end to the meeting. His prayers were answered when everyone began pushing their chairs away from the table. His cellular chimed and he smiled when he saw the number on the face plate. "Mick, Mick, Mick," he drawled and chuckled when he heard her voice. He shot Quest a devilish grin when the man heard his wife's name. "For me," he informed his brother in a wicked tone. "Yeah, Mick?" he said, tuning in to her voice. "Yeah, he's here...what? Do I have to?" Quay groaned, rolling his eyes as he looked over at Quest. "She says she loves you and can't wait for you to come to bed."

Quest's hearty rumble of a laugh roared to life. He clapped his brother's shoulder then joined in on a conversation with a few of their people and the Holtz executives.

"Listen, my contact in Savannah just had a meeting with a man named Raymond Patillo. He was the county medical examiner when Sera was killed," Mick shared.

"Mmm-hmm," Quay said, leaning back in his chair as Mick told him about the call. "What did you just say...? With her body? Dammit."

"Now calm down," Mick urged. "This is really great news. We may be on our way to catching a murderer."

"Until we hit another brick wall and the bastard continues to enjoy his freedom."

"Sweetie, cut yourself some slack. Please? You're giving this guy too much power. Try to make things right between you and Ty, all right?"

"Yeah," he said, smirking at the suggestion. "Thanks, Mick," he said, before their call ended. Remaining seated, he simply watched Ty as she laughed off one of Louie's remarks and gathered her things to leave. She caught Quay staring and, for a few moments, their gazes held. Then Ty shook her head and walked off.

Quay clenched his fists, fighting the urge to go after her. He was glad when Quest called him over to speak with one of the Holtz VPs.

Ty didn't allow the mask she wore to slip until she'd driven out of Gabron's parking lot and had taken the ramp onto the expressway. She cursed herself for being a fool—a weak-kneed, emotional woman swooning over a man's attention.

But Quay wasn't just any man, he was the only man she'd ever loved—her first lover. She cursed herself again and asked why she loved him. She was a smart woman in virtually every other aspect of her life. Why couldn't she pull herself, her heart, away from this man—the *only* man who had ever truly hurt her?

If anything, the scene a month prior should have changed her opinion of him. But, the encounter only made her want him more. She could admit that to herself. Quaysar Ramsey wasn't simply the only man she'd ever loved, he was the only man she'd ever made love with. Knowing that it was only for physical gratification on his part was killing something inside her.

She was on a mission now to work harder than ever to complete the project and get back to Colorado. It would be suicide considering what a large undertaking it was, but she knew that to stay and let herself be wooed into bed again would be just as dangerous.

"Oh, not tonight," Ty groaned when she pulled into her mother's driveway. She spotted Quay's foreboding black SUV parked a few feet away. "What is it, Quay?" she called once she'd left the SUV and he was walking toward her.

He smiled as he raised his hands defensively. "I swear that I only wanted to make sure you got home all right."

"*No,* you wanted to make sure I got home *alone,*" she corrected, folding her arms across the front of the black turtleneck she wore.

Quay simply nodded, not bothering to argue her accuracy.

Tykira's brown stare narrowed. "What is it with you? One minute hot, the next minute cold. Is this still about Wake? Or do you still just enjoy playing with my head? This isn't high school, Quay. You don't have to play that game anymore, you know."

"Ty—"

"It's confusing and it's cruel and I don't have time for it. I'm here to work and then leave," she huffed, pointing one index finger toward the ground.

Quay bowed his head and cursed himself. In his desperation to see her, he hadn't stopped to consider how she would perceive his actions. *Nice, Quay. Nice as always.*

"Why don't you use your Casanova skills on one of the many women ready to be wooed by you?" she muttered, turning to open the passenger-side door and collect her things.

"And you're not one of those women?" Quay said, speaking more to himself than to her. No, she wasn't one of those women—she had never been. She was so much more and she'd never heard him tell her that.

"No, I'm not one of those women, Quay, so stop. Just stop, all right?" she pleaded, resting her forehead against the Cherokee. "There's no need," she told him. "I didn't come here to win a spot in your life. In spite of my…eager participation, I didn't even come here to sleep with you." She ended on a whisper, sighing as exhaustion claimed her.

"Jesus," Quay hissed, mistaking her sighs for sobs and stepping close to console her. "Ty, please, I'm sorry. Please don't cry."

"Snake," she snapped, stiffening against him. "I'm not crying over you, Quay. I've done way too much of that."

Quay nodded, but made no move to back away from her. Instinctively, his hands smoothed across her slender form, moving up to fill his palms with the fullness of her breasts.

Ty blinked, her body beginning to tingle with the desire for Quay that always simmered just below the surface. Helpless to deny its power, she let her head tilt and she arched deeper into his touch.

Keeping one hand curved seductively across her bosom and the other at her hip, Quay trailed his nose across the nape of her neck. The scent of her perfume brought to mind the naughtiest acts of seduction that he ached to subject her to. His perfect teeth found the zipper that secured the chic turtleneck and tugged it down, hungry to expose more of her silky dark skin.

How she wanted him, Ty thought as his mouth traced her neck. That's all it would ever be, unfortunately—want, desire, sex-satisfying and craved, yes, but nothing more. Dammit, she hissed silently. All these years she'd felt fulfilled and successful without him in her life. Now he was here again and torturing her mind and body with his attention. With a strength she conjured from someplace deep, Ty slipped out of his embrace and headed toward the front door.

Quay seemed to snap out of his pleasure-driven state of mind as well. Leaning against the SUV, he kept his back turned until Ty had disappeared inside the house.

Chapter 7

"I love you, Quay, I love you..."

The deep right dimple appeared as Quay smiled in his sleep. Stretching restfully against crisp, charcoal-gray sheets, he smoothed one hand across the array of taut muscles upon his chiseled abdomen. He was in the midst of a delicious albeit subconscious interlude with Tykira Lowery. Her stunning dark mane flowed wildly as her body rode his. His hands traveled her strong, beautiful form with a lover's possession. On her lips, he heard her say she loved him—

Quay woke with a start, his relaxed state growing sharp with frustration. He cursed himself then, realizing the incredible scene was a fantasy—with no chance of becoming reality. He alone had accomplished that, with no help from Wake Robinson. Quay acknowledged that the man was probably on another continent, He had to know that a life behind bars awaited him if he returned.

Still, he refused to risk it.

Quay pressed a pillow across his face and groaned. He loved her so much. He had loved her forever and his feelings would never change. All the women he'd been with to try to get her out of his head were only shining examples of everything he *didn't* want.

His temper was reaching that point of no return when the bedside phone rang.

"What?" he practically growled into the receiver once he'd snatched it up. After brief hesitation on the other end, a familiar voice came through the line. "Wake?" Quay whispered, barely able to find his own voice.

"Been a while," Wake said, sounding calm yet uncertain.

Slowly, Quay pushed himself up in bed. "Goin' on three years. Where you been, man?" he coolly probed.

"You knew I had to go," Wake returned.

"Did you do this?"

Wake didn't pretend to be confused. "It's complicated, man."

"What the hell does that mean?" Quay snapped.

"It's *complicated*," Wake stressed, on edge as well by Quay's obvious mood.

"Where are you?" Quay asked, ordering himself to tone down his emotions.

"Close," was Wake's simple reply.

Quay didn't like it. "Let's meet," he suggested.

"Not now, but I'll be in touch," Wake said. "We will talk, man. But I have to be sure about the time and place. You got a lot of things mixed up and you don't know the whole story. You don't know the half of it."

"You mean about the fact that you killed Sera?" Quay pointed out.

Wake muttered a curse. "That's not a fact. It's not even *close* to a fact, man."

For a moment, Quay believed him. "What's goin' on, man?" he asked.

"This isn't a phone conversation and I think you know that," Wake reasoned. "Anyway, I already said way too much."

Quay knew he was gone before he heard the dial tone signifying the line was dead. Leaning back in bed, he closed his eyes and groaned.

"I know this is asking a lot considering all you've been through," Mick was saying as she spoke with Johnelle Black by phone.

"Emotions don't control me anymore, Michaela. I need this to come to an end," the grieving mother confided. "If something *is* buried with Sera, something that could bring answers about her death, I want it done."

Mick nodded. "We'll have to be discreet with the exhumation. The SPD may not approve of us delving into this particular area of the case."

"I understand and I'll do whatever it takes," Johnelle vowed. "Will you be there?"

"Nothing could keep me away," Mick promised.

"You've been a godsend. Thank you, Michaela."

"You take care of yourself. We'll talk soon," Mick whispered. She waited for Johnelle to hang up before she clicked off her phone and stood from the armchair in the tiny alcove of the bedroom.

From their bed, Quest watched his wife massaging her eyes and neck. "Come over here," he softly commanded.

Mick complied without hesitation, smiling gratefully when he pulled her down to the bed and began to massage her neck and back.

"Are you all right?" he asked.

"Just tired," she admitted, relishing the relief his powerful hands applied to her aching muscles.

Quest let his displeasure show, his gray eyes darkening just slightly. "What leads have you made in the case?" he asked, hoping to mask his frustration.

"We think actual physical evidence may've been buried with Sera—in her…casket."

"What?" Quest breathed, his unsettling stare narrowing dangerously.

Mick turned and scooted close to him. "Baby, I told Quay, but promise not to say anything to anyone else," she urged, smoothing her hands across his broad, bare shoulders. "The whole situation is a long shot."

"What do you think you'll find?" Quest asked, calming some beneath his wife's touch.

Mick shook her head. "Well, if it runs parallel to the file Jill found, this evidence could lead us to Sera's killer."

"Wake?" Quest probed.

"Wake," Mick sighed, her expression growing guarded.

"Michaela?" Quest called, bowing his head a bit to peek into her eyes.

"I think Wake Robinson is a part of the puzzle, but as crazy as this sounds, I don't think he did this."

"Baby, why would you think he'd be innocent in all this?"

"I don't know—a hunch? I just really believe this goes deeper than Wake."

"But why?"

"I can't make myself believe he'd have done all this and continued to live around Quay all these years." She shrugged. "I don't know…"

"Have you told Quay?"

"I haven't even told Johnelle," Mick groaned, dragging all ten fingers through her thick curls. "I don't think it'd be wise to tell your brother since he's based *all* his actions on the fact that Wake Robinson is the culprit." She folded her arms across her knees and propped her chin there. "Getting Quay to latch on to the idea of another nameless, faceless perpetrator might push him just a bit too far."

For the next two weeks, Tykira maintained her vow to steer clear of Quay. She worked herself into a frenzy to the dismay of everyone who knew her.

Her crew had seen her driven many times before, but this was even more extreme than usual. She heard nothing but her own voice pushing her to give just a little more to get the job done. Now, that voice was pushing her with another advisement: finish this job and get the hell away from Quaysar Ramsey.

She'd arrived early for the weekly meeting, mostly because she'd wound up spending the night in the office designated for her and her team. When Ty woke, she washed her face and brushed her teeth in the office washroom before heading up for the meeting.

Jasmine, Ramsey's administrative director, sent her on up to the penthouse office and the moment Ty stepped from the elevator, the sofa in the corner called to her. Minutes later, she was napping.

Quay arrived early himself that morning. He was in no mood to run into employees and be forced to engage in conversation he had no interest in. He'd been walking on a tightrope since Wake's call. He dared not tell anyone about it, not wanting to scare the man away if he was near. Each time the phone rang, Quay jumped, thinking it was his old friend.

The reality of that made him experience more than a little self-loathing. He was Quaysar Ramsey and he ran from no one. His facial muscles tightened, drawing his handsome dark features into a fierce mask. He stormed off the elevator, his anger abating when he found Ty asleep on a sofa. He moved closer and took a seat on the edge of the rich, blackberry suede.

A soft smile curved his mouth when the sound of her snoring touched his ears. Leaning close, he brushed his nose across her temple. Moving back slightly, he took advantage of the moment to watch her slumber. His fingers fondled the soft tendrils of hair that haphazardly fell from her upswept hairstyle to frame her face. He'd heard how hard she'd been driving herself and now he could see that it was true. He knew it was because of him. Arrogant thinking? Perhaps, but it was accurate. If he were her, he'd want to get as far away from him as possible. He made a mental note to ask his father how much longer Bobbie Lowery would be away on business. She'd make sure Ty took better care of herself and stayed at home instead of a hotel until the project was finished.

Quay's hand clenched into a fist at the thought. He cursed, knowing it should be *him* taking care of Tykira.

Ty awoke, frowning a bit as she sought to get her bearings. Then she found herself looking right into Quay's disturbingly dark eyes. She realized how close they were and quickly left the sofa. No words were spoken, but the tension was thick and heavy inside the room. Putting distance between them, Ty rubbed her arms across the flared sleeves of the asymmetrical mocha sweater she wore. Her sigh of relief filled the room when the elevator chimed to signal the arrival of their meeting partners.

As everyone convened near the elevator after the meeting, Mick approached her brother-in-law, who sat brooding in his private office.

"Everyone's leaving for the rail yard to survey the construction, Quay," she called, watching as he glared at the papers he held.

"Not goin'," he said, slapping the documents to his desk.

"Why?" Mick blurted, stepping inside her office. Quay's pointed look was a clear response to her question. "I can't believe you're still acting so crazy," she scolded. "You already told Ty what's going on."

"I never told her Wake is still out there somewhere," Quay argued.

"So what? What does it have to do with what you feel?"

The flip inquiry brought a hard frown to Quay's face. "I've been asking myself that very question," he admitted.

"Ready, babe?" Quest called, finding his wife in the office.

"Yeah," Mick replied idly, smiling when he pulled her back against him.

Quay walked over and planted a kiss on Mick's cheek, before quietly excusing himself from the room. Quest held her tight when she turned to hug him. He relished the gesture, but frowned a bit when he felt her leaning deep into the embrace as though she had no strength to stand.

"Hey," he whispered, leaning down to search her light eyes with his striking gray ones, "you all right?"

Mick's smile was weak, but she finally began to nod. "I'm just so ready for this case to be solved," she told him.

Quest's grimace sparked his left dimple. "Finally, we agree on something," he said, and then escorted his wife to the elevator.

Savannah, Georgia

Jill sat browsing through the Sera Black file for what seemed to be the hundredth time. She could only pray that the pieces of evidence noted in the record would actually be found with the body. She shook her head, silently acknowledging how much of a long shot it was. However, she also acknowledged that such unorthodox happenings were usually the events that cinched cases.

"Getting fed up?" Greg Youtz teased, seeing his young colleague shaking her head.

Jill blew at her bangs, before massaging her eyes. "I'm wondering if I'll be successful in fitting together all the pieces of this puzzle," she confided.

Greg tugged at the belt, completely hidden beneath the generous expanse of his belly. "What'cha workin' on?" he asked.

"An old case," Jill said, turning to face the man who occupied the desk diagonal from hers, "Sera Black? I have reason to believe it was murder, not suicide," she shared, omitting the information regarding buried evidence.

Greg lost what little coloring he had in his face. "I remember that. I'd been on the force ten years when she died," he shared. "My little girl went to school with her."

"Did you know the Ramseys?" Jill asked, folding her arms across her chest.

"Oh, I knew the Ramseys," Greg confided. "You only had to live in Savannah a few days to know the power those folks commanded here."

"Do you believe they could've been involved in what happened to Sera Black?"

"Why would you ask that?" he asked, almost defensively.

Jill suspected Greg knew more than what was in the case file. "The twins were suspected," she went on. "They're very successful now," she added.

"The twins," Greg parroted, smirking coldly. "Those boys... Let's say they were the least of Sera Black's problems."

"What do you mean?" Jill prompted, leaning forward in her desk chair. "How?"

Greg blinked, as though realizing he'd said too much. "Be careful, little girl. Black or white, the Ramseys are powerful and they claim some nasty members."

"But the case is so old now and—"

"You best believe someone's watching. Someone's *always* watching." Greg stood and reached for the suit coat to pull over his snug white cotton shirt. "You'll find that out if you dig any deeper into this." With those words, he left Jill alone.

"Quay? Quay!" Jasmine called, when she raced past the opening elevator doors. "Quay," she said, finding her boss reclining on the conference room sofa. "Why aren't you answering your line?" she probed softly.

"Because I don't want to hear any more crap, bad news or problems for at least two hours," he muttered, recrossing his loafer-clad feet where they rested atop the coffee table.

Jasmine took a deep breath and propped both hands on her hips. "Well then, you're not about to like what I'm going to tell you."

"And that is?" Quay asked, leaving the sofa to fix himself a drink at the bar.

"There was an accident at the rail yard."

A loud clamor sounded when Quay's hand weakened. The glass decanter fell, spilling contents of scotch to the pine surface of the bar. "Where's Ty?" His deep voice grated as he turned to Jasmine.

"It was Ty who was involved in the accident." Jazz dreaded relaying the news.

"What happened?"

"I don't—"

"Where is she? Is she all right?"

"All I can give you is the name of the hospital," Jazz said, already extending the card she'd scribbled the location on.

Quay hissed a fierce curse and snatched the card. He stormed out of the room and Jazz could hear him slamming his hand against the elevator's down button. She decided it'd be best to take the next car down.

Chapter 8

"She's all right. She's all right," were the first words out of Quest's mouth when Quay came bounding down the hospital corridor. "Listen to me, she's *fine*," he stressed, curving both hands over his twin's shoulders as he tried to allay the man's worst fears.

Quay's smoldering charcoal stare was unwavering. "Who's responsible for this?" he asked his brother.

Quest shrugged. "Most likely Ty herself is responsible."

"What?" Quay breathed.

"She hasn't been eating or resting," Quest shared, releasing Quay's shoulders and pushing both hands into his trouser pockets. "She lost her bearings while we were taking a side ladder up to the roof of one of the railcars. She slipped and fell crazy on her ankle. Doctor says she broke it."

"Dammit," Quay cursed, though relief was washing through him at the same time. Ty was going to be okay. "Where is she? Can I see her?" he asked.

Quest nodded and Quay removed his suit coat while making his way toward the room. He applied a gentle knock to the partially opened door before stepping inside. His heart slammed fiercely inside his chest when he saw Ty. Lying prone in the bed with her eyes closed, she looked beat, drained, like she hadn't slept in weeks. Massaging the bridge of his nose, he cursed himself for being the cause of it.

Mick had been napping in a chair next to the bed, but looked up when she heard someone else in the room. "The doctor says she'll be fine," she told him.

Quay's dark eyes were focused on the cast and sling surrounding Tykira's right foot.

"She broke it in the fall," Mick supplied.

"Was it really an accident?" Quay asked, his eyes still on the cast.

"Yeah, sweetie, it was," Mick sighed, knowing what he meant. "She hasn't been getting the rest she needs. The doctors say they're more concerned by her fatigue than the ankle."

Quay pushed one hand into his silver-gray trouser pockets. "How long does she have to stay here?" he asked.

"Not sure," Mick said, massaging her arms as she

yawned. "I know someone should be in soon who can tell you more."

"Thanks, Mick," Quay said. He tousled her curls when she walked by him. "I'm glad you were there," he told her, smiling when she rubbed his back before leaving the room.

Settling to the edge of the bed, Quay took Ty's hand and kept it pressed to his chest. He stroked her temple as he'd done earlier that day and thought how easily this accident could have been something else. When Jasmine told him Ty was hurt, he actually believed he'd lost her. *Really* lost her. Shaking his head to dismiss the thought, he leaned close and kissed her cheek.

Ty stirred, her lashes fluttering a bit as she awakened. "Quay," she whispered.

He took comfort in the fact that she knew it was him and leaned close to kiss her again.

"What happened?" she asked, grimacing at the scratchy feel of her throat.

"You need to rest, love," he advised, trailing his finger along the arched line of her brow.

Emotion flickered in Ty's gaze and she looked away. "I have work to do," she reminded him.

"It can wait," he countered, his voice firming as well. "If need be, I'll have the whole damn project postponed so you can get the rest you need. Even if you have to go back to Colorado to get it," he threatened.

Ty shuddered. "When I leave Seattle this time, I won't be back," she vowed.

"Can I do anything? Call your mom?" he offered, not wanting to argue with her.

"No, please." Ty quickly declined. "I don't need her worrying over me."

Quay disagreed. He decided to contact Bobbie on his own.

Ty tried to push herself up in the bed and gasped at the dull ache in the vicinity of her foot. Spotting the cast and sling, her mouth fell open and she couldn't believe she hadn't noticed it before. "What happened?" she cried.

"You fell at the rail yard during the tour. Do you remember?" Quay asked, stroking her arm when she nodded. "It's your ankle. You broke it," he told her.

"Nooo," Ty groaned, falling back against the pillows. Obvious dismay at being bedridden—or at the very least incapacitated—clouded her face. "Now Mommy will *definitely* come home to fuss over me. I won't get a damn thing done." She sighed then, her eyes narrowing as she contemplated the situation. "Maybe I can get one of the guys to stay with me."

Not a chance in hell, Quay decided silently.

"Quay? Is everything else all right?" she asked then, having caught the murderous expression that flashed across his face. Instinctively, she reached out to touch his hand, and cursed herself for even caring how he was. *Especially when it's my damn foot in a sling!* she quietly chastised herself.

"I just have a lot going on," he confided.

Something in his tone continued to concern Ty.

"Business?" she probed, watching him shake his head no. Clearly it was something he didn't want to discuss with her. Thankfully, there was no time to rack her brain trying to figure out what was going on with him. The nurse had arrived.

"When can I leave?" were the first words Ty uttered.

"Now, now, Ms. Lowery, the doctors want you to focus on getting more rest. They'll be in to speak with you shortly," the portly older woman announced.

"I can rest at home." Ty pouted.

"And clearly you haven't been," the nurse challenged, offering Quay an adoring look when he chuckled at her words.

Ty folded her arms across the front of the awkward hospital gown and remained quiet.

"When you *are* released, you'll definitely need someone to look after you," the nurse was saying as she fussed around the bed making sure the covers were tucked in, and recording Ty's vitals on a chart.

"Tyke, I'm gonna head out," Quay was saying then. He moved close to the bed and then leaned down to kiss her forehead. "I'll be back," he whispered.

For a moment, Ty forgot about pouting. The look in her brown eyes softened as she watched him go.

"Oooh boy," the nurse sighed, her eyes also following Quay's departure. "I wouldn't mind being looked after if *he* applied for the job."

"Detective Red," Jill answered the call absently, while riffling through paperwork at her cluttered desk.

"Miss Red, Sawyer Reynolds. Head caretaker and proprietor of Serenity Memorial Gardens."

"Yes, Mr. Reynolds?" Jill greeted. Inwardly, she groaned at the sound of the man's heavy Southern drawl and nasal tone of his voice. Clearly, Mr. Sawyer Reynolds was accustomed to respect and reverence when he announced his lengthy title. "How are you?" she asked, hoping to set an easy tone to the conversation.

"Not good. Not good one damn bit," Sawyer shared, with no interest in pleasantries. "I got an order here for exhumation. Sera Black."

"Yes, sir."

"This is a scandalous thing you doin', missy. I don't know how thangs go in Chicago, but down here we don't think it's Christian-like to make people relive painful mem'ries."

"I don't think that way either, sir," Jill said, rubbing her tired eyes as she spoke.

"You coulda fooled me, young lady. Reopenin' that case, diggin' up that girl's body just gonna wound that family all over again."

"And just for my own clarification, Mr. Reynolds, would you be referring to Sera's family or the Ramsey family?" Jill probed, not bothering to hide her disdain.

"Now you listen here—"

"Mr. Reynolds, Sera's mother wants this done. And that's the *only* family *I'm* concerned about."

"You dabblin' with powerful folks," Sawyer Reynolds warned. "Don't matter a bit if they black or not."

Jill rolled her eyes. "Mr. Reynolds, this case is far from over and until it's solved, I'm on it," she vowed.

"Be careful, young lady," the older man advised, then slammed down the phone.

Jill followed suit, looking across her shoulder when she heard Greg Youtz laughing in the distance.

"Told you so," he gloated, leaning back in his desk chair.

Jill turned, her dark eyes filled with a glare that removed the humor from Youtz's face. "If it hadn't have been for the Ramseys working to cover their asses, no one would've taken a second look at this case, but hiding evidence, making payoffs—including one to the girl's own mother—have simply caused tensions and regrets to simmer. They're about to boil over, Greg, with Sera Black's murderer coming out in the runoff. And I'll damn well be there to see it," she swore, and then shoved her chair away from her desk and stormed out of the office.

Greg's expression held a look of foreboding. "Be careful, young lady," he advised.

With the exhumation scheduled for the end of that week, Michaela was preparing for her trip to Georgia. She hoped to finish packing before her husband got home—knowing that her leaving had become a very sore spot between them. Unfortunately, Quest arrived early that evening. He was in time to not only find his wife packing, but also to see her stumble and lean over to brace her hands against the wall as though she were tying to regain her balance.

Mick was taking deep breaths when she heard the slam of the bedroom door. She whirled around to find Quest shooting his hazy gray glare in her direction.

"Hey, baby," she greeted in a light, breathless manner and cleared her throat to shed the shaky tone of her voice.

Quest didn't buy it. "The trip's out," he decided, tossing his black leather quarter-length jacket to the bed.

"Excuse me?" Mick retorted, propping both hands to her hips when her husband took a seat on the bed and casually removed his shoes and socks before deigning to give her an answer.

"I've been watching you, Michaela," he shared in a whimsical tone.

Mick's expression softened. "You're *always* watching me," she teased.

"Mmm," he gestured, flashing her a look of acknowledgement. "Well then, it shouldn't surprise you to hear me say that I've see all the little stumbles during the last couple of weeks."

Slowly, Mick's teasing expression faded.

"You've been napping all times of the day," Quest went on, watching her walk over to the dresser and lean against it. "Thanks to this case, you're not taking care of yourself and I'm sick of it."

Mick shook her head. "Honey, I swear that's not it," she said, hiding her hands inside the front pocket of the petal-pink hoodie she wore. "Everything with the case now is at a virtual standstill until Jill gets somewhere with the exhumation."

"Which you won't be attending."

"Quest—"

"That's it."

"Quest, please don't do this. Not now," Mick begged, extending her hands in a pleading gesture while walking toward him. "You know Johnelle needs me to be there."

"And I need you to be *here*," he countered, unbuttoning the black shirt he wore and leaving it to hang open outside his cream trousers. "I need you to be here long after this case is solved."

Mick had no comeback. At last, she succumbed to the weariness she'd been battling. She trudged to the bed and took a seat near the suitcase she'd been packing. Idly, she toyed with the articles that lay inside. Quest closed the space between them and pulled her against his chest. Mick was happy to let herself be held.

"She'll never go for it," Bobbie Lowery predicted into the phone as she stood in the middle of her Baton Rouge, Louisiana, hotel room.

Quay smiled. "Considering how badly she wants to be home, I think she'll consider just about any arrangement. But I need to know if you'll be all right with it."

Bobbie sighed. "No, baby, I'm afraid I wouldn't be."

"Ms. Bobbie, if—"

"Now wait and let me say this," she urged, sitting on the sill of the window overlooking the busy, rain-slicked street below. "It's not that I don't think you could handle Ty as a patient, though you probably couldn't," she added with a smile before sobering. "Quaysar, the truth is I'm sick of seeing my baby hurt and always upset over you. It's been a constant in your lives since forever and now it's so bad my Ty rarely comes home. In fact, aside from this project with your company, she *never* comes home."

Quay could hear the softness settle into Roberta Lowery's usually firm voice and knew her emotions were weighing in heavily. "Ms. Bobbie, I don't know what to say except I'm sorry. I know what I did to Ty. I know I was wrong, but I had my reasons."

"Which were?" Bobbie challenged.

Quay didn't want Bobbie any more upset. "I was wrong and I want to make this up to her more than anything. I want her in my life forever," was all he chose to share.

Bobbie shook her head. "Quaysar—"

"I love her, Ms. Bobbie. I always have and I'll never stop."

Lengthy silence covered the line while Bobbie contemplated. "What do you need?" she asked finally.

Quay uttered a hushed prayer of thanks. "I only need you to take your time on this trip. I need to be alone with her."

"Mmm-hmm," Bobbie replied, feeling she'd been told enough. "Don't hurt my baby again, Quaysar," she warned, "or you'll be dealing with me, and love, you know I'm nowhere near as syrupy sweet as my daughter."

"Yes, ma'am," Quay replied in a reverent tone, knowing the woman's words were no bluff.

Ty woke from another long nap and believed she was still dreaming when she found Quay's face looming so close to her own. She closed her eyes and opened them to see if the vision remained. It had. "What are you doing here?" she inquired groggily.

Quay grinned. Every day the same question. She'd been in the hospital just over a week and he'd made an appearance at her bedside each day. He knew she was curious and unnerved, but he had no intentions of letting her out of his sight. Ever again.

"Quay?" she probed, her doe eyes narrowing when he offered no response.

"How would you like to go home?" he asked finally.

Ty, who hated being cooped up in bed for any period of time, closed her eyes in a dreamy manner. She smiled, resting her head back against the pillows as though she were envisioning "home" just then. "That is my greatest wish," she sighed.

Quay chuckled, loving the way contentment added a different glow to her incredible features. "Well, I'm here to grant that wish," he announced.

"Huh?" Ty grunted, fixing him with a blank look.

"You'll stay with me until we get the cast off."

"No."

"Yes. Ms. Bobbie already said it was all right."

"What? You talked to her?" Ty breathed, watching him nod. "What did she say?" She had to know, lis-

tening closely as Quay told her. Ty felt her mouth
hanging open by the time he was done. Minutes
later, she was shaking her head. "I can't, Quay."

"Yes, you can."

"No...the guys—the guys can take care of me."

Quay chuckled and leaned back in the chair next
to the bed. "With you out of commission, they're
gonna be swamped with work. They can't focus on
that and worry over you at the same time."

Ty settled back. "You're right," she whispered,
tapping her chin. "I'll get a nurse."

"Already taken care of," Quay shared, standing
from the chair and moving to sit on the side of the
bed. "And I want to be there, too," he said.

"Why would you do this?" Ty questioned, dismissing the voice that called her a fool for asking.

"You need someone to look after you," he said,
trailing his fingers along her bare forearm.

Ty grimaced and folded her arms across her chest.
"The truth, Quay, just the truth."

"I feel better seeing with my own eyes that
you're safe."

Ty blinked. "Does this have something to do with
Wake Robinson?"

Quay's long lashes shielded his onyx stare from
view when he looked down to inspect a button on his
camel-colored suit coat.

"Quay."

"I don't want you scared, Tyke."

"I'm not," she finally replied, genuine courage in
her eyes. "Besides, Wake hardly knew me—and thanks

to you he never suspected we were intimate. Unless...you told him?" she subtly inquired, wondering
if he'd ever admitted his feelings about her to anyone.

Quay shook his head. "I didn't."

Ty inhaled, refusing to admit how much the confession disappointed her. Clearly she had been just
some meaningless fling that hadn't been worth mentioning. "Then there's no need for you to put your
life on hold for me," she decided, only pretending to
be cool just then.

Averting his gaze, Quay forced himself not to
admit how much he wanted and needed to be around
her. "Humor me, please, Tyke," he said instead.

Ty curled her hands into fists beneath the standard
coverings on the bed. She knew that once again
Quay Ramsey had her right where he wanted.

"Who's ready to be released?" Doctor Jonas Orvin asked upon walking into the dim hospital room.

Ty's expression brightened immediately. "I'm
more than ready! Please tell me something good."

Dr. Orvin chuckled. "Well, your vitals are far
better than when you first came to us," he said,
perusing the chart he held before his round olive-
toned face. "We still want you to adhere to strict
bedrest, though. We anticipate the cast being on
anywhere from four to six weeks."

Nodding, Ty expelled a deep breath. Thankfully,
it appeared that she'd be on her feet before the rail
was finished for the trip to Banff.

"Now, about this cast," Dr. Orvin went on, placing
his hand across the bulky creation. "I caution you

against using a hanger to get to an itch. Use a cool blow-dryer instead. You should also practice keeping it elevated and use an emory board instead of scissors to trim any rough edges that may form at the heel or anywhere else. I've got a packet here that'll go into more detail about everything I'm telling you."

Dr. Orvin was still delivering his instructions when an orderly arrived with a wheelchair. Ty's happy expression dimmed with skepticism.

"I really don't think I need that," she said.

"Tyke…" Quay called in a warning tone from where he stood across the room.

"I'm afraid it's yours until you exit the hospital doors. We've also supplied you with a lovely one to use while you're at home."

"What about crutches?" Ty suggested.

"You'll have those, as well."

"Can't I use them now instead of this wheelchair?"

The doctor was quite amused, as he was quite accustomed to this final debate by patients who abhorred being wheeled out. "Hospital rules," he said, using the tried and true argument that usually silenced the disagreement. He smiled and nodded when it appeared to work on the outspoken young woman in the bed. "Now, I'll leave you to freshen up and I'll return within the hour with your release forms." Dr. Orvin said, patting Ty's cast once more before he shook hands with Quay and left the room.

"I'm gonna bounce out of here for a minute, too, Tyke," Quay said, following the doctor's departure.

"I want to double check to make sure the kitchen's stocked with everything we'll need," he explained, tugging a quarter-length gray linen jacket across his white shirt.

Ty couldn't resist smiling. "Don't tell me you're going to cook?" she teased.

"If you'd like me to," he replied, his sensual dark gaze fixed and intense.

The look caught Ty completely off guard and she couldn't respond.

Thankfully, Quay's expression softened again in humor. "I don't think your stomach would approve of that, though," he said, pulling keys from his jacket pocket. "See you in a few."

When he was gone, Tykira expelled the breath she'd been holding. Leaning back on the pillows with her eyes closed, she questioned the intelligence of releasing herself to the care of Quay Ramsey. Despite the past, she knew she'd always be a fool for the man. But how many more times could she put herself in the line of fire and keep hoping everything would be all right, when again and again she ended up brokenhearted?

Nodding then, she decided she was just going to have to keep things on an even keel. Sure, she was in love with him, attracted to him, thought about them making love more than a few times every day and was unable to stop the excitement from pulsing through her at the idea of being around him so often during the approaching weeks....

Still, when those truths got in the way of her ability to resist his incredible charm—and that would most certainly happen—she would pull away from them. She would have to. Her very dignity and sanity depended on it.

Chapter 9

"Put that down!" Quay ordered from the driver's seat. His glare was hard and focused on the statuesque beauty as he watched her through the rearview mirror.

"What?!" Ty demanded, fixing Quay with her own glare from her relaxed position along the back seat of the Humvee.

"The doctor said no work," Quay reminded her, moving his gaze from Ty to the traffic.

"I was only reviewing some notes," Ty reasoned, already reaching for the legal pad she'd scribbled on during her hospital stay.

"Put it down," he ordered, quietly that time.

"Dammit," she snapped, tossing the pad to the

floor. "Will you tell me then what the hell I'm supposed to be doing for the next four to six weeks?"

Quay cleared his throat, eager to recite the list. "Eat three square meals a day," he began, revealing his right-dimpled smile when she groaned. "Snacks are fine, but don't get crazy, no more than four hours of TV a day. So you'll have to decide between soaps in the morning or movies at night. The rest of the time you'll be asleep."

"Mmm-hmm, and crazy inside of two days," she added, casting a despairing gaze outside the rear window. "I'll be bored to tears," she mourned.

"Then sleep will keep your mind off how bored you are."

"Oh please, shut up. *You're* not the one with your foot in a sling."

"No, that would be *you*," Quay replied, leaning his head back against the padded rest. "'Course it *wouldn't* be you if you'd been getting enough rest, so you could be more alert. But all that's about to change."

"I don't—"

"No more argument, Tyke."

Folding her arms across the front of her Colorado Rockies sweatshirt, she pouted.

Once on the freeway, Quay stole infrequent glances at her. He thanked God she'd given in and decided to let him look after her. This accident of hers had put so much into perspective. Sure, it was what everyone had been telling him—he was a fool to deny either Ty or himself what they'd both wanted. For so long he'd pretended she meant little or nothing to him in hopes of keeping her safe. His reasoning had been all wrong. He shuddered, thinking how pushing her away was more dangerous than anything else he'd done. It was a mistake he wouldn't make again. Tykira Lowery was his and it was way past time that everyone knew it.

"Am I allowed to hear music? Or is that against the orders, too?" Ty inquired, still looking annoyed in the back seat.

Quay offered no response, except to grin at her stubbornness. Dutifully, he hit the button tuned to a classic R&B station. Keith Sweat's "Make It Last Forever" was fading into another slow jam.

When Janet Jackson's "Funny How Time Flies" faded in, Ty gasped and prayed Quay hadn't heard her. Surely, he would never recall what the song meant to her, but she would never forget it.

Memories called her back to one late Savannah summer when they'd spent a private week at his grandparents' estate. Of course, Quentin and Marcella Ramsey had no idea Ty and their grandson were secluded in the private cottage across the lake that ran through their property. There was hell to pay when they finally returned from the trip. Their parents were sick with worry in spite of the fact that Quest had covered for his brother by telling everyone that he and Ty had taken an impromptu road trip with some friends.

The cottage was the last slave home left standing on the property that Quentin Ramsey's ancestors dwelled in when their master and his family deserted the plantation following the Civil War.

Quentin and Marcella remodeled the three-room dwelling and it was a private oasis for the adults only. Ty was more than excited to take part in the adventure. Just the chance to go anywhere with Quay always sounded like heaven to her. Their relationship had always been unorthodox. In fact, they'd only gone on a couple of dates, nothing serious. Quay always seemed to shut down whenever the promise to venture deeper rose between them. When they stepped inside the tiny cottage, Tykira was stunned. The place was lovely and perfect for a romantic getaway—music galore, a fully stocked kitchen, mini library/reading area with comfortable throw pillows all about and a gorgeous bedroom. They spent the entire day and much of the evening there, before Ty asked when they'd be heading back.

But he'd had no intention of taking her back just then, Ty learned. She smiled, remembering how uncertain she'd been when he suggested they spend the night.

She'd wanted to scream the word "yes," but didn't want to appear fast, Ty remembered, smoothing her hand across the Humvee's champagne suede seating. Yet Quay continued to encourage and finally succeeded in drawing a tentative "yes" past her lips. It was the best day she'd ever had. Then, one day turned into another and soon almost a week had passed. The song played the first night they made love.

"Why'd you take me there?" she heard herself ask him.

Quay shook his head against the rest and sighed. Clearly, the song had triggered his memories, too. "You wouldn't believe me if I told you. Remember what you said about me taking other girls—other virgins there?"

"So, what's the truth, then?" Ty challenged, watching streams of weakened sunlight lay across her sweatpants. "Wasn't it really because you wanted sex and I'd do because I was there?"

Quay thanked God for quick reflexes as he almost rammed the back of another SUV when he heard her question. "Is that what you've thought all these years?" he breathed, in an incredulous tone, his dark eyes fixed on her through the mirror.

Ty didn't meet his gaze. "What else could I think? The way you treated me afterwards..." her voice trailed to silence.

Now he'd come full circle in realizing the damage he'd done. What she'd gone through, what she believed he'd thought of her. Hearing that was like a knife through his side. He knew she'd be hurt; he'd prepared himself for that and said it was better than having something more hurtful befall her. But somehow, he'd foolishly not considered that she would think he thought she was nothing; that she'd only been a convenient source of gratification instead of the woman he treasured.

The drive continued with no further conversation and Tykira accepted his silence as her answer.

Clearly, Quay didn't want to hurt her feelings by telling her she was right about him. *Well, now you know, Ty, and you've got at least a month to spend with this man who sees you as nothing but a good screw.* She rolled her eyes then. She could only guess that he thought she was good. Hell, he could at least give her that. Her voice of clarity screamed that she hire a nurse and stay at her mother's. But there was more going on—more than Quay refused to say, and she was just too stubborn to let it go. For fifteen years she'd tortured herself with thinking about why Quay refused to let her into his heart. Now she had him right there, taking care of her, no less. Her determination was solid and she could only pray this time would produce the truths she'd waited half her life to hear. Shaking her head, she ordered herself to stick with the plan. Fight the attraction and love she hated to admit she had for him.

Quay pulled his Hummer right up to the entrance of the high-rise where he kept a penthouse. Ty began looking in the rear compartment for her crutches or the dreaded wheelchair. She found neither.

"How am I supposed to get out of here?" she asked when he came to assist her from the vehicle.

"Your crutches and wheelchair are inside," he informed her as though she should have known.

Ty grimaced while gingerly swinging her casted foot down from the seat. "So how am I supposed to get upstairs?"

"I'll carry you."

Ty's mouth fell open and her brown eyes began an immediate search of his black ones. She just knew he'd been teasing. "No thanks," she said at last, seeing that he was serious.

Quay was already easing his arm beneath her knees. "Don't start, Tyke."

"I'm not starting, but this is silly."

"You're right, so please stop the arguments."

Ty clamped her mouth shut and watched while Quay lifted her like she weighed nothing. *Damn him,* she thought. He was making her feel all soft and deliciously feminine without really doing anything at all. *Help me,* she prayed.

They approached the tall glass doors leading to The Loft, where scores of the top businesspeople resided. At one of the glass doors, Ty braced her hand against the jamb and shook her head.

Quay halted his steps. "What?" he asked.

"I can't let you carry me in there," she softly stated.

"Why?" he challenged just as softly.

"You can't."

"Why *can't* I?" he insisted, a smile tugging at his perfect mouth.

"You just can't," she whispered, ordering herself to look away from the sensuous curving of his mouth. "It just wouldn't—wouldn't…"

"Yes?" he probed, standing there holding her in his arms as though it were an everyday task.

"It just wouldn't look right," she argued, peeking beneath her long lashes at the people who cast interested looks in their direction.

"Your foot's in a cast," Quay reminded her, bouncing her in his embrace as he delivered the fact. "Are you saying I'm just supposed to let you hobble to the top floor?"

"It's *your* fault for leaving my crutches," Ty muttered, rolling her eyes at his playful sarcasm. "Besides, I'm sure you're gonna break the hearts of many women if they see you carrying me across the threshold—so to speak."

Quay firmed his arm behind her back, forcing her closer. "Right now, I'm only interested in *one* woman. I've bruised her heart more times than I can count and now, the only thing I care about is making that up to her."

Ty had to mentally remind herself to shut her mouth. She could scarcely focus on anything until Quay cleared his throat and stared fixedly at her hand on the door. Giving in, Ty let him walk on past the entryway. Sure enough, they drew the stares of almost everyone in the lobby. Her fist clenched at his shoulder, when more than a few men complimented Quay on his lovely burden.

"Hey, Barker, Jerry," he greeted the two security guards upon stopping at the desk. "Anything I need to pick up?" he inquired.

"No, sir," Jerry drawled, with a grin.

"Looks like you already have your hands full," Barker noted, nodding politely in Ty's direction.

Quay chuckled and nodded. "Definitely. Barker Doyle, Jerry Brown. Tykira Lowery. She'll be my guest while she's recuperating."

"Nice to meet you, ma'am," Barker said.

"Thank you," Ty whispered, shaking hands with both guards.

Quay moved on. Ty kept her head bowed and her smiles light as they strolled toward the elevator bay. *What is it with these guys and private elevators?* She wondered as Quay selected the car that went only to the penthouse.

Inside the quiet, mahogany-paneled car, Ty could almost feel Quay's probing ebony stare focused her way. Suddenly, her comfy sweatshirt and pants felt unbearably hot.

"So is the nurse already here?" she queried, desperate for conversation.

"You'll meet her in the morning since she'll only be with you during the weekdays," he announced, laughing when he heard Ty gurgle a mournful sound in her throat.

"I wanted to take a bath and I needed her help."

Quay shrugged. "I'll help you."

"No."

He slanted her an innocent look. "I promise to be a gentleman."

"Mmm-hmm, unless I tell you not to be, right?" Ty retorted, knowing the words would be the next out of his mouth.

"You need your rest," he said instead, his sleek brows rising when he noticed her surprise. "Besides, I'm not quite *that* low down."

"Yeah, right. Whatever."

The car stopped and the doors opened into the

penthouse living room. Ty forgot her unease and was immediately taken by the decor. She easily could compare it to the office at Ramsey. The twins clearly adored the dark, masculine decor. Ty hoped Quay couldn't feel her shiver as she took in the savagely beautiful masks and etchings on the brick walls. There were aquariums in each room and they accounted for much of the lighting in the place.

Quay didn't set down his burden until they were inside her bedroom. Ty wondered when the trip would end. After all, she'd be the first to tell anyone that she wasn't the lightest woman in the world. Quay seemed quite content, though, as he carried her through the massive dwelling.

The room that was to be hers was mellow and dim—much like the rest of his home. This room, however, was decorated with sweet creams and pastels. In addition to the pillows and linens, other feminine touches gave it another kind of warmth.

"I just had it redone," Quay made a point of telling her while trying to read her reaction. "I hope I got your size right," he was saying while setting her on the bed where her suitcase rested. When he moved away, Ty noticed that the walk-in closet across the room was filled with clothes.

"What did you do?" she breathed, blinking rapidly as she took in the array of pieces.

Quay shrugged, and then folded his arms and glanced toward the closet. "I figured you'd have a time getting in and out of your clothes." He cleared his throat softly at the way the words sounded.

"Anyway, I had some stuff picked out. You'll find some new pj sets that should go on easy over that cast."

Ty had already hobbled across the room and was peering through the clothes and gasping at how lovely they were.

"Tags are still on. I didn't want you to think they belonged to anyone else," he said when she fixed him with a curious look.

Ty shook her head and turned back to the clothes. "This was so sweet and thoughtful," she whispered, not quite believing he'd done that for her. "Thank you," she added finally.

"Why don't you get settled in," Quay suggested, not wanting to get sucked in by the moment. "Press six on the cordless when you're ready for your bath," he instructed and turned to leave.

Ty only nodded and watched him go. When the door closed behind him, she left the closet and fell back to the bed, covering her eyes with both hands. If Quay intended to play the charming host for the duration of her stay, she was definitely in trouble. She realized it was far easier to handle—or conceal—her needs as long as he remained cool, distant or arrogant. When he switched gears that way, not only was he irresistible, he was downright confusing.

The truth was, she didn't want to believe anything he said—*any* excuses about why he did what he had to do. She didn't want to even consider that his feelings for her were more than just a desire for another sexual conquest. She recalled what he'd said about bruising her heart. If he told her something else, something more than she wanted to hear… But then again, if he told her something more and then went cold again after letting her glimpse into *his* heart, it would kill her.

Less than an hour later, Quay returned to check on his houseguest/patient. He found her asleep with her suitcase opened and partially unpacked. Smiling, he crossed the room, pulled her arm off the case and situated her more comfortably. Then, he finished unpacking her clothes and afterwards he pulled a blanket across her sleeping form. He had all intentions of leaving, when he heard the bed shift as she stirred.

"Quay?"

"Shh…go back to sleep," he urged, holding the door partly open.

"No," she whined, leaning up on her elbows. "I want a bath and I'm hungry."

"All right, well, let me bring something up to you, but forget the bath until the morning," he bargained and prayed she'd go along. He didn't want to think about having to help her settle into a bath he couldn't enjoy with her.

"Quay, please," she insisted, "I just feel so grimy after all those sponge baths at the hospital. I just want to sink into a bubble bath for a while," she sighed, closing her eyes and smiling as though she were envisioning that very thing.

Averting his gaze, Quay smothered a groan and

prayed for strength. Of course, he could understand her desire for a hot bath. "All right, I'll go get the water run." He gave in.

"With bubbles," Ty called, before he could walk out the door.

"Get undressed," he said, gritting his teeth as he spoke the words.

"Quay," Ty called again, pointing when he finally turned. "The foam bath is in the overnight case on the dresser," she told him.

He mouthed a soft curse and practically snatched the bottle from the bag before leaving the room. On his way to the connecting bath, Quay prayed that he'd be able to remember that Tykira was recovering. She didn't need him coming on to her. That seemed fine as a thought, but as a deed, it was murder on other more sensitive parts of his body. *Play it cool, Quay,* he said to himself. Knowing that Ty didn't trust him had to be his top priority. Again, the words sounded fine in his head. Remembering them, when all he wanted was her entwined with him beneath the black satin sheets on his king-size sleigh bed, would be an almost impossible feat.

"Yeah?" he replied, hearing Ty calling to him from the bedroom.

"Bring me a towel, please!"

Groaning, he bowed his head and uttered a hushed, "Help me."

He returned to the bedroom in time to watch her maneuver the wide legs of her black sweats across her ankle cast. Leaning against the doorjamb, he watched her intently. His seductive black stare slid across the sensuous long length of her legs and he grimaced, actually jealous of her hands where they smoothed along the molasses toned thighs. How he longed to replace her hands with his own.

Ty gave her hair a quick toss and was about to pull the sweatshirt above her head when she realized Quay had returned. She smiled when she heard Quay clearing his throat, and extended her hands for the towel he waved.

"Thanks," she said and pulled the shirt over her head.

Quay commanded himself to turn his back before he caught a glimpse of anything. He stood in the doorway, his back turned, and was about to walk out when she called again.

"I'm ready to go to the tub," she said.

He kept his eyes closed for a second or two and then turned. Every single one of his hyperactive male hormones responded to the sight of her on the bed in nothing but a towel—*and that damned cast*—with her gorgeous hair tumbling to the middle of her back. No way could he let this woman walk out of his life. He would not survive losing her again.

Tykira's stare was narrowed inquisitively as she focused on the expression tightening his face. "Are you okay?" she asked.

Hell no! he snapped silently. "I'm good," he managed aloud. "Let's do this," he said, and then smirked and tried again. "Let's get you to the tub."

"Quay?" Ty whispered, pressing a hand to his chest when he leaned closer. "Are you truly okay with me staying here? I can be quite a handful," she admitted.

Don't I know it, he acknowledged silently, taking note of how much a "handful" she was. Her supple curves, the full breasts, firm, ample-sized mounds that a man could lose himself in. "Your water's getting cold," he said, knowing that his thoughts were taking him into dangerous territory.

Ty was only focused on a hot bath and a good meal. She had no idea how she was affecting the man she leaned on. The trip to the tub was achingly slow and Quay cursed and savored every minute. Tykira Lowery struck every man she met as the quintessential independent woman. She had the body and face of a goddess yet one could quickly see that she was a force. She was not someone who could literally be pushed aside without very harsh consequences like a black eye or bruised…extremity. But as overt as that aspect of her persona was, there was that subtle aura of intense femininity. As she leaned on him, her hands curled trustingly around his forearm, her temple brushed his shoulder and she pressed her lips together and looked every bit the determined little girl while hobbling her way to the tub.

With gentle hands, Quay coaxed her into the bathroom. Once there, Ty stopped, her lips parting as a gasp escaped them.

"What'd you do?" she asked, her eyes widening.

Quay shook his head. "I figured you'd want to enjoy your bathtime."

Ty was speechless after that. The room was already exquisite and spacious, but now it possessed the added effect of sensuality. Candles lit the perimeter of the sunken black and gray marble tub. Their delicious unique aromas swirled throughout the air. Soft music just barely vibrated from the speakers and the huge tub overflowed with coconut-scented foam.

"You didn't have to go to all this trouble."

"I don't wanna hear it," Quay grumbled softly, knowing she'd appreciated it. "Just don't get too wild in here. You have to keep this cast dry. It's crazy to even think about a bath, anyway."

"Thanks, anyway, for helping me bend the rules a bit," Ty quietly said.

She looked up at him, her gaze soft and lingering. Quay knew she only had to ask and he'd do whatever she wanted.

Her mind still on the bath, Ty straightened and let the towel slip to the floor.

"Tyke…" Quay breathed, almost losing his hold on her arm.

"Are you okay?" she asked, surprised by his reaction. The raw emotion in his stare had taken her by complete surprise. "You've seen me naked before," she said.

"You don't have to remind me," he spoke through clenched teeth.

Ty nodded, deciding silence was best. Quay finished helping her into the tub of foamy water. He propped her casted foot on the stack of fluffy bath towels he'd perched on the edge of the tub.

"Do you need anything else?" he asked, coming to kneel beside the tub.

"There's a hairpin on the towel," she said, looking past him, "could you...thanks," she said, when he placed the clamp in her palm.

Quay watched, helplessly fascinated as she wound the magnificent black mane into a loose up-do and pinned it tight.

"Mmm...thank you," she sighed, then reclined in the sunken tub.

Quay didn't vacate his spot. He longingly studied the bubbles, wanting to delve just one hand beneath their surface and stroke her with his most intimate touch. He wanted to watch her lashes flutter and her lips part as she enjoyed the pleasure he would bring.

"I'll be fine," Ty said, feeling his stare fixed on her.

He nodded once and patted his hand against the tub. "Call me when you're done," he advised, motioning toward a navy cordless phone that was mounted to one side of the black-tiled wall above her head. Standing then, he reluctantly left her alone.

Chapter 10

"I'm sorry," Quest uttered for the fifth time before the weak apology was followed by another round of laughter.

Quay needed something to keep his mind off the woman lounging naked in his tub. It was either call to vent to his brother or have a few drinks and build up the nerve to go and take what he wanted. Of course, he realized the latter option would probably earn him a busted lip or a shove down the stairs.

"Thanks a lot, Q," he sighed, his dilemma not stopping him from chastising his twin's bouts of chuckling.

"I *am* sorry, man. For real," Quest swore and cleared his throat in hopes of swallowing what remained of his laughter. "I just can't believe you left her up there without making a move on her."

"I'm losin' my edge, Q."

"No, you're not. You're gaining one, if anything."

The perception didn't put Quay at ease. "Gaining what, man?" he snapped. "Some punk mentality? Maybe a better word would be stupidity."

"Wrong. You're gaining a sense of what it means to love and respect one woman so much that you put what she needs above what you want."

Quay massaged his eyes. "What the hell does that mean, Q? I've always loved and respected Tyke."

"But not enough to keep her close—to be honest with her, right?"

Silence.

"You're in a different place now, my man," Quest pointed out. "This time you won't be able to just walk away. Not for any of the thousands of reasons you could find to justify it. You're gonna stay and you're gonna fight to keep her."

"What if she doesn't want to stay?" Quay had to ask. "What if she's finally had enough?"

"Dammit, man, just tell her how you feel. No beating around the bush this time. Tell her. If that doesn't convince her...you're in trouble."

"Thanks," Quay spat.

"There're no easy answers here, Quay. You really screwed things up royally. I can't blame Ty for being suspicious."

"Speaking of Ty," Quay said after he was silent for a while. "I asked her to call me when she was ready to get out of the tub. Q, man I need to go," he decided, knowing Ty would most likely try to get out on her own.

On the way back upstairs, Quay recapped what his brother had said. He had to come completely clean with her. Of course, he knew why he hadn't. It was something he could only admit to himself. He was afraid. Afraid that she really wouldn't believe him and then he honestly wouldn't know *what* to do. Shaking the unsettling thoughts from his mind, he took the steps two at a time, until he was on the wing to the guest bedroom.

He approached the bathroom from the hall entrance and knocked. "Ty? Tyke?"

There was no answer and he guessed she'd gone and gotten out of the tub on her own. He twisted the knob and stepped inside the bathroom. Sensual shock washed over his face when he found her still in the water and asleep. The bubbles were long gone and there was nothing covering her svelte dark frame lying prone beneath the fragrant water.

"I can't do this," Quay whispered, backing away from the tub as he spoke. "Ty?" he called, hoping to rouse her without having to touch her. "Ty?" he tried again.

She never stirred.

"Dammit," he muttered, kneeling beside the tub then. He bowed his head in a vain attempt to keep his gaze averted. She was in a deep sleep; tiny snores slipped past her throat as she slumbered.

Quay rolled his eyes and faced the obvious—

there was no way he could leave her there any longer. He took a bath sheet from one of the unfinished oak cabinets and carried it to the bedroom. Then, he tossed another across his shoulder.

"You're a gentleman, Quay," he chanted. "You're a gentleman," he kept telling himself as he removed his watch and rolled the sleeves of his shirt above his muscular forearms. Effortlessly, he took her from the lukewarm water. His every hormone sizzled in response to what he was viewing—what he was holding.

Ty had obviously washed her hair, for it was wet and hung in wavy, black ribbons. He held her close to his chest and carried her from the bathroom. His grip was firm in order to prevent her slick form from slipping from his grasp. The sound of his own teeth gritting filled his ears as he fought to keep his composure.

Tykira didn't stir once during the brief trip that seemed to last for an eternity to Quay. He placed her on the bath sheet he'd spread upon the bed, and would not allow himself the treat of letting his eyes linger over her incredible form. Instead, he focused on the cast she wore and remembered that she was recovering. Dutifully, he began to rub the other bath sheet across her body. He performed the task in a brisk, efficient manner until his baser instincts strengthened. Then, the strokes slowed and became more lingering. Soon, he was smoothing the bath sheet across spots he'd already dried.

Ty fidgeted in her sleep and mumbled something incoherent, before tossing one arm above her head.

The movement thrust her breasts more prominently upon her chest.

Quay stopped pretending to still be focused on drying her and simply watched. The bath sheet fell from his hand when he lost patience with sight. One hand clenched into a fist and hid deep inside a trouser pocket, the other traced the curve of one breast with the tip of his index finger. He leaned close, pulling the hand from his pocket and bracing it against the bed while brushing his mouth along her temple. He palmed the plump, chocolate mound of her breast more possessively. His thumb just barely grazed a tender nipple.

"Mmm...." she responded in her sleep.

The sound was like a dash of cold water to Quay. He snatched away his hand, muttering harsh curses to himself. Quickly, he found a cute, but concealing pair of pajamas. He dressed her rapidly, gritting his teeth again as he eased a pair of lacy panties over her hips. Once done dressing her, Quay almost sprinted from the room.

Ty woke about two hours later, content yet mildly confused as she studied her surroundings. Then, she remembered she was at Quay's. She remembered something else, too—she'd been in a tub of bubbly water. Now, she was deliciously cozy in a new pair of pj's. She couldn't recall making the transformation, so he must've done it for her.

Her groan filled the room then. She experienced her embarrassment posthaste as she thought of what a sight she must've been—all seductively nude with a big cast on her foot.

But what of Quay? Had he taken advantage of her submissive state? She didn't think he had, sure she would have felt certain aftereffects. Should she ask him? Would she embarrass him? Hmph. It'd serve him right for making her stay with him, knowing all he had to do was look at her long enough and she'd most likely beat him to the bedroom.

Gingerly, Ty pushed herself up and swung her legs across the side of the bed. Switching on the nightstand lamp, she smiled. Her crutches and wheelchair waited across the room. Tossing her hair, which had dried to a wavy mass down her back, she made her way to the crutches and headed out the door.

"What are you doin'?"

Ty was halfway downstairs when she heard him bellowing to her from the bottom.

"I don't believe you," Quay ranted, curving a hand across the banister as he glared, "coming down here in a cast, on crutches and by yourself no less. Do you want that damn ankle to heal, Ty?"

"I can't stay up there all night. I have to eat," she argued, unfazed by his voluminous reasoning.

"I was going to bring it to you," he said, coming up the stairs to finish helping her down. "You can relax in the living room while I get everything heated."

Ty's hand tightened around his. "I hope you weren't waiting on me to eat?"

"I wasn't hungry," he insisted softly, leading her

to a huge, worn black suede armchair. He set a pillow behind her back and made sure she was comfortable before leaving.

Ty dozed in and out, completely at peace in the mellow room, with Marvin Gaye crooning in the background.

"It smells great," Ty complimented when Quay came to collect her from the living room about thirty minutes later. "Did you cook?" she teased in a suspicious manner.

"I never cook." He eased her curiosity with a haughty look. "That's Quest. But my ordering skills are gourmet."

Ty laughed, allowing him to help her from the chair and out to the kitchen. Quay had set the cozy round table for two and the meal it carried looked as wonderful as it smelled. Quay had ordered Italian and there was a veritable feast. For the next ten minutes, they contented themselves on filling wineglasses and loading their plates with Chicken parmesan and angel hair pasta tossed with perfectly seasoned steamed vegetables.

"I can't seem to remember getting back into bed after my bath." Ty mentioned after they'd been eating a while.

Quay continued eating and only offered a shrugged shoulder for reply.

"Do you happen to know how I got there?"

The bath was the last thing Quay wanted back at the forefront of his thoughts. It had been there for the better part of the evening.

"Quay?"

"Hell, Tyke, yes I know how you got there. Who else would've gotten you out? I'm the only other person here."

But Ty was taking great pleasure in torturing him, seeing him so out of sorts. Besides, she had a nagging curiosity to hear him tell her *exactly* how he'd managed.

Quay could feel her staring and gave in. Muttering a curse, he slapped his fork to the table. "I took you out of the tub, I dried you off—"

Ty smiled when his onyx stare wavered and he coughed.

"I, um, I dressed you."

Slowly, Ty nodded. "Thank you."

Quay bowed his head, slicing another morsel of the succulent chicken parm. "I did what had to be done."

"Mmm…and you always do what has to be done?"

"Mistaken again, that's Quest. I'm far more selfish."

"Ha! You get no argument from me there," Ty blurted, taking a swig of merlot.

"It wasn't intentional," he said, setting aside his fork, "not where you were concerned."

Ty kept her eyes trained on her plate.

"Our conversation in the car," he continued, folding his arms across the front of his shirt, "you asked about the weekend—if it meant anything to me? Did I just want sex from you because you were there?"

"Quay, stop," Ty urged, looking up from her plate then. "You don't have to—"

"You asked if my taking you there was really about Wake Robinson. You asked if I was trying to protect you then, too."

"Quay, I mean it," Ty insisted, her warm brown gaze now fiery with determination. "I don't want you to get into that. I should've never brought it up in the first place," she said, forcing her chair away from the table. "I don't need an explanation. I don't *want* one." She stood and immediately stumbled on her cast. She waved a hand toward Quay when he moved to help her. She shook her head and hobbled over to the hutch where the crutches leaned.

"Fool," Quay growled, knocking a fist to his forehead when Tykira left the room. What was he thinking, hitting her with that her first night out of the hospital? She probably thought he was about to lay another line on her. A few seconds later, he heard a thump followed by a curse.

"Dammit, Ty," he chastised when he left the kitchen and found her seated on the stairs where she'd taken another stumble.

"I'm fine," she insisted, tugging on the frosty pink top to her pj's. "Quay, no," she again insisted when he lifted her against his chest.

Of course, he didn't release her, but carried her to the guest room. He tucked her in before taking a seat on the edge of the bed.

"I'm sorry," he said, his dark eyes filled with

genuine regret as he voiced the apology. "I was wrong to come at you with that. Especially tonight. I mean that."

She nervously trailed a hand through her hair. "I just don't need you feeling like I need you to explain. I was wrong for bringing it up in the first place. It doesn't matter anymore."

Quay brushed his thumb around the curve of her mouth. "That can't be true when it made you so upset just a little while ago."

Ty couldn't look at him, and kept her eyes on her lap.

He didn't push. "Get some sleep," he told her instead, pushing a lock of her hair behind her ear when he kissed her cheek. "Good night," he said before moving back. "And don't come downstairs in the morning. I'll bring breakfast to you."

Ty only smiled and waited for Quay to pull the door closed behind him. Then she flopped back in bed and pulled the covers above her head.

"Hey!"

"Hi, you sound out of breath, did I catch you at a bad time?"

Mick switched the phone to her other ear. "Not at all. You caught me on my way out of the study. What's up?"

"Good," Jill sighed. "I know it's late, but—"

"Are you kidding me? It's only 9 p.m. here. Besides, I've been on pins and needles waiting to hear something," Mick cried, then cast a quick glance across her shoulder to see if Quest was near. "How did it go?" she asked more quietly.

"I tell you, getting this exhumation approved almost sounded the end of things. But everything went through incredibly well."

"And?"

"Jackpot."

"You found something?"

"Mick, *every* piece of physical evidence that was somehow *separated* from the official reports was found with Sera's body."

"My God," Mick whispered, feeling a nauseous rumble float through her stomach in response to Jill's news. "What exactly did you find?" she asked.

"Let's see." Jill spoke as though she were looking through the evidence then. "Aside from the clothing she wore on the night of the murder, there're samples—lab samples all labeled nice and neat. Whoever wanted this information out of the way wielded some mighty influence."

"How could Patillo have managed this—to hide evidence this way?" Mick asked.

"From what I understand through conversations with members of the staff when Patillo was C.M.E., the man ruled that place like it was his own private kingdom. He had free rein to do as he wished—no questions asked. Not to mention the caretaker at the cemetery—Mr. Sawyer Reynolds and Patillo were old fishing buddies. It was probably no trouble at all for him to convince the man to…assist him in hiding the evidence. The only question now is, what or who could've persuaded Patillo to put his career on the line this way?"

"Yeah..." Mick replied, her thoughts wandering. "How long will it take to get the evidence tested?"

"I'll get to work on it right away and call you ASAP."

"Thanks for everything, Jill...yeah, we'll talk soon." Mick set the phone aside and thought about what she'd just discovered. She tried to shake off what she was thinking, but it wouldn't go away. Again, the nausea roiled in her stomach and that time it sent her sprinting for the bathroom.

Ty dressed in the private guest bathroom the next morning. She'd selected one of the lovely sundresses Quay had supplied her with. She had no idea the lavender chemise-style frock would favor her curves so adoringly, but it was too late to change now.

"Tyke! Breakfast!" Quay bellowed from the bedroom.

Sighing resolutely, she grabbed her crutches and headed down the short corridor which connected the bath and guest room.

"Will you join me?" she offered, watching as he placed a food-laden tray upon the bed. "Looks like you've got enough," she noted wryly.

"I'd planned on it," Quay said with a bashful grin, "but thanks for offering."

Silently, they took their places on the bed. Quay's dark gaze was hooded as he watched Ty move around in the dress. He cleared his throat and focused on selecting a muffin when she looked up and found him staring.

"Thanks for making me feel so at home, Quay," she said, hoping to dispel some of the heavy emotion in the room. "You're quite the host," she complimented, tucking one foot beneath her when she sat on the edge of the bed.

"Truth is, I never entertained a houseguest before," Quay shared, adding a few slices of cantaloupe to his plate.

"Bull," Ty sang, selecting a plate and fork.

"I didn't mean I've never had an overnight guest before, but I've never had one I've *wanted* to stay longer," he clarified.

"Thank you," Ty drawled, smiling over the way he tried to smooth the admission.

For a while the twosome ate in a peaceful silence. Then Quay hissed a curse when he noticed the time.

"Gotta bounce, Tyke. Another meeting with the Holtz Enterprises," he explained, setting aside his plate.

"Oh," Ty said, obvious disappointment reflected in her brown eyes, "another meeting, huh?"

"Yep," he confirmed, hearing the next question before she even spoke a word.

"Quay, do you think I—"

"No."

"But—"

"No."

"Dammit," she snapped, pounding her fist on the bed. "Won't you let me finish?"

"Not if you're about to ask to go to this meeting," Quay said, about to leave the bed.

"Please," she said, folding her hand across his wrist to prevent him from rising. "Please, Quay," she begged, scooting closer to him. "I'd just be sitting there. What harm could it do?"

Quay shook his head while watching her intently. He knew he was seconds away from giving in.

"Please," Ty urged once more, inching as close as she could.

Losing all ability to restrain himself, Quay leaned in to kiss her. The surprised gasp Ty uttered in response afforded him the opportunity to simultaneously deepen the kiss and position her neatly in his lap. Her casted foot dangled next to his trousered leg while she straddled him. Quay moaned when he felt her cupping the rigid, pulsing part of his anatomy that most wanted her attention. The kiss went on, growing deeper and hotter. Quay's hands applied a penetrating massage to her hips and the small of her back. He settled her closer, groaning when Ty became an even more eager participant in the kiss. Her fingers toyed with the open collar of his shirt, teasing the powerful cords in his neck, before her hands curved around his shoulders. Quay couldn't resist palming and fondling her breasts, manipulating her nipples to stiff peaks beneath the satiny bodice of the sundress. He played in the heavy darkness of her hair as tirelessly as he splayed wide palms across her thighs. When he would have pulled away, she kept his hands where they were and urged them higher.

"Tyke…" he moaned, breaking the kiss to rest his forehead against her shoulder. "The nurse will be here soon. She's got a key. I'll see you later." He quickly delivered the words while setting her away. Then, he was gone.

Hearing the door close, Ty grabbed a hearty apple walnut muffin. She slathered it with butter before chomping voraciously in a weak attempt to clear the encounter from her thoughts.

Chapter 11

Tyke Designs had completed its work. The guys
had agreed with Quay that it'd be best not to keep
Tykira in the loop despite her many requests for information when she'd called in to the office. The
construction crews, architects and interior designers
were at peace with the final plans and she would only
find new worries to interfere with her recuperation
time. As the mechanical building and engineering of
the train had already been underway, the group was
looking for total completion within two months.

Holtz felt that the rail's maiden run should be
something special. They wanted the Ramsey clan on
board along with everyone involved on the project.
The *Holtz Destiny*, the name chosen for the train,

would reside at the new Banff Tower in Canada. It was Holtz Enterprises' plan to have all parties involved with the creation of the resort to be on hand to enjoy the resulting vision. Needless to say everyone was terribly excited and could hardly wait for the event to commence.

"How's it goin'?" Quest asked when he'd pulled his brother aside following one of the morning meetings.

"One night and I'm about to lose it," Quay confided, his deep voice muffled as he dragged a hand across his face. "I have to keep reminding myself that she's off-limits." He grunted and shook his head. "I have to remind myself all the damn time. I want her, Q. Boy, do I want her." His eyes narrowed as visions of Ty lying naked in a tub of bubbles filled his mind. "But if her heart isn't part of the deal..." He trailed away.

Quest didn't hide his smile. "This is what I like to hear."

Quay shook his head and allowed his brother to gloat.

"You think you can handle it?" Quest asked.

Quay's expression was skeptical. "Last night was the first night any woman ever spent the night in my home and woke up the next morning without having been in my bed."

"And it felt like hell?"

Shaking his head at his brother's question, Quay grinned. "Not hell. Not heaven, either, but definitely not hell."

"Damn, man, you're growing up. I'm proud," Quest teased, pulling his twin into a bear hug.

* * *

"Well, this is a treat," Catrina Ramsey declared, while pulling her daughter-in-law close for a hug and kiss on the cheek.

Mick's father-in-law Damon was next in line, bestowing his kiss to her cheek and forehead as he escorted her into the living room. "We were so happy to get your call," he told her.

"I know how busy you both are," Mick noted, squeezing her hands as she took a seat on one of the gold love seats in the living room.

"We're never too busy for you, sweetie," Catrina said.

Mick nodded. "Thanks, because this is something I couldn't put off any longer."

Damon and Catrina exchanged concerned glances.

"Sweetie is…everything all right between you and Quest?"

"Oh!" Mick started, realizing how confusing her words may've come across to her husband's parents. "No, Catrina, no. No, everything's fantastic between Quest and me. This is something else," she said, her amber stare clouding again. "It's something that's not very pleasant, I'm afraid."

Damon and Catrina were silent.

"Sera Black," Mick said, noticing the immediate change in the couple's expression.

"Are there any new leads?" Damon asked after clearing his throat.

Mick told her in-laws everything, holding nothing back. She saved the announcement of the newly discovered evidence for last. When she told them how it'd been uncovered, Damon and Catrina were clearly stunned.

"Obviously someone wanted that evidence out of the picture. I guess they—whoever *they* are—never intended on Raymond Patillo having a crisis of conscience on his deathbed," Mick said.

"And you want to know if we were responsible for the evidence being misplaced? If we paid someone off in hopes of protecting our sons in the event one of them—or both of them—were guilty?" Catrina asked, her lovely dark face a picture of calm.

"I'm so sorry to come to you both with this," Mick apologized, fiddling with the leather ties on her denim jumper, "and I'm not accusing or standing in judgment of anything," she rambled. "But I have to know. If it helps, I can understand why this was done. I'm not a mother, but I know I'd do anything to protect my child...."

"Well, then, love, I'd say you've already learned the first and most important thing about parenting," Catrina commended, reaching out to pat Mick's knee. "But, honey, we didn't do this," she said, before her expression tightened. "*I* didn't do this," she clarified.

Mick and Catrina looked to Damon, who graced them both with a double-dimpled grin.

"Love, I'd be the first to admit that I'd do any-thing—*anything* to protect my boys," he addressed Michaela. "I've already protected them to a great extent." He shrugged. "Perhaps it was wrong, but a parent's love can be a powerful and sometimes misguided thing. Unfortunately, it never occurred to me to do this. When they told me they weren't responsible for that child's death, I believed them."

"Even though Quay was drunk, passed out and couldn't remember a thing?" Mick probed.

"Even then," Damon admitted, with a solemn nod. "Guess that makes us a couple of saps, huh?"

Mick smiled. "No, just a couple of loving and trusting parents."

Catrina elbowed her husband's arm. "Uh, baby, isn't that loving and trusting stuff equal to saps?"

The threesome burst into laughter that greatly lightened the mood. Shortly, however, Damon's expression darkened.

"Even though we weren't responsible, I think it's safe to conclude that this was done by someone in the family," he stated. "Only a Ramsey would have had the means and the motivation to pull off a cover-up like this."

"Who?" Mick wanted to know, her eyes narrowed in confusion. "Who else would have reason to? After all, this hidden evidence, whatever it proves, would've protected Quest and Quay. That's *your* job."

Catrina and Damon exchanged glances over their daughter-in-law's naiveté.

"Sweetie, in such a large family it's natural to protect one's own," Catrina said. "What affects one, affects all."

"You're right," Mick sighed, realizing the woman's point. "I still wonder who, though."

Damon leaned back against the sofa he shared with his wife. "I got a good idea," he said.

"How are you?" Quay asked when he knocked upon Tykira's bedroom door that evening.

"Bored," Ty snapped, without looking his way.

"Nothin' on the tube?" Quay asked.

Ty shrugged, smoothing her hands across the arms of the thermal knit top of her pj set. "I really wouldn't know. This is only my first movie."

"Is that right?" Quay drawled, taking a few steps into the room. "Because I know you watched the soaps earlier today, so I'm pretty sure you've gone over your TV limit."

"Quay!" Ty whined, balling her fists on the bed. "I'm about bored out of my mind. What else do you expect me to do? I begged you to take me with you to the office this morning, if you recall."

"Yeah, I recall," Quay admitted, his expression tensing as he tried not to envision the sultry scene that followed her request. "You hungry?" he asked, noticing Ty watching him.

She softened a little. "I told the nurse I'd wait for you."

"How's pizza sound?" he asked, pulling both hands from his trouser pockets when she nodded. "I'll go place the order. Be right back," he said, watching her snuggle down in bed before he headed out of the room.

Out in the hallway, he prayed for more strength

to keep his hands off her. He dutifully placed the order, took a quick shower and changed clothes, hoping the food would be there by the time he was done. Just chatting with Ty could be dangerous. He was beginning to care less and less about the cast she sported.

Ty clapped when Quay returned to the room carrying a large square box, paper plates, napkins and a six-pack of soda. He set it to the night table while she made room for him on the bed.

"I'll just eat over here," Quay offered, motioning toward the easy chair across the room.

Ty's brows drew close. "But you won't be able to see the movie from over there," she complained.

Not wanting to call more attention to his uneasiness, Quay didn't argue. He prepared two plates filled with three slices of the sinful, cheesy vegetarian pizza for himself and Ty, topped off by two cans of sparkling 7UP.

"What is this?" he asked, referring to the movie about to begin.

"I hope you won't be too bored. It's a mystery-movie marathon. Tonight they're featuring Agatha Christie."

"I hope they start with a Poirot," Quay was saying as he bit into a gooey slice of the pie.

Ty watched him with an incredulous gaze. "What do you know about Poirot?"

Quay leaned against the pillow-lined headboard and smirked. "You're surprised?"

"Quite," Ty admitted with a shrug. "I wouldn't have pegged you for a mystery lover."

"Why not?"

"I don't know," she sighed, taking a swig of 7UP. "You don't seem the kind to sit down to read a book, much less sit still for a two-, two-and-a-half-hour movie. Especially one that requires paying attention to more than foul language, sex or a series of explosions."

"Damn, Tyke, is that what you think of me?"

"Hmph." Ty gestured, helping herself to another bite of pizza. "It's the way you've always been," she cited, having no regard for the stunned expression he wore. "Fast paced, wild, testosterone driven, that's Quaysar Ramsey."

When Quay chuckled and shook his head, Ty's brows rose inquisitively.

"You're surprised?" she queried. "I'm sure I'm not the only woman who has that perception of you," she said, eating heartily as she spoke. "You're fun and incredible to be with—but only for a time. You're not exactly a 'long haul' kind of guy."

Quay didn't know why the description bothered him, but it did. Especially when it was Ty who held that perception.

"Tyke—"

"Shh, shh…it's starting," she ordered, then patted his arm. "Looks like you'll get your wish to see Poirot. They're showing *Murder On The Orient Express*," she announced.

Quay settled back and tried to focus on dinner and

the movie. Unfortunately, he found that spending an innocent evening next to the leggy dark goddess was murder on every part of his body. He wanted her every way he could take her. But, of course, she'd be expecting that—just that and nothing more meaning-ful.

After all, he wasn't a "long haul" type of guy.

A tiny furrow formed at Michaela's brow as she turned onto her back. She moaned softly, feeling herself being caressed by the sweetest touch. She arched upward upon feeling her nipples being suckled and then bathed with lingering strokes. Un-fortunately, the feeling that truly caused the furrow in her brow was a subtle roiling in her tummy. The discomfort grew more unbearable even as the sweet caress continued.

"Mick?" Quest called, pulling away just slightly when he felt her struggling against him.

Mick writhed amidst the covers only a few sec-onds more before she woke. Then, she was bolting from the bed with one hand clamped over her mouth. Quest rested on his elbow, frowning, as he watched his wife race to the bathroom. Slowly, he left the bed and followed her.

Leaning against the doorjamb, Quest folded his arms across his bare chest and watched Mick heav-ing and vomiting into the toilet. The episode lasted at least three minutes.

"Something you ate?" he asked when she was done.

"I—" a totally unladylike burp interrupted her "—I don't think so," she said, sitting on the floor and leaning back against the toilet as she closed her eyes.

Quest pulled a phone from its cradle on the marble countertop. He pressed the button that speed-dialed the family doctor.

When Mick realized who he was speaking with, she waved her hand to get his attention. "Quest, no!" she hissed.

"Just a minute, Doc," Quest said, and then holding his hand across the mouthpiece, he fixed his wife with a firm look. "Hush," he ordered.

"When was your last period, Michaela?" Doctor Lucas Sims asked.

Mick blinked and then flashed a quick glance toward her husband. "I don't...I don't remember," she admitted, crossing one sneaker-shod foot over the other while wringing her hands in her lap. "But, it's usually irregular," she saw fit to share, "especially when I'm stressed or under the pressure of a deadline."

"Is that the situation now?" Dr. Sims inquired.

Mick shook her head, and then rolled her eyes toward Quest when he cleared his throat. "Not exactly, but I *am* working on a case. It's been pretty demanding."

"I see," Dr. Sims replied, and only made brief responses as Mick spoke.

The doctor reached into his bag and Mick and Quest watched as though he were about to extract a magic antidote. When Dr. Sims produced a home pregnancy test, Mick backed away as though it were a poisonous snake.

"Doc? What is this?" Even Quest sounded a bit unnerved as he spoke.

Dr. Sims only waved his hand. "I only want to cancel out the obvious first. Michaela, humor me," he requested, holding the box in her direction.

Quest was right on his wife's heels as she shuffled to the bathroom.

"Quest, what if—"

"Shh...let's just get the test out of the way first," he suggested, even though he was just as rattled as she.

In the bathroom, Mick handled her business and finished up while Quest took the test and placed it on the counter. The only sound in the room was the click of the second hand from the wall clock and Quest's wristwatch, not to mention the methodic tapping of Mick's foot as she sat on the toilet cover. She was seconds away from voicing her impatience when she saw Quest reach for the test box. He read the back and then looked at the test lying on the counter. Then, it appeared as though his legs were about to give and he braced his hands around the rim of the sink.

"What?" Mick called in a frantic whisper. Both her feet were tapping as she practically bounced on the porcelain toilet cover.

In response, Quest turned and flashed his wife a brilliant smile.

* * *

Quay and Ty had already spent three weeks together. It was at times tense and uncertain—and at other times easy and quiet. Through it all, Quay's emotions strengthened and solidified. The problem? He still couldn't verbally admit to wanting a meaningful relationship with Ty, and it was like a knife through his heart every time he looked at her. He'd never given a damn about whether a woman thought he was the relationship type or not. If he wanted a bed warmer—and that's all he'd ever wanted—he had one. Now, though, he wanted more, and it was becoming painfully clear that his "want" would not be fulfilled.

Music touched his ears the moment he left the foyer. He followed the lilting sounds of the violin concerto drifting from the speakers. He found her snuggled on what had become her favorite lounge. Quay's black eyes narrowed as he watched her on the cushioned chair, her fingers toying in locks of her lengthy hair, her toes wiggling where they appeared at the opening of the cast.

Tykira gave a start when she heard him clear his throat. She looked up and greeted him with a lazy wave.

"You and that chair are becoming inseparable," he noted softly while stepping into the living room.

"Mmm, yeah, I'll miss it when I'm gone," she said.

Quay winced, his hand flexing into a fist. His expression turned fierce at the mere mention of her leaving.

"Bad day?" Ty asked, noticing the look upon his darkly handsome face.

"It's not that," he sighed, managing to conceal his mood. "Things are going pretty smooth, actually."

Ty sat up a bit on the lounge. "That's what I've heard. The guys have *sort of* been keeping me in the loop," she shared, smoothing both hands across her arms, bared by the thin straps of her black tank top.

"What's that tone for?" he asked, watching her roll her eyes.

"I get the feeling they're trying not to make me feel left out and pitiful because I'm stuck at home with a broken ankle. I got a call from Louie Danoue earlier and he even sounded like he felt sorry for me."

Quay's grin revealed his right dimple and he shrugged. "Come on, Tyke, they're just tryin' to look out for ya."

"Well I guess I'm just not used to that."

Eyes narrowed, he found her words strange. After all, he'd been protecting her for over fifteen years, hadn't he? The question lodged in his mind and caused him to ponder it for a moment. Maybe he *hadn't* been protecting *Tykira* at all. With that loaded possibility in mind, he went to fix himself a drink at the pine wall bar and then went to join her on the edge of the lounge.

"Having a man look out for you can't be that extraordinary, can it?" he asked, bracing elbows to his knees, while cradling his glass in both hands.

Ty leaned her head back. "Pretty much," she told him.

"Bull."

"Why?"

"Ty, look at you."

She followed orders and did just that, looking down at her black tank top and comfy white cotton sweats. Then, she shrugged and fixed him with a bewildered look. "What?" she asked.

Quay grimaced; he was that perturbed by her confusion. "Woman, do you ever look in the mirror? A man would do almost anything to have you on his arm. Hell, I swore off tall women when I lost you. You were that deep in my system."

Ty blinked, her cool expression turning to something more inquiring. "When you *lost* me?" she probed, her gaze faltering when Quay set down his glass.

"Yeah, when I lost you," he confirmed, turning to face her fully on the lounge.

She was silent for several moments as though debating on whether to speak her mind. "Quay, in losing me, you would've just been making a mistake. You let me go and that was a choice."

"By choice or mistake, I was an idiot for letting it happen."

Bracing her hands on the arms of the lounge, Ty angled her legs over the side. "I'm heading up," she decided.

Quay looked on helplessly as she stood and prepared to hobble out of the room on her crutches.

"I love you. I always have," he said, watching her stop in midstride. "I know you don't believe me, but I have no intentions of stopping."

"Dammit, Quay, you don't know what you're saying," she whispered, turning to face him.

"Why can't I say it when you feel the same?" he challenged.

"And what good did it do for me to love you, Quay?" she countered, her sparkling brown eyes appearing more brilliant from unshed tears. "You say you've always loved me. Do you realize how hard it is for me to believe you felt that way back then? To not be scared out of my mind that…"

"What?" Quay urged, stepping closer to her. He stopped when she backed away.

"I'm going home tomorrow. I won't be here when you get back from work," she announced, already turning away.

Quay commanded himself not to stop her. He'd taken a huge step in telling her how he felt. He watched her until she was gone from view and prayed for the strength he would surely need to make her believe in him.

For *both* their sakes….

Chapter 12

The following weeks went by in a blur. Tykira had her cast removed and had made a full recovery. The family was ecstatic to discover Quest and Michaela would be delivering the newest Ramsey in the summer of the following year. Of course, Quay was already strutting around as the proud uncle and everyone loved the show he put on. When he was alone, however, his every thought centered around Ty.

He hadn't seen or spoken to her since their emotion-filled discussion so many weeks prior. He'd remained absent from several of the meetings, not wanting her to feel uncomfortable around him. He kept abreast of things through Quest, who knew what a rough time his brother was having. Quaysar was thankful for his twin's silent support, but wished he had some verbal advice to see him through the confusion.

The railcar was complete and everyone was looking forward to the celebration party, which would take place aboard the *Holtz Destiny*. The train would be taking its maiden voyage to Banff, Canada. Arrangements to accommodate the group had been in place for months. Around 4:00 p.m. one chilly autumn afternoon, the passengers began to arrive. For a while, everyone simply marveled at the finished result. The majority of the Ramsey clan were in attendance, as were several members of the executive staff and their families. Contessa had even made a special trip from Chicago to enjoy the festivities.

Tykira felt like a proud mama as she accepted all the accolades that were bestowed upon her. She almost couldn't believe it herself as she gazed upon the stunning bi-level railcar. A luxurious glass-domed gallery overlooked a gracious lounge, that could be used as a ballroom. An adjoining dining car would offer passengers fine cuisine in luxurious ambience. Ty couldn't fathom that such a creation had first taken shape in her mind and had developed from simple sketches. Nothing she'd ever done compared to this and it was quite a feeling to be part of such a grand accomplishment.

Porters rushed to and fro, taking bags and directing passengers. Their quarters were all spacious, fully equipped cabins that offered breathtaking views from the widest windows.

Ty decided to head to her own cabin, but stopped just short of taking the steps into the car when she saw Quay. Weeks of not seeing him were like losing a part of herself. She'd missed him terribly, but knew it had been best to leave when she had. Staying would have been far too costly a price for her emotions. He loved her. He'd said it with no subtle coaxing from her about his feelings. For a while, Ty allowed herself to imagine that it was real. That *he* was for real and that the things she'd always dreamed they could share together would really happen. Then, the side of her persona that was responsible for kicking sense into her made her remember the hurt Quay was capable of invoking with his confusing behavior. From that point, all she could focus on was when he'd turn cold again.

After all, she'd heard those words before.

She wanted to move on, but her feet had a mind of their own and refused to budge. Quay caught sight of her, his dark eyes narrowing when he saw her. He dropped his bags where he stood and looked ready to bound toward her.

"Ms. Lowery? Ms. Lowery?"

Ty broke her gaze from Quay and looked down at the young woman calling to her. She could barely hear the girl for the ringing in her ears. "I'm sorry?" she said to the young woman.

"No, Ms. Lowery, forgive me for stopping you. I'm Corin Forest. I've been hired by Holtz to conduct tours of the train."

"Yes, yes of course. It's a pleasure to meet you," Ty said, stepping down from the train to shake hands with Corin.

"The pleasure is mine, Ms. Lowery. I can't tell you how proud I feel to be working on this train, a train designed by a woman."

Ty's smile was genuine. "That's so sweet of you. Thanks, Corin. I know you'll have your work cut out for you."

Corin's expression seemed to dim with a shade of unease. "Actually, that's what I'd like to speak with you about. This train is so big," she sighed, her brown eyes widening as it scanned the creation. "I only have a few questions. If you could spare a few moments?"

Ty was already focused on Quay, who was now speaking with the conductor of the train. She was grateful for the out granted by Corin, but knew she couldn't avoid Quay for the entire trip. Still, it was a large train...

"Ms. Lowery?"

"I'm sorry," Ty gushed and cleared her throat. "Of course, you can ask me anything. Why don't we discuss it on the way to my cabin?"

Corin was delighted. She was already rambling off a dozen questions as she and Ty made their way onto the train.

Ty gasped when she entered her cabin suite. Though she pretty much knew what to expect, she was still awed by the completed product. She hadn't visited the site since before her accident, and, after recovering, decided it would be better to be dazzled once the project was finished. Pleased she'd made that decision, she inspected the area. Unconventional comfort was what Holtz had wanted. They didn't want their passengers to feel cramped or lacking any convenience during their voyage aboard the *Holtz Destiny*. In addition to plush, big beds, all the cabins featured full showers, toilets, storage cabinets, TVs, DVDs, desks and telephones with beautiful throw rugs and matching pillows on the sofas and desk chairs. The effect was topped off in a rich, cherry-wood finish.

Surrendering to the feel of total contentment, Ty removed her boots and took a seat Indian-style on the bed. With the folds of her beige suede skirt surrounding her, she indulged in staring out the window. Of course, at the moment the view from her side of the train mainly consisted of the conductor, engineers, porters and members of her crew seeing to last-minute crises before the train departed. Ty looked past them, staring up at the sky, and imagined gazing up at the stars over rivers and between mountains as the train chugged closer to their destination.

A clicking sound tugged her attention away from the view and she saw a lever turning on one of the doors. When it opened and Quay stepped inside, Ty was stunned. Her legs went immobile and she couldn't even leave the bed.

"What are you doing here?" she managed to ask.

"Um—" his deep voice seemed to vibrate in the

area "—I was just exploring and decided to try the door. I had no idea…"

He trailed off and Ty knew he was just as stunned as she. "Probably Quest and Mick up to something," she predicted in a wistful manner.

Quay smoothed one hand across the front of his mocha-colored sweater. "I fully agree," he muttered.

"I was only teasing."

"I wasn't. I'm pretty sure my twin and his wife are responsible for the coincidence."

"Sorry," Ty whispered, looking back out the window.

Quay waved his hand. "Not your fault my brother and sister-in-law are just pitiful matchmakers."

The word forced Ty's breath to catch in her throat, but she offered no comment. Quay left it alone as well.

"This place is incredible, Tyke," he said, deciding instead to compliment her work.

"Thank you, Quay," she whispered, without realizing how much his approval pleased her.

From the overhead speaker, the announcement was made. The train was set to depart. Ty finally left the bed and joined Quay where he stood at the window to watch the train depart.

As they enjoyed the sight, however, Ty could feel Quay's smoldering ebony stare wholly fixed on her. She would have turned and moved away, but he held her upper arm fast.

"Quay…" was the only word she could pronounce in hopes of refusing. Sadly, every part of her body was highly sensitized to his touch and she trembled noticeably beneath his hand.

Quay was ruthless, offering no escape as he kept her there near the window. He cupped his hand beneath her chin and held her still for his kiss. His mouth slanted across hers and he kissed her tenderly at first before his tongue plundered deep inside. He feasted on the sweetness of her mouth as though drinking in the very taste of her. Moans sounded, but it was impossible to tell who was more affected.

The moment was as explosive as ever, but Tykira could sense an urgency in Quay she'd never felt before. Tiny sounds of desire passed his lips and she was awed by the helplessness she heard in them. His head angled from right to left as if he could not decide which way he enjoyed more. Ty felt as though he were trying to convince her that he was what she needed. Of course, she already knew that and the realization made her melt against him.

Being in such close proximity to a bed did nothing to quell Quaysar's more devilish hormones. They unnecessarily informed him that she was offering no resistance and that this was the time to take what he'd been obsessed with having. He whispered her name then, burying one hand deep within her luxurious hair while his other hand cupped a full breast straining beneath the fabric of the chic suede blazer that hugged her torso adoringly. When she pushed more of herself against his palm, he almost lost the ability to stand.

Somehow, he managed to resist the irresistible.

His hand weakened on her bosom and he broke the kiss to hide his face in the crook of her neck.

"I'll see you tonight," he told her in a voice that was as soft as it was deep.

Ty trailed her lips across his, hoping for just a bit more of his attention. He'd removed his hands, however, and stood waiting for her to uncurl her fingers from the collar of his shirt. Reluctantly, she complied.

Quay's dark stare was knowingly intense. He smiled and watched as she focused her eyes on the carpeting beneath their feet.

Ty didn't move until she heard the door close behind him. Then she turned and pressed her forehead against the window.

Mick had been trying to decide between the two outfits she'd placed on the bed, when the soft chimes of her cell phone filled the cabin. Stunned that the thing was even picking up a signal, she retrieved it from her leather tote. "Michaela Ramsey," she greeted slowly.

"Mick? It's Jill."

Mick began to laugh, ecstatic to be hearing from her friend.

"Is this a bad time?" Jill asked.

"No, no it's a wonderful time!" Mick assured her.

Now Jill was joining in on the laughter. "I suppose any time is a wonderful time when you're expecting a little baby."

Mick rolled her eyes then. "I can see you haven't heard of morning sickness," she teased, indulging in only a few more seconds of laughter before she sobered. "So tell me, can we get to the dirt now?" she requested.

"We can."

"I assume you've had luck?"

"You won't believe how many times I've been stonewalled, Mick," Jill sighed, her frustration coming through clearly in her voice. "No one wanted me to test that evidence and I tell you it was quite a chore in light of how old it was."

Mick sat on the edge of the bed. "But you found something?" she asked, nervously easing her feet in and out of her fuzzy bedroom slippers.

"I did, Mick," Jill admitted, her voice clouding with disappointment. "Honey, I don't think you're gonna like it."

Mick felt the roiling in her stomach that had nothing to do with morning sickness. She couldn't even open her mouth to ask Jill to go on.

"There was semen taken from her thigh, skin from her nails and saliva from her chest," Jill continued, prompted by Mick's silence. "I was able to make a DNA match for two of the specimens—the saliva and the skin. Blood found on one of the pillows was a positive DNA match for the saliva. Thankfully all the guys who attended the party were tested and that was documented in the file—preventing me from having to chase anyone down."

"Mmm, and we both know where that would've gotten us," Mick noted sourly.

"Well, in addition to the blood on the pillows,

there were also trace amounts on the carpeting. I couldn't find a match among the boys at the party," she sighed in frustration. "Anyway, when the murder occurred the two prime suspects were Quest and Quaysar. Like everyone else they were fingerprinted and blood was drawn in light of the fact that a possible rape could have taken place. I even found the actual blood samples in the evidence box."

"I still find it hard to believe they even took blood at the scene, much less the fact that the samples were actually buried with Sera," Mick mentioned.

"Well, there may've been a reason for that."

Mick closed her eyes. "Go on," she said.

"The blood linked to the saliva is a positive match to Quay."

Mick expelled a shaky breath. "Jill, are you sure?"

"I'm afraid so, honey. I even ran the tests more than once to be sure. That's another reason it took me so long to call with the results."

Mick pressed her hand to her mouth and forced herself to calm. "You said you linked two pieces of the evidence. The skin? Who did that belong to?" she forced herself to ask.

Jill understood her friend's concern. "It wasn't Quest, honey."

Mick's entire body loosened as a great deal of tension left her. "Then who?" she asked, after sending up a prayer of thanks.

"The skin was a match for Wake Robinson."

"Wake?" Mick breathed, her mind reeling from

the revelation. "I was beginning to think he'd been a scapegoat."

"Well, I'm not so quick to point the finger at Quay either," Jill told her. "Remember there's still one key piece of evidence with no owner."

Mick nodded. "So what happens now?"

"Now, the ball's in your corner. I need you to talk to Quay. See if he can remember *anything*. The answers may be there and he only needs to unlock them. Whatever happened in that room happened before Quest got there and Quay's the only one who can tell us what that is."

Contessa Warren was already working her magic on the room. The myriad stuffy business conversations mingling around the celebration cocktail party seemed surprisingly *less* stuffy with Contessa's personal flair for gab.

"Tell me, Ms. Warren, is your publishing company targeting any other wealthy families?" Marcus Ramsey asked when he wangled a private moment with her.

"My company doesn't target wealthy families, Mr. Ramsey," Contessa replied, her easy aura never fading. "In fact, the majority of those families come knocking on *my* door looking to tell their stories. The book was my idea," she admitted, her almond-shaped eyes sparkling as beautifully as the row of sequins lining the scoop neckline of her curve-hugging crimson gown.

Marcus nodded. "Your idea?" he parroted.

Contessa smiled. "Mmm...I find your family fascinating, but I too can understand your desire for privacy."

Marcus kept a moderate rein on his tongue. Somehow, he knew his usual overbearing manner wouldn't play well with the no-nonsense young woman he spoke with. "Ms. Warren, *no* family wants *all* their dirty laundry aired before the public," he said.

"I can certainly understand that," Contessa agreed, leaning a bit closer, "especially with regard to your family's situation and all."

"Situation?" Marcus inquired, something dangerous flickering in his dark eyes.

"Sera Black," Contessa specified, her lips curving into a faint smile as she watched the man's dark face grow ashen.

Marcus leaned closer so that he was practically towering over Contessa. "I would suggest you watch how you throw that name around."

"That name may be thrown around a lot more before long, Mr. Ramsey. I've got a feeling a killer is about to be brought to justice." She stepped back and fixed him with a gleaming, albeit phony smile. "Good night, Marcus," she said, and then strolled on to find more interesting conversation.

"Now there's a young lady who doesn't bite her words."

Marcus bristled when he heard Damon's voice. "She's just like her friend," he told his brother.

"Ah, yes, my Mick's somethin' else, isn't she?" Damon commended his daughter-in-law. "She's got drive, spunk, courage," he tirelessly boasted. "I got a feeling you'll have the chance to see lots of that one day," he predicted, clapping a hand to the shoulder of his brother's tuxedo jacket.

Marcus narrowed his eyes and turned. "What the hell are you talking about?"

Damon pretended not to notice his brother's agitation. "I think your sons will gravitate toward those sorts of women. Mine did."

Marcus smirked. "That's because you never stressed that they marry well. A *lady* befitting the Ramsey name."

"The Ramsey name?!" Damon bellowed and threw his head back to laugh. "A family that helps its members get away with murder."

"Dammit, if your sons were to blame you would've—"

"What?" Damon inquired, his brother's words stopping his laughter cold. "What's really goin' on here, Marc?" he breathed.

"I don't know what you're talking about," Marcus said, scanning the semicrowded lounge.

"Nah," Damon drawled, his onyx stare narrowing as he shook his head, "none of that this time, Marc. I know you were the one who covered that evidence."

Slowly now, Marcus turned.

"You didn't know it still existed, did you?" Damon realized, seeing the confusion in his brother's eyes. "Raymond Patillo," he said, smiling when he saw Marc swallow. "You convinced him to *misplace* that evidence, didn't you?" Damon asked when Marc opened his mouth to speak and produced no words. "He didn't get rid of it, Marc, he just hid it with Sera's body. Too bad for you, he wanted to clear his conscience before he died."

"Bastard," Marcus sneered. "How the hell can you accuse me of somethin' like that?"

"Save it, I'm not buying, Marc," Damon sneered right back. "Which one of your boys did it?"

Marcus seemed to calm then and surveyed his brother with a critical eye. "You always looked the other way, Damon. As far away from the family as you could. Especially when one of us was in trouble."

"Now you can just stifle that, Marc," Damon advised, his index finger raised in warning. "You seem to forget all the times I tried to cut corners to *help* you fools hide your messes."

"Yeah, I remember. But in family that's a never-ending task, and when you decided you didn't want it anymore, *I* had to step in."

"This is murder we're talking about, Marc."

"And you wouldn't sacrifice one of your own any more than I would."

Damon searched Marc's dark eyes with his own. "Which one? Which one did it?" he probed.

"So blind," Marc said while shaking his head. "You haven't been able to see anyone or anything since you had those boys."

"They're my children," Damon reminded his brother in a tone of disbelief. "I want you to stop beating around the bush and talkin' in riddles. What the hell is going on?"

The request went unanswered as a round of applause filled the room. Tykira had just arrived and the elegant bar lounge was alive with cries commending a job well done. Marc chose that moment to blend into the crowd, smoothly ending the tense conversation.

From across the room, Quay maintained his position at the bar and watched her bask in the success. He thought about all he'd put her through and how he'd darkened a relationship that could have been nothing but joy. Now, it was up to him to change things. Ty would be his, she'd believe in him again, he vowed to himself.

"Playing shy tonight, I see."

Mick's voice in his ear brought a smile to his face. He squeezed her hand when he felt her rub his shoulder.

Quay kept his eyes on Tykira. "Just trying to give her some breathing room," he said.

Mick elbowed his arm, "Why now?" she teased. "Not in the best mood, huh?" she asked when his smile tightened and he offered no comeback to her question.

"Not in the best mood at all," he confirmed.

"Then I won't feel so bad about sharing my news," she sighed, smoothing both hands across her arms left bare by the wispy straps of her empire-waist gown.

Quay turned, his inquisitive stare turning dark when she announced that she'd spoken with Jillian Red. Quay was stunned, but continued to listen as Mick told him everything she'd learned. For so long, he'd tried to believe it was Wake who'd been solely responsible. Now, there was evidence. His own DNA had been at the scene, not to mention confirmation of a third party.

"Do they suspect Quest?" he had to ask.

"He was tested back then along with you, remember? They've ruled him out as the third party," Mick shared, seeing relief wash Quay's face. "Sweetie, do you remember anything, *anything* that happened before you passed out?" she pleaded, her amber eyes intently searching his onyx ones.

"I can't," Quay admitted, grimacing at how helpless he felt.

Mick bowed her head, sending a slew of curls into her face. "Then, I'm afraid we're all in the dark until Wake comes forward."

Only to himself could Quay admit that he was more than a little terrified to hear the man tell him what part he'd played in Sera's death.

"Will you tell Ty?" Mick asked, smiling as she looked over at the woman laughing with Holtz executives.

Quay shook his head. "Not tonight."

"Will you pull away from her?" Mick asked.

Again, Quay shook his head. "Not ever again."

Ty was waving off someone she'd been speaking with when a pair of steely arms slipped about her waist.

"Congratulations," Quay spoke against her ear, loving the way she felt in the sleeveless black wool jersey dress. The V-neck bodice emphasized her

stunning bosom while the uneven flare hem and
open-toed sling-back heels accentuated the lovely
length of her legs.

Ty snuggled back against him, deciding to enjoy
all the closeness she could.

"I have to say it again, Tyke, this train is unbe-
lievable."

Ty fiddled with his tuxedo sleeve. "I'm glad
you're impressed."

"I was impressed before you drew one sketch," he
said, trailing his nose along her nape bared by the
elaborate up-do she wore.

Ty turned in his arms then. Instantly, she could see
that all was not well. "What's wrong?" she whispered.

Quay shrugged, cursing her perception. "Probably just motion sickness."

"That was your worst lie yet," she criticized, purs-
ing her lips as she watched him. "Come on, what is
it?"

Debating, Quay quickly decided it was best to
keep quiet for the time. "I will tell you this," he said,
gathering her even closer. "I'm never leaving your
side again. You're never getting rid of me," he
vowed.

Tentatively, as though she feared he would pull
away, Tykira eased her hands across the crisp
material of his tuxedo jacket. "I never wanted to get
rid of you," she confided, linking her fingers behind
his neck. "You always seemed intent on leaving,
though."

"That's because I was a fool and I wouldn't deserve you if I allowed that to happen twice in a lifetime," he said, smirking when he noticed Louie Danoue trying to get their attention. "I think your public is waiting," he told her.

Ty barely glanced behind her. "What about you? Where are you going?"

"Not far," he swore, curving his thumb around her cheek, "we *are* on a train in the middle of nowhere, remember?"

Ty tugged on her bottom lip and seemed reluctant to leave him alone. But she decided not to press it and joined the Holtz team on the other side of the room.

Weary and tired of socializing, Quay massaged his eyes and headed back to his compartment. Along the way, his steps slowed and he took time to stare out the glass dome of the corridor leading back to the cabins and seating area. He could tell they were nearing the upstate toward the mountains. Trickles of snowflakes were tumbling from above. They'd be in the thick of it by morning, he predicted. With a sigh, he reached his compartment. Once inside, he didn't bother to turn on the lights, deciding to continue to enjoy the passing scenery.

Quay had been relaxing for a while, and was obviously far more relaxed than he realized, for he was shocked to his soul when a male voice greeted him in the darkness. Turning in the leather swivel chair before the desk, he saw Wake Robinson emerging from the shadows.

"Don't freak out, man. I only came to talk," Wake continued. "I only want to tell my side of things and nothing more."

"Why now?"

"It's time," Wake said.

"You've had plenty of time," Quay remarked dryly, "and I can think of far better places to clear your conscience."

"I need to say this, man."

"By all means," Quay drawled with an airy wave. The room was still bathed in darkness, but his eyes focused steadily on Wake.

"How long had we been friends, Quay?" Wake asked, removing both hands from his jeans pockets as he sat on the leather couch on the other side of the desk.

Quay smiled in the dark, remembering. "Since your mom brought you with her to Ramsey when she interviewed to be my uncle's assistant."

"And have I ever lied to you?"

Quay grunted and removed his tuxedo jacket. "Considering the circumstances, I'd say that's a yes, and this trip down memory lane is getting old. Before you think about sharing the lie you came here with, I should tell you the cops have matched certain pieces of DNA to forensic evidence they uncovered from the murder scene. They've matched me to saliva and you to skin found under Sera's nails." Quay clasped his hands atop the desk and leaned forward. "You understand what I'm saying?"

Wake nodded. "I do. You think I killed her."

"You're here to tell me I'm mistaken?" Quay challenged.

"Very mistaken. If anything, I tried to save her life."

"What?"

Wake's gaze narrowed in the moonlight. "You really don't remember, do you?"

"I really don't. And I'd hate for you to sit there and tell me—"

"I tried to save her life and that's the truth."

"And a truth like that caused you to disappear for the last two, going on three years?"

"No one would've believed it."

"I wonder why?"

"There was a fight, Quay," Wake sighed, massaging his temples as he leaned forward. "You were drunk out of your head and willin' to take Sera up on her offer."

"Bullshit. Sera wasn't one to give it up like that."

"She was bent on revenge—"

"Against who?"

"Against the man she was sleeping with. The same one who dumped her."

In addition to being confused, Quay's anger had reached the boiling point. "I'm not in the mood for riddles," he warned his old friend.

"Look, Quay, after you and I fought—it was nothing more than a punch in the mouth, which probably explains the blood they found. I got the upper hand and you were out cold, but Sera was determined to wake you up. She kept saying she was going to have a Ramsey—one who was free to have her back. She kicked and scratched at me, which is probably how my skin got under her nails. I had scratches for weeks."

Quay smirked. "So I was passed out and you helped yourself?"

"It didn't happen that way," Wake swore.

"Then what way did it happen? Because you obviously know and won't talk," Quay accused. In spite of the dark, he could hear the man's voice shaking terribly.

"Just know this, Quay. The man Sera was seeing came to the room soon after we fought. He told me to leave and I did. When I saw Sera again she was lying on the concrete eleven floors down."

"So you just left her in the room with some guy?" Quay asked, his disbelief clear.

"Dammit, Quay, I was working for that guy. I had been for years."

Quay leaned forward. "Working for him?" he asked, seeing Wake nod in the moonlight.

"I was a cleanup man, so to speak. I *never* killed anybody, but I...*persuaded* several young women to leave certain Ramseys alone."

"Persuaded..." Quay breathed, closing his eyes as so many things began to come together—the disappearances, girls moving away. "This man, the man Sera was seeing, did he have something against me? Since every woman I'd ever shown interest in had conveniently left or been removed from my life."

"This man hates you and Quest very much."

Quay swallowed past the foreboding lump in his throat.

Wake continued. "What happened with Sera was between the two of them. But when it parlayed into a chance to get you and your brother out of the way, he jumped at it."

"What the hell does he have against us?" Quay demanded, standing so quickly he almost sent the heavy leather chair to the floor.

"It's not so much you and Quest as it is your father." Stunned, Quay was already poised to ask his next question when a soft knock sounded against his door.

"Quay? It's me."

Tykira's voice sent Quay's anger fading fast. He forgot about Wake Robinson as he went to answer her knock.

"Hey," he greeted quietly, his dark eyes roaming her face with sweet intensity when he opened the door.

"Are you all right?" Ty whispered, curving her fingers just inside the door as she stepped close.

"I was fine. I'm a lot better now seeing you," Quay said, already leaving his cabin to escort Ty to hers.

Inside her compartment, Quay turned on a couple of lamps and then prepared to leave. "Don't worry about me," he said, brushing his mouth across her brow.

Ty took hold of his wrist. "Will you please stay?" she asked, not ready for their evening to end and not completely sure that he was okay.

Quay cupped her lovely face in his wide palms and smiled. "You can't know how much your concern means to me, but I'm fine. I'll be back, I promise," he said and had every intention of keeping his word.

Eventually, Ty nodded and accepted that his decision was final.

Again, Quay kissed her forehead and backed out of the cabin suite making sure the door was secure before he walked away. Immediately, his thoughts returned to Wake. Unfortunately, Quay found the man long gone when he returned to his compartment.

His anger returned in a second. Hands clenched, he searched for something to slam, which would only upset things. Besides, Ty would surely hear him from her cabin and he needed to keep this quiet. Wake couldn't leave the train and would be like a caged animal before too long.

Quay left his compartment, intent on finding the security chief, conductor and Quest. He saw his brother and Mick strolling the corridor shortly after he'd left his cabin.

Quest took note of his twin's mood the moment they stood face-to-face. "What?" he asked.

"Wake's here."

"Wake? How?" Mick whispered, stepping between the two brothers.

Quay explained briefly, but gave an accurate account of his conversation. When he was done, Quest ordered Mick to her cabin and she didn't argue. After making sure her door was secure, Quest went with his brother to find the chief and the conductor. They made a pit stop in the lounge to collect their cousin Moses who had coordinated the train security with contacts made through his organization of bounty hunters. Quay and Quest were calm as they briefed the men. They emphasized the importance of keeping things quiet. The last thing they needed was a panic on a train ascending a snowy mountainside.

"Quay, I don't think you should leave Ty alone," Quest advised on their way back to the compartments.

"Way ahead of you, Q," Quay said and moved on down the corridor.

Quay had the porter let him into Tykira's cabin. He doffed his clothing quickly so as not to awaken her. Slowly, he slipped beneath the bed's crisp coverings.

Ty stirred, gasping when she felt his arms encircling her—his lips against her ear. She tried to turn.

"No, go back to sleep," he urged, his hold tightening.

Still, Ty tried to turn. "I don't want to," she argued softly.

Quay understood. He was just as starved for her as she was for him. "Wait until the morning," he promised her, brushing his mouth across her cheek. "Right now, I only want to sleep with you."

Chapter 13

A steady snow began to fall during the earliest morning hours. It continued on through a hazy dawn and blanketed the environment in a scene of winter white. Ty opened her eyes and focused on the wide window that held her entranced by the passing view. She was filled with a sense of contentment—and something else. She was very warm and it had nothing to do with the bed coverings. Moreover, it was the steely embrace surrounding her.

It took some doing, but she managed to turn, and gasped when she found herself staring into Quay's strikingly handsome face. He was awake and watching her with an intense emotion that radiated from his dark eyes.

"Are you all right?" were her first words. Her nails grazed his jaw as she spoke.

"I'm good," he muttered, his mellow voice seeming to resonate in the room.

Ty studied every inch of his face. "I want to know what's going on," she said.

"I don't want to talk, Ty."

"But I—"

"Tyke, right now, talking is the last thing I want to do with you."

Tykira's questions faded like mist as his words melted her amidst the luxurious covers. "Quay..." she breathed, her fingers weakening on his cheek.

Taking both her hands and pressing them close to his chest, Quay lavished her mouth with quick, soft kisses. The innocent pecks grew hotter and wetter in their urgency until he'd kissed a path down the column of her neck and the swell of her breasts.

Ty tugged her bottom lip between her teeth and surrendered to what occupied most of her waking thoughts. Quay paid special attention to the budding nipples that were already firm in anticipation of his touch. He tended to one with maddening thoroughness. His tongue bathed the rigid peak with languid strokes before he suckled fiercely. His long brows were drawn close as he focused all his concentration on the task. Persuasive fingers grazed the other nipple. He alternated between squeezing the dark tip and soothing it with his thumb.

Ty arched and moaned, surrounded by a sea of sensation. Quay partially covered her with his lean,

muscular frame. His hands now encircled her waist
when she arched upward. He never ended the maddening assault on her breasts. The glorious mastery
of his lips and tongue was wholly centered on her
nipples. Tykira's gasps of utter delight in his ear
fueled his determination to take her to the cliffs of
satisfaction with the simple caress.

Quay settled himself snuggly beneath her thighs
and almost lost all ability to reason when she raised
herself against him. The torturously erotic friction
forced a moan past his lips. Ty shuddered, feeling his
helpless cry against her breast. Her hands gradually
gained strength and she stroked the crisp silkiness
of his hair. Unconsciously, she drew his head closer
to her chest. Quay switched his attention to the other
breast, ravaging it with his tongue and teeth. His
hand cupped and fondled the mound as he drew
more of her satiny molasses flesh into his mouth.

Ty's breathing was basically a series of shuddery
sighs as she struggled to relay her need. Quay knew
how affected she was—he felt the same. Her unconsciously sensational grinding against his manhood
was slowly driving him out of his mind. His head
was filled with visions of burying himself deep
inside her then. He wanted to plunder the soft cream-
iness of her sex until she had nothing left to give.
Still, he wanted to savor the moment and knew that
would be a lost fantasy if he gave in to his basest
urges then. But he had to see her, smell her—feel her
on his mouth.

Ty cried out her disappointment when he left her

chest and showered his kisses across her abdomen. Her hands fell away from his back to lie weakly against the pillows cradling her head.

At the joining of her thighs, Quay simply trailed his nose across the light dusting of tight black curls he found there. He grazed the most sensitive area of her femininity, the devilish right-dimpled grin appearing when she responded with a delighted shriek. Her hands came to his shoulders. The pleasure was so overwhelming she didn't know whether to pull him closer or push him farther away.

Quay made the decision for her. He held her hands to the bed and only feasted on that overly sensitive bud of flesh. Tirelessly, he nibbled and stroked there without a care for her breathless pleas for mercy. Ty strained against his hold. Never had she been so affected. Her hips rose from the bed and eventually Quay released her wrists to hold her thighs in place.

Ty buried her fingers in her hair and submitted to the sinful pleasure he eagerly provided. She'd climaxed more than twice and knew not whether she could survive the eventual treat of their lovemaking.

Quay offered her a brief respite. Of course, Ty would've been the last one to call it that. He ended the scandalous kiss after plunging his tongue deep inside her only once. Then he was turning her onto her stomach, tonguing a wet kiss down the length of her spine. Then he rose to cover her with his body. He pushed her thick hair over her head, exposing her neck, and feasted on her nape. Ty pressed her face into a pillow and snuggled her bottom against the impressive extent of his thrusting power. Quay's hand curved over her hip and disappeared between her thighs. Ty sobbed when his fingers entered her one, two three at a time. They stroked deep and rotated in an ever increasing wealth of moisture. Quay's kisses to her back grew more ragged as Ty continued to grind her bottom against him.

Completely weakened by desire, he could barely retain his grip on the condom packet he'd taken from his trouser pocket. Ty saw it fall to the pillow in the line of her gaze and she could feel him trembling behind her. Just as overwrought as he, she turned over and managed to remove the condom from its packaging and eased it in place. The simple act took far longer than she'd anticipated. Her eyes widened at the sight of him; his length and girth made her mouth dry with desire.

Quay could waste no more time. His powerful hands curved around her upper thighs, pulling them apart as he thrust forward. He squeezed his eyes shut and clenched a fist that he pounded against a pillow. Never had he experienced such sheer desire for any woman. But Ty wasn't just *any* woman. She was the woman he dreamed of every night and day.

They made love throughout the snowy morning. Quay took his time pleasuring her and allowing himself to be pleasured. Ty felt ravished and welcomed the feeling of being overwhelmed by the powerful dark male she had desired all her life.

"Quay?" she called, when they lay spent and satisfied amidst tangled covers.

Immediately, he raised his head and blinked when he spied the unease in her stare. "What's the matter?" he asked, his concern clearly evident.

"The night we were together...after the club," she clarified, seeing his dark gaze grow haunted by memories of that evening. "I hadn't been with anyone since that night we first made love."

Quay's sleek onyx brows drew close and now his eyes held a look of stunned disbelief. In his wildest dreams he couldn't fathom this beauty virtually locking herself away because of him.

"Ty, I'm so sorry for the way that night ended. The way I made you feel..." he trailed away, grimacing as though the words put a sour taste in his mouth.

"I've never been able to imagine myself with another man," she confided, her eyes lingering on snowflakes trying to cling to the window. "Whenever my platonic relationships took that turn, I'd end them before things went any further. I cursed you so many nights. I cursed myself for feeling so deeply for you that I couldn't let another man touch me. I was sure you didn't have that problem where other women were concerned."

Quay winced. "Tyke—"

"No, no, don't," she soothed, curving her fingers

around his jaw. "There's nothing to be sorry for or to regret. You owed me no loyalty. I only wanted you to know those nights meant so very much to me. I love you. I always have. I fear I always will."

"Fear?" Quay parroted, appearing hurt.

"When it came to being hurt by you, you never disappointed me. To believe it may really be a thing of the past scares me. I'm so afraid that I won't be able to handle it if it happened again."

"Ty, listen to me—"

"Shh…" she requested, hugging him close when he lay sprawled across her. "Later. I don't want to talk about this anymore now."

Quay raised his head from her shoulder, not misunderstanding the meaning in her words. He began to love her every bit as passionately as before, but with an added urgency. It was laced with tenderness, as though he were trying to tell her that he'd never stop until she was happy, and the amount of time that would take would do nothing to discourage him.

Afterwards, they lay staring out the window with Quay's head resting gently against Ty's chest.

"I always wanted to protect you," he said. "I felt that way even when I felt girls were yucky instead of yummy." He chuckled. "Quest always treated you like you were one of the boys, like you could handle yourself. And you could, but something made me want to keep you safe."

"That's probably why I fell in love with you," she whispered, stroking his temple.

"That didn't stop me from being a selfish jackass, though," he admitted, his voice growing rough in the wake of his agitation. "I knew I was hurting you by being so cold, but doing what *I* felt was right was my only concern. Truth is, I was only protecting myself and *my* feelings." He turned over and looked down at her. "*I* was the one who'd had girls disappearing and dying on me. *I* was the one who didn't want to lose my heart. *I* was the one who couldn't handle knowing I was the reason you were in danger or the possibility of losing you. *Really* losing you, Tyke, was something I couldn't think about."

Ty braced herself on her elbows and watched him closely. "And now? Are you saying you don't feel that way anymore?"

"I know you don't believe me," he said, his right dimple appearing when he smiled, "but I can't let you walk out of my life this time. As important as your safety is to me, living without you a minute longer is a reality I can't live with a second longer." Inching closer, he cupped one hand around her cheek. "I know it's going to take you a long time to trust me and I'll wait as long as that takes. You've always meant everything to me and I only ask that you please not shut me out while you make your decision."

Ty felt the slight pressure of tears behind her eyes. She smoothed the back of her hand across his cheek and whispered his name.

Catrina Ramsey was adding cream to her hazelnut coffee when a shadow slanted across her table.

"Houston," she greeted, smiling up at her brother-in-law.

"I only stopped to extend my congratulations on your future grandchild. You'll be the most beautiful grandmother I know," he said.

Pleased by his comment and overjoyed by talk of her grandchild, Catrina laughed. "Why, Houston, thank you so much. Damon and I can't wait until Michaela has the baby, and she's not even showing yet!"

Houston managed to chuckle at the comment. "Yes, it looks like you and Damon are doin' it up as usual—the first grandparents," he noted, his tone mildly biting, as he thought of his son and daughter, Taurus and Dena.

"Well, I'm sure you'll experience the same joy soon enough," Catrina predicted. "Besides, I never thought either of my sons would fall deeply in love with one woman and become content in making a life with her." She shook her head. "It's wonderful to see two ladies' men like my sons finally get it together."

Houston appeared confused. "Are you saying Quay has also found someone special?" he asked, sliding into the opposite side of the booth.

"Mmm...found her *again* would be more appropriate. I pray he and Ty will be next."

"Tykira?"

Catrina nodded, her clipped silver locks bouncing around her lovely dark face.

"I had no idea there was anything between them."

"There always has been, since they were kids. Then Quay started showing his ass and wanting to sow royal oats. But I think he's finally matured to the point that he realizes pushing Ty away would be the biggest mistake of his life."

"Well my, my, don't y'all look cozy!" Damon's playful bellow drowned out his brother's next question.

"Well, *my, my*, Damon, still possessive of your toys, huh?" Houston retorted, taking personal offense to his brother's tease.

Damon noticed Catrina's hand curve into a fist and he covered it with his own. "You had your chance, Hous. Don't blame me because I got the prize," he said wryly.

Houston moved from the booth so quickly he almost tripped.

Catrina shook her head, watching the man bolt away in a huff. "Children," she chastised.

Damon shrugged and reached for his wife's coffee mug. "He started it," he muttered.

A few booths away, Quay and Ty sat talking with Quest and Mick. Of course, the topic of discussion was Wake Robinson and his visit. Impossibly, it seemed the man had disappeared from the train, as all searches had turned up no sign of him.

"Do you guys have any idea who this other man Wake mentioned might've been?" Mick asked, watching the twins shake their heads simultaneously.

"He didn't give me one damn clue," Quay said softly. "But he did say whoever it was hated me and Q with a passion."

Silence settled as the foursome stared unseeingly at the snow-white beauty past the windows.

"Mick?" Quay called, having worked up the nerve to ask the question that had been nagging him since the night before. "How long will Jill hold off on what she discovered about the evidence?"

"Oh, honey," Mick soothed, reaching out to rub his hand, "I understand your concern, but we can trust her. She won't make a move until she hears from me."

Silence settled once more and then Quest nudged his wife's arm. He nodded once toward Quay, who sat with his legs extended across the booth while Ty leaned back against him. The couple wore pensive expressions, and Mick agreed with her husband that they'd probably want time alone. She and Quest quietly excused themselves and left the dining car.

The moment they were alone, Quay expelled the heavy sigh he'd been holding.

Ty turned, watching as he massaged his eyes. "What is it?" she whispered.

Quay rested his fist under his chin. "I'm scared," he admitted.

Ty blinked, never believing he could feel such an emotion. She toyed with the comfy material of his black knit turtleneck sweater and realized that he was more than entitled to feel that way. She wanted to reassure him, but decided that he only needed her to be there.

"Isn't this somethin'?" she said, turning to lean

back against him. They watched the gorgeous winter view from the train's huge windows.

Banff, Canada

The *Holtz Destiny* reached its destination later that afternoon. The view from the mountaintop was a vision that could not be described. Bags were taken from the train and deposited in the specified rooms. All the while, the passengers stood mesmerized by the scenery.

Girard Holtz, founder and president of Holtz Enterprises arrived to greet his guests and told everyone he prayed future visitors would be as taken by the view as they were. The group was treated to hot cocoa topped with marshmallow crème while they breathed in the crisp mountain air. Girard covered his plans for their stay: tour the property via sky lift, skiing, ice skating and games. There were also libraries, a movie theatre and several cafés for their enjoyment. All features would be accessible for the trial visit.

Everyone felt right at home and eventually the group began to disperse. Ty had gotten separated from Quay and found herself pulled aside by her crew chief Samuel Bloch.

"So, is Quaysar Ramsey the one?" Sam asked, after he and Ty spoke briefly about the inn and their grand accomplishment.

Ty rubbed her yellow mittens across the arms of her heavy white ski jacket. "Yeah, it's Quay. It's always been Quay."

Sam nodded. "I can't say I'm not disappointed, seeing as how I always thought it'd be me." He feigned despair and joined in when she laughed. "I thank God you aren't doomed to be a beautiful lonely woman for the rest of your life. And don't tell me you were *alone* and not lonely," he ordered when she opened her mouth to argue. "I know what lonely looks like," he said, tugging on the tassels of her knit cap.

Smiling, Tykira nodded. "You're right. I worked and worked to keep myself occupied and even though you guys kept me close, I could never quite escape the feeling."

"I get the feeling there's a lot of hurt there?" Sam probed softly, his arms folded over his chest as he watched her closely. "You sure about him?"

Ty laughed. "I'm not sure about *anything,* but I know I can't walk away from it. I've wondered for too long what being with him would be like. I can't wonder any longer, you know?"

Sam nodded. "I know," he said, and pulled her close for a hug. "I wish you everything good," he told her while pressing a kiss to her cheek.

That afternoon, Mick found her husband seated at the spacious walnut desk in their suite. His laptop was on, but his gray stare was focused past the window. The champagne-colored drapes had been opened and Quest was staring over the rolling expanse of snow-covered land.

"Quest?" Mick called softly, already closing the

distance between them. She stood behind the chair he occupied and then leaned down to link her arms around his neck. "You okay?"

"Are *you* okay?" he preferred to know.

"Uh-uh, mister. I asked you first. Are you on edge about Quay?"

Quest felt every muscle he possessed tighten a thousand times. "I know he's innocent, but the reality is, the evidence puts him there with Sera. If that evidence surfaces... Without Wake to come forward and confirm what he told Quay, Quay will take the fall."

"But Jill—"

"Love, Jill Red may be a good friend, but she's a cop first," Quest warned. "She's not going to sit on that evidence forever. Remember, everyone already thinks the Ramseys have been getting away with murder."

Mick didn't want to think about it. "What about the other person Wake mentioned? The one who he said hired him?" she said, hoping to add a tone of assurance to the conversation.

"Unfortunately, we still need Wake to resurface and confirm that to someone besides Quay."

"Well, have you been able to think of anyone since breakfast? Anyone who could hate you guys like that—business associates, former friends...or cousins?" she asked, massaging his shoulders beneath the hunter-green sweater he wore.

Quest was already shaking his head. "I can think of several business associates, but none who knew us since high school. As for cousins, in spite of all the drama in the family, we've managed to stay close."

When Mick uttered a heavy sigh, Quest turned and had her sit on his lap. "I don't want you worrying over this."

Mick's smile was melancholy. "I'm afraid I will until something presents itself in our favor."

"Baby, I believe the Ramsey luck and double dealing has finally run its course."

Mick's arms tightened around Quest and they shared the snug embrace for the longest time.

On the other side of the mammoth-sized inn, Tykira found Quaysar in the same pensive mood that his brother was currently battling. He held a glass of scotch perched on the arm of the chair he occupied. The sitting room was lit only by the snowy grounds and inside by a fire roaring in a grand stone hearth.

Ty kept a mug of hot tea cradled in her palms as she neared Quay.

"If you sit anyplace but my lap, I'll be very unhappy," he called out to her.

Ty smiled at his undying humor and followed his instructions. She set down her mug and snuggled into his lap, smiling when he grunted his satisfaction.

"You seem unhappy," she noted quietly.

Quay didn't deny it. "Unhappy and unnerved— not because of what the evidence showed," he said, when Ty turned to look at him. "I was there and I played my part in not conducting myself the way I should have. But, it's knowing that there's some fool out there with this old grudge against me and Q."

"Have you thought anymore about who it could be?" Ty inquired, folding her arms across the front of her navy-blue hoodie.

"No one who goes that far back," Quay said.

"What about jealous cousins?" Ty asked. "Ones who were outside the closest circle you grew up with?"

Quay gave a slow shrug and then shook his head. "I can't see it. Besides, none of them lived that close. We only saw each other during reunion time—if then."

Ty bit her lip, toying with a lock of her hair as she debated. "What about someone else in the family?" she asked finally.

Quay's sleek brows drew close when he heard the question. Then, his expression cleared as though he were grasping the true meaning of her words. "You think it could've been one of the elders?"

"Have you ever considered that?"

"No," Quay responded quickly. "We never had a reason to…" His voice trailed away. "I mean, we've had our run-ins, but they usually rose from basic teen-age crap—nothin' to frame a person with murder over."

"Maybe *you* don't think so."

"Uh-uh," Quay denied the possibility by shaking his head, "I can't make myself believe that."

"All right, it's all right," she soothed, feathering kisses across his brow. Snuggling deeper into his embrace, they enjoyed the snowy view for a time.

"I'm not a nice man, Tyke," Quay said after the silence had grown lengthy.

"Hmph, you're tellin' me." Ty didn't lift her head from his shoulder as she uttered the teasing remark.

"I'm serious, Ty. I mean, damn, I've done everything to get you out of my life, out of my mind, out of my heart over some foolish need to protect you."

"All you had to do was be straight with me," Ty said, raising her head then to stare at him. "You could've saved us so many years of heartache if you had. But," she sighed, replacing her head on his shoulder, "your reasons...I can understand them, but Quay, please stop punishing yourself for doing what you felt you had to do." She reached for his hand and planted a kiss in his palm. "I love you. You love me. It's all that matters."

"What about your business?"

Ty shrugged. "What about it?"

"Tyke, your business is gonna be the hottest ticket after word spreads about this project."

Ty snuggled deeper into his embrace. "I'll have time for my business and you, too."

"In Colorado?"

"We'll work out something."

"I don't want to work out something," Quay argued, the muscle dancing fiercely in his jaw. "That'll get old quick," he predicted.

Ty blinked, unease finding its way into her thoughts. She feared he was grabbing for excuses to keep them apart. "Quay, what are you saying?" she forced herself to ask.

He waited for her to turn and face him. "I'm asking," he corrected, placing a hand over her heart, "I'm asking you to make room for me—for us—to have a life together, Tyke. I'm asking you to be my wife."

Tykira was stunned speechless. Seconds—though they seemed closer to minutes—passed before an incredible smile illuminated her face.

Quay blinked, his features softened by relief. "You have no idea how long I've waited to ask you that. I pray you won't wait too long to give me an answer." His brows rose as he lowered his gaze. "If the answer's no, I won't like it, but I'll accept it."

"Yes," Ty whispered, searching his dark eyes with her vibrant ones.

Quay closed his eyes as though he were praying. Then, he leaned in quick and provided her with a devastating kiss.

Chapter 14

Mick got a late start that morning. She wasn't surprised to find Quest gone, she'd been sleeping later and later, due in no small part that she was now sleeping for two. When the knock sounded on the door, she celebrated having a reason to motivate herself out of bed.

"Good morning, Mrs. Ramsey," the valet greeted in a shy tone from his position on the other side of the door.

"Good morning," Mick returned just as another yawn claimed her. "Sorry," she whispered.

The young man smiled, glancing down at his shoes before looking back toward the petite dark beauty that stood before him. "That's quite all right, madam. A package for you," he announced.

Mick's amber stare brightened as she watched the short Hispanic man produce a small wrapped package from the valise he carried. She signed the pad he extended and then found a ten-dollar bill inside one of Quest's jackets on the coatrack.

"Have a good day," she bid when the young man thanked her for the tip. Sighing then, she closed the door and tore into the package. Finding the name Sera Black scrawled on the front of what looked to be a small book forced a gasp past her mouth. Her heart began to race frantically when she realized the book must've been the other half of the girl's diary.

"I'd almost forgotten," Mick whispered to herself. Immediately, she opened the book and began to scour the cream-colored pages trimmed in a floral print. Closing it then, she decided to call Sera's mother and thank her for never tiring of the search.

Johnelle Black answered her line and Mick relayed her appreciation. Johnelle's reaction, however, was not what Mick expected.

"It's wonderful news, Mick, but for the life of me, I don't know how you got it. I've been searching and rechecking places I'd already looked, but I haven't come across it."

Mick's hand went limp around the phone. "Then who?" she whispered, wondering who in the hell could have sent it.

"I have no idea… Does it shed any more light on the case, though?"

Mick trailed her fingers across the spine of the diary. "I haven't really read it yet, but I'll keep you posted."

"Thanks so much, Mick."

"You take care."

The call ended and Mick reached for the book. She held it reverently as a pensive look came to her face.

Tykira smiled as she snuggled deeper within the covers of the gorgeous king-size bed with its royal purple dressing and champagne linens, which was the basic color scheme of the elaborate suite. Snow trickled past the windows, reminding her of the morning she and Quay had spent making love aboard the *Holtz Destiny.* Delicious smells wafted beneath her nostrils then and she saw Quay arriving with a silver food tray in hand.

"What's this?" she asked, pushing hair out of her eyes as she leaned back against the bed's cushioned headboard.

"Breakfast. I hope you're hungry," he said, placing the tray upon the covers and taking his place on the edge of the bed.

"Well it certainly smells good. What is it?"

"Something I hope you'll love forever."

The strange comment brought a curious smile to Ty's face. She observed the tray. A single red rose lay across two covered platters. A smaller platter sat atop the larger and Ty decided to check it first.

"Quay," she breathed, seeing a breathtaking marquise-cut diamond ring sitting on a cushion in the middle of the saucer. "What have you done?" she gasped as he took her hand and eased the sterling silver band onto her finger. "Why didn't you give this to me yesterday?"

"Yesterday was so crazy," he recalled, brushing his thumbs across her fingers as he stared at his ring adorning her hand. "I wanted us to start today off better. Is this better?" he asked, looking up and smiling when Ty began to giggle her agreement. Tugging on her hand to draw her close, he kissed her deeply.

When Quay pulled away, Ty noticed the drawn look clouding his dark face. Tilting her head, she cupped his cheek. "What is it?" she asked.

Swallowing, Quay took her hand and kissed the center of her palm. "I need to tell you about Zara."

"No. No, you don't," Ty said, having no desire to discuss the girlfriend he'd flaunted in her face during high school. "Why would you even mention her now?" she asked with an uneasy laugh.

Quay took both her hands in his. "You need to hear this."

"Quay, no—"

"Shh…" he urged, pressing a kiss to her mouth. "I need to say this, all right?" he pleaded, giving her hands a quick shake and smiling when she nodded.

"You remember us together?" he asked, waiting for the nod which she reluctantly gave. "She went missing the summer after our junior year—do you remember that?"

"Yes, Quay, but why—"

"I blamed myself for that."

Ty blinked, as a confused frown marred her lovely features. "But…why?" she asked.

"The week I kept you with me, I was so desperate to have you," he confessed, staring down at her hands as though the action were giving him strength to continue. "I don't know what I would've done if you'd refused to go. I knew that I was taking a chance even going there with you, but it was a chance I had to take."

Ty scooted up in bed and focused on him more closely. "Why'd it have to be a—a *chance?*"

Quay squeezed his eyes shut, then his jaw clenched and he looked up at her. "Because...two other girls I knew had already gone missing during our Christmas break sophomore year."

"What? B-but how?"

"I don't know," Quay whispered, his onyx stare narrowing as if he were concentrating. "At first, I only told Q about what I suspected. Then we got Ma and Dad in on it. Q was sure the girls—both of whom had fathers working for Ramsey—just moved away or relocated because of something with the company. We checked with Pop and that wasn't it." He swallowed, clutching Tykira's hands a bit tighter. "Then there was you. Always there—always caring about me, even when I started treating you cold to make you want nothing to do with me. That week with you was about me taking what I wanted—what I'd *always* wanted—and knowing I could never have again."

Ty smoothed the back of her hand across his cheek. "Quay..."

"Anyway...Zara," he sighed, massaging the

bridge of his nose. "Zara was always there, too. She always made it known that she was *available* to us. I don't know how many of us gave in to her, but I knew she'd be the perfect one to show you I was serious about it being over with you and me."

Ty leaned back against the pillows lining the headboard. "The way she used to hang all over you...I figured you guys had something really close."

"Close," Quay grimaced. "Yeah, sexually, and that's all it was. Zara wanted it to be more. All of a sudden she wanted to be in love and I was the lucky guy. She was always telling me how she felt and wanting me to say it back, but I couldn't, and then..." he shrugged while shaking his head. "One day I was finally honest with her. I blurted out that I loved you—that all this was to make you stay away because it was safer for you. She asked if I cared about *her* safety, but she didn't wait around for me to give an answer. I never saw her again."

"Quay..." Ty soothed, moving to her knees and leaning close to kiss his temple.

"Then there was Sera, a girl I'd barely known, was barely close to, and she wound up dead," he said, keeping Ty close as he spoke the words. "The reason I'm telling you all of this is because I want you to be sure. I won't lie to you. Having you in my life—letting it be known that you're mine—it scares the living hell out of me." His hold tightened around her slender frame. "I want you to be sure."

Ty inched back to look at him. "I'd rather live a full life with you, no matter how brief it may be," she vowed, cupping his face when he grimaced at her

words. "I'll take that *any day* over some half exis-
tence without you. I love you, Quay—only you—
only you forever."

The grimace left Quay's face and was replaced by
his dimpled grin. "Forever. You mean that?"

Ty settled herself across her fiancé's lap and
linked her arms around his neck. "You betcha," she
confirmed before snuggling down within the luxurious covers. Quay followed her example and they
spent the rest of the morning making love.

Later, Quay had lunch sent up for them to enjoy
in bed.

"Quay?" Ty called even as she arched into the
erotic kisses he rained across her thighs.

"Hmm?" he replied, his kisses growing wetter as
they fell to her inner thigh.

"Do you have any ideas about the wedding?" she
managed to ask.

Quay was caressing the sensitive flesh of her
femininity with the tip of his nose. "You can have
whatever you want. All I want is you for my wife,"
he said, and treated her womanhood to a lengthy
stroke from his tongue.

Ty's lashes fluttered as she submitted to the sensual power of the scandalous delight. His expertise
made her orgasm within minutes, and it was quite
some time before she spoke another word.

"Could we have the wedding at your grandparents' place in Savannah?" she asked when they were
finally dining on the delicious lunch.

"Are you sure, Tyke?" Quay asked, his handsome face a picture of stunned uncertainty.

She shrugged. "Why not?" she countered, and began to munch on a cherry tomato.

"That's where things started to go wrong for us," he reminded her.

"I don't see that," she disagreed, pushing her plate aside and focusing on him. "I see it as the place where my love for you reached a new level and now it's happening again and I can think of no other place where I'd want to become your wife."

"I love you," Quay swore, pulling her from the bed to kiss her again. "You're about to be mine forever," he whispered, gliding his hands across her dark figure and reveling in the way their bodies were a perfect fit. "I better start preparing this thing," he said suddenly, as though he'd just been struck by an idea.

"You're going *now?*" Ty cried, already anticipating more of his touch.

Quay needed no further persuasion. He pulled her with him to one of the armchairs set before the frosty windows. Taking his place there and having her straddle his lap, another sensuous scene ensued.

Quest's gray eyes narrowed when he returned to the suite. He'd assumed Mick had been up and about hours ago and therefore hadn't returned to the room. Finding his wife sprawled out and asleep sent his concern mounting. He went to kneel next to the bed, where he toyed in the dark curls covering her head.

"Michaela?" he whispered, waiting as she opened her eyes and focused in on his face. "Are you all right?" he asked quickly.

"Mmm...fine. Just taking a nap, I'm fine," she assured him with a lazy smile.

Quest leaned close and kissed the mole at the corner of her mouth. "Dinner's in a couple of hours," he told her.

"Quest..." Mick groaned, turning her face into the pillow. The last thing she wanted to do was leave her reading that had proven to be so interesting. "Can't I just eat up here?"

"Why?" he asked, her simple request triggering his suspicion.

Slowly, Mick began to push herself up in bed. "I've been catching up on work I—I just didn't want to break into it," she said, watching as Quest thumbed through the material littering the bed. She snatched away the diary just as he reached for it.

"What's wrong with you?" he demanded, his unsettling gaze narrowed toward her.

"Dammit, Quest!" Mick snapped, leaving the bed in a huff. "I'm pregnant! Does that answer your question?!" she raged, faking a hysterical fit and praying he'd buy it. "Jeez, I think I'm entitled to behave strangely and completely *not all right*," she grumbled and folded her arms across the front of her burgundy empire-waisted nightie. "Would you please leave me alone now? I promise to be ready for dinner."

Knowing it was completely useless to argue,

Quest ordered his own temper to cool. Throwing up his hands, he left the suite, muttering below his breath. Closing her eyes in relief, Mick flopped down on the bed and clutched the diary to her chest.

Quaysar had sent special invites out to the members of the Ramsey family in attendance. One of the glorious top-floor dining rooms of the inn had been specially prepared for the event.

As promised, Mick was ready for dinner and sat looking lovely yet troubled—a fact that didn't go unnoticed by her husband. Quest sat directly across from her. Mick spent the better part of her time fidgeting with the asymmetrical collar of her tan silk frock and staring blankly around the room. In spite of the fact that she'd barely spoken two words to the woman, Mick was grateful to have Contessa seated next to her and chatting away. Contessa's rambling was perhaps the only thing keeping Quest from grilling her, Mick thought.

Contessa, unfortunately, was far from pleased. Her best friend was barely reacting to a thing she said. If there was one thing Contessa Warren hated, it was not receiving adequate reactions to her sly, outrageous comments.

"I'll bet I'd get your attention if I ripped off this gown and pranced naked up and down this table," she scoffed, folding her arms across the scooped neckline of her ample bosom.

A moment later, she felt a soft touch brush the nape of her neck. Turning quickly, she glanced up and froze.

He has to be a Ramsey, Contessa thought. She swallowed, knowing her words had deserted her when she studied the man whose magnificent caramel-toned face held her in awe.

Fernando Ramsey leaned down a bit, his soothing fingers still brushing Contessa's skin. "You may not have Mick's attention, but you definitely have mine," he said, and then walked away as coolly as he'd approached.

Thoroughly embarrassed, Contessa was silent following the brief encounter. Thankfully, the guests of honor arrived. Quaysar and Tykira were the epitome of beautiful chic. He was in a gorgeous black tux with a three-quarter length jacket that made his powerful torso appear more massive. She was alluring in a figure-flattering black gown with flaring long sleeves and thigh-high splits on both sides. Open-toed black heels had straps that hugged and accentuated her ankles and toned calves.

Quay helped his fiancée into her chair at one end of the long table, and then he took the chair opposite her.

"What's this about Quay?" Marcus had to know.

"Patience, Marc," Quay urged, getting comfortable at the table.

"Patience," Marc retorted as though it pained him to pronounce the word. "Is that what you told our clients when they asked how long we were going to wait before dining with them?" he admonished, leaning forward in his chair to rap his knuckles against the table. "It's ill-mannered and bad for business to exclude our hosts," he added.

"I've already spoken to them. I told them why we wanted time alone with the family."

Feeling foolish for voicing his criticisms, Marc let the subject drop without another word. Michaela was watching the man so intently, she almost missed her husband's gaze focused as intently on her.

"Come on, Quay, enough suspense. What's up?" Yohan Ramsey asked his cousin.

Quay's right-dimpled grin flashed and then he was looking at Ty. "I finally wised up and asked the goddess at the end of the table to marry me. She said yes."

At once, the room grew even more lively as the sounds of best wishes and cheers filled the air. Even Quest forgot his mood and bestowed congrats on his brother and future sister-in-law. Conversation and laughter filled the room. A short while later, the servers began to arrive with a hearty meal.

Through it all, Mick was still quite unresponsive. Contessa decided that enough was enough.

"Does this have anything to do with the baby?"

The question effectively pulled Mick from her doldrums. "The baby?"

"Mmm-hmm. You *are* pregnant, right?"

"Contessa—"

"I mean, you're sitting over there *not* talking to me, *not* laughing at my jokes. What? Don't you like Tykira?"

Mick rolled her eyes at the absurd question. "I love Ty. She's exactly what Quay needs and the only woman he's ever really loved."

"Then dammit, what the hell is wrong with you?" Contessa practically growled.

"I know who killed Sera Black."

The hushed statement caused Contessa's hazel eyes to widen. "You know, but—but who? How did you find out? Have you called the cops? Do they have Wake?"

"Contessa, Wake Robinson hasn't done a thing except help keep a murderer free."

"Who did it?" Contessa asked, carefully pronouncing her words as if Mick were dense.

"I can't say just yet."

"Mick!"

"All I have is circumstantial evidence. At least I think it's circumstantial."

"And what is this evidence?"

"The diary," Mick shared, watching Contessa lean back against her chair. "Johnelle Black was right—there were two diaries. But of course Sera couldn't write down her murderer's name in the diary, so there's nothing binding that links the murderer to her."

Contessa shook her head to relay confusion.

"She was having an affair with a married man."

"Ah!" Contessa bellowed, glancing across her shoulder. Thankfully all the other conversations in the room were an effective cover for hers and Mick's words. "So much for innocent lil' Sera. What?!" she cried, when Mick slapped her thigh.

"She didn't deserve to die, Contessa."

"Obviously his wifey didn't think so."

Again, Mick looked toward the other end of the table. "It wasn't his wife. In her diary, Sera wrote that she'd threatened to reveal the relationship if he didn't leave her. If we can tie him to that semen evidence taken from her body, maybe…"

Contessa's eyes narrowed almost to the point of closing. "It's someone in the family, isn't it?"

"Everyone, could I have your attention please?"

Contessa's question went unanswered as silence filled the room and everyone looked toward Quay, who had spoken.

"During our train trip up here, I got a visit from Wake Robinson," Quay shared, allowing voices to raise as the group expressed surprise. "We kept it quiet, but we did have Moses and his boys on it," he said, nodding toward his cousin.

All ears and eyes were riveted on Quay as he divulged every aspect of the conversation he'd had with Wake aboard the *Holtz Destiny*. The family listened in awe as he spoke on the newly discovered evidence and how he'd remained hidden.

From then on, the dinner went downhill. The meal went unfinished as appetites were lost and everyone just wanted out of the dining room. Amidst it all, Quest's entrancing silver-gray stare was trained on Michaela. She'd barely noticed that they were virtually alone in the room. When at last she pushed back her chair and stood, Quest was right by her side.

"Bedtime," he announced.

"Quest, please don't pull the overbearing husband routine right now, I—"

"Then you're ready to tell me why you're walkin' around here lookin' like you just lost your best friend. You hardly ate a thing."

"Neither did anyone else," Mick pointed out in a meek tone. She swallowed when the muscle danced wickedly in Quest's jaw.

"I have no more patience left, do you hear me, Mick? You say you're not sick because of the baby, but I wonder about that. You won't tell me what's going on and I'm not about to take a chance with your health or our baby's."

Mick bowed her head and said nothing more. She let Quest lead her back to their suite. There, he undressed her and selected nightclothes which he put her into himself. Then he tucked her in for the evening and forced himself to leave her be.

Still, Mick couldn't stand seeing him so uneasy and caught the edge of his tuxedo jacket before he moved away from the bed.

"I have the other half of Sera's diary," she confided.

Like his legs were deflating beneath him, Quest flopped to the side of the bed. He looked completely drained and Mick scooted close to hug him.

"Sweetie, don't. It's not Quay. He didn't do a thing," she assured, still hugging him close.

Quest tilted his head and watched her. "Wake?"

"No."

"Mick—"

"Shh," she soothed, pressing her fingers to his mouth. "Baby, please just let it go at that for now.

Nothing is for certain yet and I don't want you more upset. Just let me handle this for now, okay?"

Quest pressed his lips together, sparking his left dimple as he debated. "I don't like the toll this is taking on you," he said finally.

Mick agreed. "Do you think it'd look bad if we left a few days early?" she asked, her eyes downcast.

"I don't care what it looks like," Quest returned. "We'll leave in the morning."

Everyone, in fact, felt much the same. After the dinner scene the night before, the beauty and luxury of the inn had worn thin on them as well. The Ramsey jets arrived by midmorning the next day. From Canada, it was a nonstop flight to Seattle. Both jets remained void of heavy conversation. Pensive moods struck everyone hard. Even Contessa, who was usually never at a loss for words, had little to say. She stared idly out her window without really seeing any of the gorgeous blue sky or luminous clouds. With her legs crossed and her hands folded primly in her lap, she had no idea how closely she was being studied.

After a while, however, her senses peaked and she turned toward the muscular caramel-toned male seated diagonally across from her. Surprised to feel a smile tugging at her lips, Contessa cleared her throat softly. She took note of the man's slanting stare, which raked her legs in a repetitive and scandalously erotic manner.

Contessa recrossed her legs and waited.

The man took his time, but eventually his translucent caramel stare rested on her face.

"I hope I meet with your approval?" Contessa said, once their gazes locked.

He smiled, stroking his goatee with a light touch. "I have no complaints."

Obviously, she thought. She refused to let his blatant appreciation excite her. After all, she was Contessa Warren. She was no stranger to men staring at her.

"Who are you?" she asked, believing he was a Ramsey but not knowing which one.

"Fernando Ramsey," he supplied.

Contessa nodded. "The black sheep," she added.

Fernando's eyes crinkled adoringly when he grinned. "That label does little to set one apart in a family like mine."

"Mmm, indeed," she agreed and leaned forward to extend her hand. "Contessa Warren," she said, mildly surprised by her response to his hand enveloping hers.

"Ah, Mick's friend. The publisher."

"That's right."

Fernando appeared impressed. His mesmerizing stare was focused like a lion on his prey. "Busy profession."

Contessa toyed with the diamond stud adorning her earlobe. "Busy, but rewarding."

"And draining?"

Thinking about Mick, Contessa's easy mood vanished. "It's *very* draining," she admitted.

"And you don't think Mick should be putting so much of herself into this investigation?"

Contessa blinked, stunned by the man's perception. "You're right. I don't. I do pray that Sera's murderer will be caught soon." Her gaze faltered when Fernando just continued to study her intently.

"You shouldn't worry," he said finally and rested his big hands on either arm of the chair he occupied. "Mick's strong and one has to keep up a strong front to be part of this family, blah, blah, blah…"

Contessa laughed, surprised that someone who appeared so intimidating could be so animated. "I've noticed that," she told him, her expression sobering. "Kind of sad, don't you think?"

Fernando shrugged. "I never looked at being strong as a sad thing."

Contessa made a tsking sound and stood. "Mr. Ramsey, one should never have to keep up a strong front for family. Excuse me," she whispered, leaving Fernando staring after her as she walked away.

"How is she, Quest?" Ty asked when she and Quay arrived for dinner one evening.

Quest closed the front door and then turned to hug Ty and shake hands with Quay. "We had to bully her into staying in bed. The Doctors forbid her to do anything more," he told them.

It had been one week since the group had returned from Banff. Mick had been conducting what work she could from the comfort of her bedroom, before finally deciding she needed to share what she knew.

She'd arranged a dinner party, asking Quest, Ty, Quay, Catrina and Damon to attend. Clearly, Quest was on edge about the gathering in light of her health.

Ty sat tapping one of her flat leather riding boots to the carpet. "I'm going to check on her," she decided, standing from the sofa.

"It's okay, girl, I'm here," Mick called, making her way downstairs just then. She walked right over to Tykira and hugged her tight. "Congratulations. I'm so happy for you," she whispered, pressing a kiss to Ty's cheek before doing the same to Quay.

"All right, Mick, enough with the sappy stuff. Exactly what's all this about?" Quay asked, keeping his arm around his sister-in-law's shoulders.

The bell sounded before Mick could explain and she was glad. Damon and Catrina were just arriving. Hugs, kisses and idle chatter were in order again. When the conversation settled on wedding arrangements, the twins exchanged incredulous gazes.

"Enough!" they bellowed simultaneously.

"Mick, out with the secret," Quay ordered.

Nodding, Michaela agreed this needed to be said *before* dinner. "Everyone sit down," she requested, waving the group toward the living room.

"Sweetie, are you feeling well?" Catrina asked, once she and Damon were sharing the butter cream leather love seat.

Mick nodded. "I'm fine," she said, smoothing both hands across her red silk lounging pants and taking a deep breath. "I'd feel a lot better, though, if

I knew why your brother-in-law hates Quest and Quay so much."

Damon and Catrina watched each other for several moments and seemed to reach their decision in silence. Clearly, Mick had most of her answers and only needed their confirmation.

"I came into the Ramsey family on Houston's arm," Catrina said, smiling at the surprise on her sons' identical faces. "We'd been seeing each other for two years before he decided to introduce me to his people. Not that he wasn't proud of me," she interjected, smiling as she remembered. "He treated me like a queen. Actually, he seemed less proud of himself. Even with his own family he was always on edge. Especially around his brothers. He hated Damon. I could see that right away. At first, I thought it was because Damon was the youngest, but it went deeper than that."

"I was the laid-back one of the group," Damon boasted, winking at his sons when they laughed. "Things always seemed to come easy to me with little or no effort—grades, girls, our parents' love," he said, his expression sobering.

"Damon caught my eye right from the start," Catrina shared, her lovely features bright with love for her husband, "but I never had an intention of hurting Houston. One day, I—I found myself alone with Damon where he, um, made his attraction known," she explained, shaking her head when Quest and Quay whistled and commended their father.

"Anyway," she sighed, "I told him I wasn't interested, but he wouldn't back off. After that, it was only a matter of time before I'd fallen for him completely."

"What happened to Houston?" Mick asked.

"I refused to leave him in limbo, so I told him about my feelings for Damon."

"Ugly scene," Damon said, leaning forward as one hand clenched into a fist. "It could've been worse had I not arrived when I did."

Quest and Quay's gazes narrowed in unison.

"Did he touch her?" Quest asked.

Damon grimaced. "I walked in just as he'd knocked her to the floor."

"Son of a bitch," Quest hissed, both his large hands fisted.

"He's dead," Quay muttered, already out of his chair.

"Quest! Quay! Boys, please," she cried.

Damon caught Quay's arm and pulled him close. "Believe me when I say I took great pleasure in handling it," he said, pushing Quay back to his seat and massaging both his sons' shoulders before returning to his own seat.

"We never spoke on it again," Catrina went on. "We've managed to be civil to one another over the years, but I know the hatred is still there and simmering."

"Simmering more than you know," Mick said. "It's why he pushed the book so much. He was determined to see Quay or Quest pay for Sera's death."

"He was pretty much the same when the murder took place," Catrina noted.

"Yeah, for a while he was really pushing the cops to look into it," Damon added. "We knew it was because the room where Sera was found was in the boys' names, but then one day he just let up and never mentioned another thing about it."

"It was because he knew there was even stronger evidence against him."

The group seemed stunned by Mick's revelation.

"Evidence against Houston?" Quay asked.

"Sera was having an affair with a married man. That man was Houston," Mick said.

"Houston?" Ty cried in disbelief.

No one could believe it. Damon told everyone about his conversation with Marcus aboard the train. He remembered accusing his brother of covering for someone, but had assumed he was trying to save one of his sons, Moses, Yohan or Fernando.

"Not his sons, but his brother," Ty replied, then shook her head. "Why'd Houston kill her, Mick?"

"According to Sera's diary, she wanted him to leave his wife. He wouldn't," Mick shared, recalling the words scribbled angrily into the girl's diary. "She said she wouldn't give up until he left Daphne—said she'd go tell her if he didn't."

"Do you really think he killed her, Michaela?" Catrina asked.

"I don't know," Mick sighed, trailing her fingers through her curls while leaning back in her chair, "but if the semen matches his, he'll be the prime suspect."

"So what now?" Quay asked.

"*Now* he'll have to be tested, and I doubt that'll happen in Seattle," Mick warned. "Perhaps we'll have a better chance in Savannah. After all, they'd have jurisdiction, right?"

"And how do we get him there?" Catrina asked.

"The wedding," Quest figured.

Damon nodded. "If we could get him down there, he'd be somewhat off-kilter and it could be to our advantage."

"Honey, this is your brother," Catrina whispered to her husband.

Damon kissed the back of her hand. "My brother wanted my sons to pay for a murder *he* committed."

While everyone mulled over the best way to get Houston to Savannah, Quay left his chair to kneel before Tykira.

"How do you feel about this?" he asked, brushing his thumb across her mouth. "This is your day. Everyone here would understand you not wanting it marred by some sting operation."

"That's right, Ty," Mick called, having overheard Quay's words. "This can be handled in a whole other way."

"Thanks, Mick," Ty said with a smile before turning back to Quay. "It's *our* day and we could've been together so long ago had it not been for all this. That jackass deserves to pay," she decided, biting her lips when the words passed her mouth. "Sorry, Mister D," she whispered, wincing toward

Damon, who graced her with his striking double-dimpled grin.

"No apologies are needed, love," he told her.

Ty nodded and then squeezed her fiancé's hand. "Let's do this."

Chapter 15

Savannah, Georgia

The home of Quentin and Marcella Ramsey had been the meeting place for virtually all the family's happiest gatherings. After the scandal that had rocked them, and with Quentin and Marcella's deaths, the family scattered. The beautiful estate was infrequently used or maintained.

Tykira Lowery was determined to change that. After all, this was the place where she and her future husband first made love. Today, it was to be the place where they would vow to love each other forever. The property, which had been a prosperous antebellum plantation, was a picture of life. Busy caterers, musicians, florists and valets rushed about seeing to the needs of the arriving guests as well as food and entertainment. The brisk mid-November chill added a cozy feel to the festivities. The event would culminate with the wedding, to take place the following evening.

"You mind?" Damon asked Marc, having found his brother in one of the sitting rooms that had been stocked with a full bar.

"Hmph, father of the year," Marc cajoled with a tired grin. "Can't believe you're about to have *two* married sons."

Damon knew the remark wasn't meant as a compliment. "Care to elaborate?" he asked, determined to keep his cool.

Marc shrugged. "Hell, what's there to elaborate on? Those two? Their lifestyles and attitudes…neither is the marrying kind."

"Be that as it may," Damon sighed, pouring a glass of Hennessey, "my boys know how to love."

"And what the hell does *that* mean? That some dig at my sons?" Marc snapped.

Damon took a swig of the liquor. "Not at your sons, just at their upbringing. You raised them to be suspicious of everyone—even their women," he said, fixing Marc with a knowing look. "You treated Josie like a possession and taught them to do the same with their women," Damon remarked, referring to Marcus's wife Josephine. "I've watched all three of them lose wonderful ladies because they treated

them like possessions—objects for their pleasure."
Damon shook his head and turned back to the bar.
"Thank God they're finally growing up and seeing
the error in their ways."

"Who the devil do you think you are, D?" Marc
snarled, leaving his stool at the bar. "You come in
here actin' all big to run down how I raised my boys?
Why? 'Cause yours finally decided to walk down the
aisle? Hell, I give both those marriages four years
tops," he predicted with a haughty sniff.

Damon finished his drink and prepared to leave
the bar.

"Hell, I see why Houston hates your ass," Marc
still rambled. "Possessions. Ha! You wanna talk to
me about possessions? That's a laugh, considering
how you treated Catrina. You took her for your own
when she was on your brother's arm."

"Speaking of Houston," Damon interjected, refusing to be riled by Marc's words, "did you know how
far he was willing to go with Sera before she died?"

Marc appeared to stop breathing. "What are you
getting at?" he asked.

"There's proof that could link Houston to her
death."

"You lie."

"Marc, please don't waste my time acting like
you didn't know that. After all, it's the reason you
went to such lengths to protect him all these years,
isn't it? Did you know what Houston was planning
to do to that child?" Damon whispered when his
brother remained silent.

Marc's deep-set eyes narrowed with menacing intent toward his younger sibling. "That *child* was about to rip this family apart," he sneered.

Damon stood. "She was a baby—not even eighteen!"

"She was a conniving *woman*," Marcus corrected. "Slut, if you will. To let a man use her like that and then threaten to publicly expose him with adultery."

Damon shook his head, trying to will his heart to stop its frantic beating. "So you *did* know he was going to kill her?"

Marc smirked and turned away. "Your good-son routine has no authority here, D. You ain't the police."

"Oh, so you'd prefer speaking with them? They're on their way, you know?"

Marcus turned swiftly. The smug expression he wore vanished instantly.

Damon checked his watch. "They should be coming up the driveway any minute."

"What have you done?" Marc breathed.

"What should've been done long ago to give that girl's family some peace."

"Where's Houston?" Marc demanded.

Damon closed the distance between them. "I suggest you worry about yourself. The law don't look too kindly on accomplices, either."

"Son of a bitch!" Marc raged, slamming the beaded whiskey glass he held against the bar. "This isn't over," he promised.

"It is for our brother," Damon said, before Marc stormed out of the room.

* * *

Tykira was going over last-minute music selections for the reception when the door to Quentin Ramsey's study closed behind her. "Hey, Houston," she greeted with a cool smile. "I'm so glad you decided to come down."

The curiosity on Houston's face was a perfect match to the tone of his voice. "I was anxious to see how the place looked. You've done a wonderful job," he commended.

Ty nodded and looked around the study. "Well, truth is, I have to give most of the credit to your nephew. Quay's been more of a part of this thing than I have. What?" she queried, noticing the look Houston sent her.

Smoothing one hand across his closely shaved head, he grinned. "It's hard to picture Quay married. Are you certain about him, Tykira?"

"Why Houston, what an odd question," Ty said, pretending to be shocked.

"Sweetheart, forgive me. It's just that Quaysar Ramsey isn't exactly known for being a one-woman man."

"I'm aware," Ty admitted, watching Houston approach her.

"Forgive me," he urged, spreading his hands in a defensive gesture. "The last thing I want to do is cloud your day, but you *are* a very beautiful woman," he said, his eyes roaming over her body with unmasked appreciation. "You have a lovely personality and I would hate to see a dog like Quay ruin you."

"Dog," Ty repeated, her brows rising. "Well, Houston, I've hated Quay a long time. I hated him because all those years ago I loved him and I believed he didn't love me," she said, turning back to rummage through the pile of CDs and vintage albums cluttering the desk. "It wasn't until I finally went back to Seattle that I discovered he was trying to protect me."

"Protect you?" Houston repeated, his eyes narrowing inquisitively.

"Mmm…against a *shameful bastard* who had a vendetta against Quay and Quest because of some old grudge he held against their parents. The *shameful bastard* wreaked havoc," she continued, still riffling through music as she spoke, "especially on Quay, because he couldn't touch his real enemy—Damon. Quay was so outspoken, so outwardly confident—just like his father. So in order to drain him of some of that confidence, the *shameful bastard* started targeting the women Quay was interested in. He'd get 'em to leave town or just disappear. Then came Sera Black—who wanted a Ramsey and was quite interested in Quay. Then she met the same *shameful bastard,* who proceeded to have an affair with her without a care for his wife and kids. He had a real good time, too, until Sera demanded he leave his wife or else." Ty shrugged. "Then she, too, had to go. You can see how all this would affect Quay. He wanted nothing to do with me because he wanted me to hate him, to leave him alone, to get me as far away as possible before the *shameful bastard* realized he had another victim."

Once Tykira finished her theory, Houston could barely contain himself. His chest heaved beneath the worsted fabric of the three-piece light blue suit he wore. His hands shook noticeably as he tugged upon the white tie around his neck. "Tykira, are you trying to tell me someone—someone else was responsible for Se—Sera's murder?" he managed to ask.

"Precisely," Ty confirmed, tossing her hair across her shoulders.

Houston cleared his throat. "But without proof—"

"Oh, there *is* proof, Houston."

"May I ask what?"

Ty took her selected CDs to the shelving near the door. "Oh, proof that was buried—not destroyed, like the *shameful bastard* and his equally shameful brother thought. Thankfully, the man who agreed to do away with said evidence had a crisis of conscience on his deathbed," she went on, turning to stroll back to the center of the room. "Then, there's Sera's diary, which names the *shameful bastard*," she concluded.

Fighting a losing battle against trying to maintain his cool, Houston shuddered. "Shall I guess who, Miss Lowery?"

Ty smiled. "Why, no, Mr. Ramsey. You know all too well."

"Houston Ramsey?"

The study door opened and Detective Jillian

Red arrived with several uniformed and plain-clothes officers.

"Houston Ramsey, we have a warrant for your arrest and we'd like you to come with us, sir," Jill requested.

"I'll do no such thing," Houston lashed out. "What's the meaning of this?"

"Sera Black," Jill announced, nodding to two of the officers who went to stand on either side of Houston. "We have some questions for you regarding her murder."

Houston still feigned confusion. "What would I know about that? Whatever your questions, you can save them for the appropriate party," he decided, his voice beginning to tremble. "Now get out of my parents' home."

"Very well, Mr. Ramsey. If you'd just come with us," Jill repeated.

"On what evidence?" Houston thundered.

"Based on evidence we have that you and Miss Black were having an affair and semen taken from her body on the night of the murder, we're also requesting a DNA sample. This will hopefully rule you out as a suspect, Mr. Ramsey. It would look far better if you cooperated without being summoned by a court order."

"Preposterous!" Houston raged, knowing he was running out of time. "I'm a married man. How dare you accuse me of—" He stopped himself, watching as Michaela entered the room and handed something to Jill.

"Sera Black's diary," Mick explained to her husband's uncle. "That and a positive match to the semen should help the D.A. form her case."

"Thanks for your help, Mick," Jill said. "Let's go, everyone."

"You little bitch!" Houston hissed, charging toward Michaela. The uniformed officer stopped him cold. "How dare you turn this around on me! I came to *you* with this!"

"Mmm, all a part of your plan to frame the nephews you hated, right?" Mick surmised.

Houston struggled against the officer's restraining hold. "You scheming little—you were never good enough for this family. You—Marc?! Marcus!" he cried, having spotted his brother barging toward the room.

Marcus fought his way past the officers filling the doorway. It seemed the rest of the family had gotten wind of the uproar, for the entire corridor was filled with people.

"Marcus!" Houston literally cried. Tears pooled in his eyes and wet his cheeks. "Do you see what they're doing? Help me! Marc!"

"I'll take care of it, Houston, calm down!" Marc urged his brother, fighting against the officers who kept him from reaching Houston. "Go and answer their questions and I'll be there when you're done," he bartered, watching as the officers ushered his brother out of the house. Marc would've left behind them, but he caught sight of Mick. "It was you," he sneered.

"No, it was your brother," Mick corrected, folding

her arms across her tasseled sweatshirt. "I would suggest you get him a lawyer."

"A good one," Ty added.

"You little whorish bitches!" Marcus snapped, turning his fury on Mick and Ty. "Mark my words, you two sluts will pay for what you've done to my family."

Quest and Quay had been virtually silent as they stood side by side and viewed the scene from the study's wide doorway. Hearing their uncle say such vile things to the women they loved stoked their anger in unison.

"Whoa, guys," Damon urged, clutching each of his sons by the elbow. It did little good as his children kept moving forward, practically dragging their father behind them.

Just as the twins reached their uncle, they were shoved aside by an even greater force.

The crowd watched in stunned silence as Yohan caught his father by the neck and lifted him clean off the floor.

"Son of a bitch!" Yohan raged, his loss of temper long overdue. "I will not listen to you speak to another woman this way! You hear me, Pop?!" he bellowed, now both his massive hands encircling Marcus's neck. "I let you run Mel away with this haughty bullshit so long ago. I won't let you do this again!"

No one, not even Yohan's older brothers, dared intervene just then. The massive, darkly beautiful young man rarely lost his temper. Those who'd seen it happen before felt a shudder of fear for Marcus. The group watched as Yohan carried away his father.

The study cleared as almost everyone followed on their heels.

The argument spilled into the ballroom. Yohan shoved his father inside none to gently. The caterers and florists who were there preparing for the wedding needed no coercion to leave the room. Fernando and Moses assured the family everything would be fine and closed the ballroom's double doors on their questioning faces.

"Han, please," Josephine Ramsey urged her son, her hands clasped as she prayed frantically.

"Come on, Yo," Fernando urged, using his own considerable strength to restrain his younger brother. "You don't want to do this, man," he whispered.

Moses tried as well. "He's right, Yo. He ain't worth it, man."

Marcus's dark eyes narrowed in surprise. He looked upon his sons with renewed realization and saw no trace of love in their eyes.

"Yohan, please," Josephine cried.

"You knew, didn't you?" Yohan grated, his hands still gripping Marcus's neck. "You knew what Houston did to Sera, didn't you? Didn't you?!"

"Afterwards," Marcus gasped. "Later—much later, please—" he sputtered and coughed to catch his breath. "Please believe me, son."

"I don't believe a damn thing you say," Yohan growled, his grip beginning to loosen. "I never would've lost her if I hadn't believed every word that came out of your lying mouth," he lamented, his thoughts returning to his estranged wife, Melina.

"But Mo's right," he said, stepping away. "You ain't worth it," he muttered.

"We have to stick together," Marc was saying, clearing his throat while massaging his sore neck. "The family—"

"Aw, Pop, save that crap," Moses urged.

"Yeah, Pop, I don't think you got a leg to stand on with that family honor bull anymore," Fernando guessed.

"What will happen to Houston?" Josephine asked her husband in hopes of shifting the conversation and steering male tempers from another flare-up.

"Ma, I think Hous is done for," Fernando answered for his father.

"In light of this evidence, I'd second that," Moses added, clapping Yohan's shoulder as they stepped away from Marcus.

"You think they'll match him to this semen?" Josephine asked, watching her sons nod.

"It'd be pretty foolish of him to refuse giving the cops a DNA sample," Moses continued. "It'd be almost like admitting his guilt. And then there's Wake Robinson and Sera's diary."

"Where the hell did it come from is what I'd like to know," Fernando said.

"Sera's mother probably gave it to Mick," Moses surmised.

Josephine stumbled suddenly, as though she were losing strength in her legs. Her boys rushed to her side.

"Are you all right?" Yohan whispered, kissing her temple.

"Mmm," Josephine nodded, managing a faint smile. "Just a bit light-headed," she said.

Fernando's gaze was intent as he studied his mother. His hand clenched unconsciously and he was suddenly overcome by the same rage that had held his brother moments earlier.

"Fernando?" Josephine called when her middle son rose quickly to his feet. "What is it?"

Fernando leaned down to kiss her hand. "You relax. I'll be back before the wedding. I promise."

"Where you off to, man?" Moses asked.

Fernando slanted a glare toward Marcus, who kept his distance on the other side of the room. "Something I need to look into," he said.

Quaysar and Tykira remained in the study long after everyone took off after Yohan and Marcus.

Ty stood close to the door, shaking her head as she replayed the earlier scene in her head. Quay shook her ponytail in his hand before pulling her back against his chest.

"Wanna tell me about it?" he asked her.

Ty continued to shake her head. "I don't think I could put it into words," she marveled.

Quay bowed his head and inhaled the softness of the perfume that clung to the fuzzy raspberry sweater she wore. "You sure you wanna be part of such a dysfunctional group?" he asked, realizing he was reluctant to hear her response.

"No, Quay, I'm not sure," Ty whispered, missing the helplessness and hurt that flashed in her fiancé's beautiful deep-set eyes. After a moment, she turned in his arms. "But I am sure that I want to be a part of *you* and since your family comes with the package, I'll have to accept that."

Quay closed his eyes as though he were giving thanks. "I love you," he vowed, gathering her close.

"I love you, too," Ty returned, giggles rising when she felt Quay's fingers beneath her sweater. "What are you doing?" she laughed.

"Well, if you gotta ask, I guess I need to try harder," he decided, his lips brushing her cheek, before they suckled her earlobe.

Ty arched closer to enjoy the caress. Her nails grazed the back of his head and she shivered when his hands cupped both her breasts. Quay sought her mouth and favored her with a throaty kiss. Their moans rose in unison. Ty was loudest, her cries infrequently muffled as she thrust her tongue eagerly against his.

Quay's brows drew close as a swell of emotion rushed through him. Slowly, his fingers slipped beneath the waistband of Ty's jeans. A second later, he'd unsnapped them and was lowering the zipper.

"Quay!" Ty gasped, pulling back at last. "Wait," she urged. "Quay, we can't now."

The determined look he wore offered no clue to whether he heard her or not. His tongue nuzzled within her mouth again, completely taking Tykira's mind off her protests. A shuddery sound lilted from her throat when his middle finger slipped inside her panties. He stroked her femininity with deep possessive thrusts that drenched his finger with her desire.

"Quay," Ty called, trying to triumph over the sensational feelings stemming from the erotic caress. "Sweetie, there's a houseful of people."

"And?" he challenged, backing her against the study door while his fingers continued to work their magic.

Ty surrendered briefly to the delicious thrusts that were drenching the middle of her panties and forcing her to powerful orgasm.

Quay's sinfully gorgeous face was a picture of satisfaction. "You want me to stop?" he teased relentlessly.

Ty took several seconds to respond. "I—we should go check on things down there."

With his free hand, Quay propped up her chin. "I have everything I care about right here."

The next morning, Tykira woke to the sound of her mother's humming. Bobbie Lowery flitted around the master suite removing wrappings from her daughter's wedding gown, shoes and other accompaniments. Hearing her daughter's yawn drew her attention instantly.

"Hey, sleepy, you excited about the big day?" Bobbie called, strolling toward the bed. "And just to be clear, I'm talking about your wedding day, not that mess yesterday."

Ty chuckled. "I know, Mommy."

"Listen, honey," Bobbie was saying as she took a seat on the edge of the bed. "I have no doubt of your love for Quay and I know he feels the same for you. But you have to know that in marrying him you'll be claiming *all* the Ramseys, and they ain't an easy lot to belong to."

Ty was nodding. "I know, Mommy. I had this very talk with Quay yesterday. Don't worry," she said, patting her mother's hand. "The Ramseys won't be in my door every night."

"Precisely—and there are those in that family who dislike being shut out. Keeping to yourself, having your own life, being content with your husband without their involvement, can rattle lots of feathers. You're getting a pretty decent mother- and father-in-law, but you watch yourself with the rest of those jackasses and be careful."

Ty laughed. "Mommy! What would your employers say if they heard you?"

Bobbie waved her hand. "Forget 'em," she drawled, joining her daughter in laughter as they shared a tight hug.

A sharp curse sounded in the otherwise silent area of Quest and Mick's guestroom just a few doors down from where Ty and Bobbie chatted. Michaela heard her husband's outburst clearly. Her face was a picture of curiosity when she came rushing out of their adjoining bathroom. Quest was on the phone and Mick waited. She listened, not able to gain much from the disturbing cell phone conversation. The moment he ended the call, she raised her hands to prompt his explanation.

"They lost Houston."

"What? How?"

Quest shook his head and tapped his index finger to Mick's chin. "This is Savannah, baby. The family's got a lot of *well-meaning* friends down here."

Sadness clouded Mick's features and she took a seat on an armchair near the bathroom door. "I so wanted to tell Johnelle that we had Sera's murderer behind bars."

"I'm sorry you heard me on the phone," Quest whispered, kneeling to capture her hands in his. "I didn't want this upsetting you."

Mick smiled, watching him press kisses to the backs of her hands. "I'm fine. I'm fine," she repeated when he looked up at her. "I worked hard to give Johnelle answers and she knows more today than she did before. Now the only mother I'm concerned about is me."

Her words like music to his ears, Quest closed his eyes and rested his head in her lap.

Quay had journeyed to his grandfather's smoking room for a drink alone. He'd been there a little over fifteen minutes when his father found him.

"You better not be having second thoughts!" Damon teased, joining his son in the intimidating maple-paneled room. "Tykira's too beautiful to let get away. Besides, I've been rooting for this since you two were younger," he shared.

"Dad!" Quay grinned, surprise tingeing his words. "Since way back then?"

"You shouldn't be surprised," Damon said, pouring a bit of burgundy and then waving the decanter in Quay's direction.

"I'm good," Quay said.

"Anyway, it was easy to see how you two felt about one another."

Quay's lashes fluttered down over his eyes as a wave of rage pierced through him. "Thank God Houston didn't see it," he said.

"Do you really think he would've hurt her?" Damon asked, leaning against the bar.

"I really do, Dad," Quay replied without hesitation. "Girls I was interested in before Ty...he played a part in their disappearances, too. I know it."

"I never realized he could be capable of an evil like that," Damon breathed, shaking his head as he strolled over to his son. "I'm proud of you, boy," he said, clapping Quay's shoulder. "You kept the woman you love safe from a monster."

"And I almost lost her in the process."

Damon leaned down, cupping the back of Quay's head. "The operative word being *almost.* Just don't let it happen again," he ordered, and landed a playful slap to Quay's jaw.

They shared a close hug for several moments and then Damon pulled back.

"Let's go get your lady," he said.

Quest and Michaela decided to keep Houston's sudden disappearance away from the family until all the festivities had ended. In truth, they hadn't thought much else about it since the wedding events began.

The entire group was elated and truly happy for the bride and groom. People mingled, danced and ate from the huge preceremony spread. The gathering was made even more lovely by the fact that Marcus had decided not to attend. Many thought little of it and it seemed that no one really missed him or Houston.

Tykira and Bobbie arrived in the entryway to the room where the vows would be taken. Ty stood mesmerized by the enchanting scene that met her eyes. It was to be a night wedding and the sunroom was a vision of candlelight that flickered and danced all about. The room of glass windows and ceiling offered a captivating view of the starry evening sky. A cello, flute, violin and oboe quartet completed the fairy-tale ambience.

Ty was a vision of classy chic in a creation of chiffon and satin. The gown itself was straight and accentuated her tall, svelte figure. The empire waistline cinched right below her breasts to emphasize their fullness. The sleeves were long and tapered to her wrists while a straight coat of chiffon trailed behind. The coat's upturned collar flattered the graceful line of her neck that was adorned by a thin silver necklace, her only jewelry.

Bobbie barely managed to keep her tears at bay. Tykira looked down at her mother and chuckled at her emotional state. Bobbie uttered a quick "shhh" in response.

"My big girl," Bobbie cooed, pulling Ty close then. "All my love and happiness. You've waited so long," she said, fiddling with the spiral curls that fell from Ty's upswept coiffure to frame her face.

"It was worth the wait, Mommy," Ty swore, sniffling when she and her mother pulled apart.

Bobbie cupped Ty's cheek, and then turned to signal the quartet leader, who segued the group into the wedding march.

Satisfied, Bobbie nodded and winked at her daughter. "Let's go get your man," she said.

Arm in arm, the two strolled down the aisle. Everyone "ahhed" or grew misty-eyed over the beautiful picture Ty made as well as the fact that her mother was giving her away.

Tykira prayed she wouldn't stumble when she caught sight of Quaysar. He stood between Quest— the best man—and the minister. He was riveting in a gorgeous black satin tux. His gaze was smoldering and intent and he watched Ty as though there were nothing and no one else in the room.

Side by side the bride and groom turned to the minister who had married Quay's parents. Sniffles could be heard from the audience as the minister delivered his sage words. The minute pop and crackle of the candlelight sounded every so often. Then, the minister announced that the couple had vows to speak. He instructed Tykira to begin. Smiling demurely, she took a deep breath before turning to Quay.

"I loved you the first time I met you. Security and protection always surrounded me whenever you were near and somehow I always knew that no bad thing would ever touch me as long as you existed. My love for you never died or dwindled even through our darkest times." She squeezed his hands tightly. "The only place I will ever want to be is by your side. I'll love you forever."

The minister nodded, and then instructed Quaysar to begin.

"Tyke, I believe I loved you before I knew I even liked girls. There've been so many ups and downs, and I've done so many things to make myself forget you when our darkest times seemed like they would never end. But I could never stop loving you. Now and forever the *only* place I will ever want you to be is by my side." He raised both her hands and pressed a kiss to the back of each. "I love you. Always."

The minister cleared his throat to speak his binding words. "Now by the power vested in me by the state of Georgia, I now pronounce you husband and wife. Quay, you may kiss your bride."

Cheers rose seconds after Quay pulled Ty into a crushing embrace.

"Sisters and brothers may I present Mr. and Mrs. Quaysar and Tykira Ramsey," the minister announced.

Everyone rushed to their feet with more cheers and applause. Quay already had his wife in his arms and was carrying her down the aisle amidst a sea of colorful confetti and best wishes.

"Quay, where are we going?" Ty inquired, breathless from laughing. She saw that her husband hadn't stopped walking. He headed right out of the house and down the majestic front porch steps to the carriage that waited out front. "I thought we were taking a car to the airport?" she said.

Quay's midnight eyes twinkled gleefully as he settled her into the carriage. "Patience, Mrs. Ramsey," was all that he would say.

Thoroughly content, Tykira snuggled next to her husband when he joined her inside the cozy carriage. The walkway was lined with brass lamps that shed golden light to mark their path. Eventually, Ty realized they weren't headed for the road, but deeper into the estate. She steeled herself against asking more questions and waited. Her eyes narrowed when she spotted a construction coming into view.

"Quay," she gasped, finally realizing where they were. "I had no idea it was still here. I didn't even want to ask," she said, clutching his hand while looking upon the quaint cottage where she and Quay had first made love so long ago. It had obviously been completely refurbished, for it looked newly built and freshly painted where it sat in the middle of the moonlit forest.

Quay left the carriage and walked around to open her side. He cupped her face, holding her still before she could exit. "This place, *our* place will always be here and *we'll* be here for at least a week," he shared and dropped a kiss to her nose.

"An entire week?" Ty marveled, as he pulled her from the carriage and into his arms once more. "Just the two of us," she added, smoothing her fingertips across his jaw.

Quay shrugged. "With the exception of the caretakers and security guards who know they'll be taking their lives into their own hands if they even think about disturbing us."

Ty looked back toward the cottage. "I never dreamed the next time I saw this place, I would be your wife."

Quay stopped walking then. He planted a tender kiss just below her ear. "My wife, my love, my life," he vowed.

Leila Owens didn't know
how to love herself let alone
an abandoned baby
but Garret Grayson knew
how to love them both.

She's My Baby

Adrianne Byrd

(Kimani Romance #10)

He found *trouble* in paradise.

Mason Sinclair's visit to Barbados was supposed to be about uncovering family mysteries not the mysteries of Lianne Thomas's heart.

EMBRACING
THE MOONLIGHT
(Kimani Romance #12)

Wayne Jordan

AVAILABLE SEPTEMBER 2006

FROM KIMANI™ ROMANCE

Love's Ultimate Destination

Available at your favorite retail outlet.

**Introducing an exciting appearance
by legendary
New York Times bestselling author**

DIANA PALMER
HEARTBREAKER

He's the ultimate bachelor…
but he may have just met
the one woman to change his ways!

Join the drama in the story of a confirmed
bachelor, an amnesiac beauty and their
unexpected passionate romance.

"Diana Palmer is a mesmerizing storyteller
who captures the essence of what
a romance should be."—*Affaire de Coeur*

**Heartbreaker *is available from Silhouette Desire
in September 2006.***

Page-turning drama…

Exotic, glamorous locations…

Intense emotion and passionate seduction…

Sheikhs, princes and billionaire tycoons…

This summer, may we suggest:

THE SHEIKH'S DISOBEDIENT BRIDE
by Jane Porter

On sale June.

AT THE GREEK TYCOON'S BIDDING
by Cathy Williams

On sale July.

THE ITALIAN MILLIONAIRE'S VIRGIN WIFE

On sale August.

With new titles to choose from every month,
discover a world of romance in our books written
by internationally bestselling authors.

HARLEQUIN *Presents*

It's the ultimate in quality romance!

Available wherever Harlequin books are sold.

www.eHarlequin.com   HPGEN06